THE MARK OF SATURN

A BLOOD LUMINARY NOVEL

JOSEPH EASTWOOD

Third Edition Copyright © 2015 Joseph Eastwood
First edition was published © 2012 under the title "Lumen".
All rights reserved

ISBN: 1495979962
ISBN-13: 978-1495979965

This is a work of fiction. All characters and events portrayed in this novel are fictitious and are products of the author's imagination and any resemblance to actual events, or locales or persons, living or dead are entirely coincidental.

For Tonya.

ACKNOWLEDGMENTS

Since the first edition of this book, I've acknowledged and thanked several people. I'm not the same person I was back in 2012, I would like to think I'm currently the best version of myself, and that wouldn't be possible without everything I've been through and everyone I've met since then. So thank *you*.

I don't have a huge team of people working with me behind the scenes, but with what I do have and who I do work with, we've created the best possible book for you. The start of an adventure into Templar Island and beyond.

I want to thank *you* for reading, for occupying a fantasy headspace of mine. I really hope you enjoy '*The Mark of Saturn*', and I hope you'll leave a review.

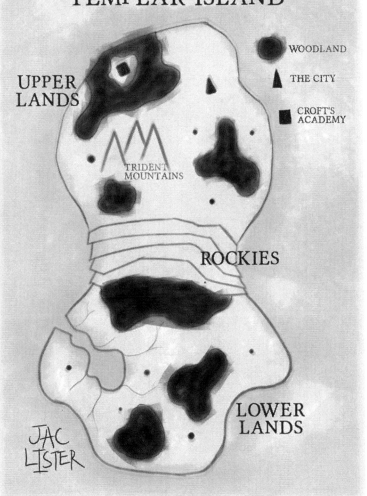

CONTENTS

Enjoy your stay in *my* fantasy land.

PROLOGUE

DEATH is a contract signed at birth, it's a truth agreed upon, and once you're born your name goes in a book. Life is measured in time, an hourglass to each person. Each time is different, some hourglasses can last a century, while others can end before death is even a concept. There's purity in that, dying so naïvely, the purest of deaths are tainted with innocence.

Daniel was four years, three-hundred and sixty-four days old. He giggled to himself as he ran around the coffee table with a miniature blue plane tucked between his fingers. His father sat back with a smile, engrossed in the whooshing sound Daniel made in dipping the plane.

"We don't have those here," his father said, "apparently they're huge beasts that fly, high, *high* in the sky." His smile grew as he reeled away childhood memories of the tales his father had told him.

Daniel fumbled and stopped at his father's feet. He rubbed at his chin and itched at his temple. "Um—uh d—d—daddy, that—that's silly! B—but this is so tiny." He pawed at his father's knee and pushed the plane up to his face. "See." He grinned a goofy half-toothed smile before running off again.

His father grinned down at him. "My dad brought that back from another island, a *huge* island, far *far* away from here."

Daniel's mother's laughter filled the air from the kitchen. "Don't fill the boy's head with nonsense, Erik, nobody has ever set foot off the island."

"It's true, Roan." He grabbed his son and pulled him into his arms, hugging him tightly. "It's true, Daniel, it is." He tickled his son and took the plane from him, holding it out in front of them. "Do you want to fly one of those when you're older?" Daniel giggled.

He snatched the plane from his father and ran with the toy in his hands. He watched it in awe, dipping and raising, letting the little air in the back of his throat tingle and dance in his lungs.

"Do you?" His father leaned forward in his chair. "Daniel? Look at me."

Daniel circled the tree stump table, over and over. He ducked and dipped with the plane in his hand, baring down on his bottom lip.

His father called out to him again, watching as a long white thread fell from the back of his t-shirt. Erik reached out to grab it. "Come here." He pulled at the string and tugged it free. "Daniel," he whispered, rubbing the string between his forefinger and thumb.

Erik's eyes fluttered shut. The thread was pure energy and it flushed up in Erik's cheeks and bounced around his body. He opened his eyes to witness the string his son had created, fall thicker, leaving a trail. And then the first fluffed feather slipped out.

"R—R—Roan!"

"Stop pining at the boy, he's not gone deaf."

"Honey." He watched as Daniel weaved a circle. "Come through I—I need you to look at something."

She huffed and poked her head out. "What is—it?" She froze by the doorway with thousand more questions swollen in her throat.

"The change?" Erik cleared his throat. "Right?"

Roan locked eyes with her pasty-faced husband. "Oh—" she coughed, "of course."

"I thought it would happen overnight?" he said.

She pressed a forefinger and thumb into the collar of her neck and swallowed hard. "Better late than never." She smiled, closing her eyes.

Erik's shoulders settled. "Thank the Luminary."

Roan moved her hand to her chest and grabbed at the seven-pointed star on her necklace. "Thank you," she whispered.

"Hun."

"He'll be fine."

Daniel ran faster; absorbed in a world of his own. He jumped and dipped, letting the feathers fall from his t-shirt. The t-shirt tore at the seams and dropped to his waist like excess skin.

Roan and Erik glanced to each other, their jaws dropped and they shared a silent gasp. The t-shirt revealed two thick white stumps of bone protruding from the top of his shoulder blades. Pockets of blood had burst around them.

Roan wobbled on her legs as she leaned against the chair and fumbled around for her husband's hand. "He's fine." She blinked back some tears and took a deep breath.

The blood from Daniel's back coated feathers and dripped down his pants, freckling the stone floor. The thin feathers grew in bunches around the base of the bone, clumping and falling as he moved.

They watched Daniel move in the syrupy air, locked in languid strokes, where seconds settled as minutes. Daniel slipped on the mess he'd created and yelped. He fell to his knees,

4

throwing the plane into the wall ahead. From his knees he fell to his chest in a small pile of feathers. The protruding bones on his back crumbled and congealed with the blood in a lumpy paste.

Roan kept a tight grasp of her husband's hand, tightening as He shuffled in his seat. "We don't want to intervene," she sniffled. She reached up to her neckline and found her necklace again. She gripped it until it cut her palm.

Erik closed his eyes and shook his head. He massaged the bridge of his nose and pushed back the tears. "Can we—" he began before Daniel screeched.

Erik pulled his hand from his wife and dropped to his son's side. "Daniel," he said, with his hand hovering above his son's back.

Roan's voice croaked with concern. The whites of her eyes turned pink as she went through her mind of all the times she'd saved lives as a nurse.

"Hush, Daniel, hush," his father said cowering over. He stared up at Roan. "They—they can't, they can't decide his fate. We have to do something. We have to help him pull through."

She pinched at her lips with her teeth and rolled her eyes. "No." She pulled her husband up from under his arm. "No."

Blood had pooled inside Daniel's ears, engulfing sound. He screwed his eyes shut. He was trapped in his skin.

His parents hushed him as he cried out to them, and they cried out to the Luminary. Daniel coughed up bloodied phlegm, spitting it out and turning his lips red.

There was as a sigh of defeat. A deflation in his chest and shoulders as he relaxed on the floor. This wasn't *his* fight.

CHAPTER ONE

DANIEL'S yellow feathered wings unfurled from his back, catapulting him to the ceiling. His fingers slipped into grooves, worn away through the years to fit his hand placement perfectly. He stayed still and took a couple deep breathes before finding himself conscious and clinging to the ceiling in his bedroom. Again.

The bedroom door opened and in rushed his mother, panting with a hand on her chest and a cloth in hand to press against her forehead. "Daniel, get down!" She snapped the cloth up at him. "Come on now, we have a guest."

A long drawn out sigh left him. "It's been happening a lot," he said.

She stood with her hands on her hips and raised an eyebrow at him. "We don't have time for this today," she said.

"Nice to know you care."

"Oh, shut up and stop being silly," she said. "Come on then, there's a guest downstairs."

Daniel rolled his shoulder blades and the wings on his back molted away; the feathers danced in spirals until they reached the floor, leaving the skeleton of his wings behind. He gripped the brick harder as the bones thinned back into his body.

His mother tapped her foot. "Come on," she said, shaking her head. "And clean this up."

He released his grasp and fell back on his bed. Feathers bounced around, attaching to his skin. "See, cleaning," he said. He laid there for a moment while stray strains of energy rekindled with his body. "How's that for control?"

"Neat trick, how about not waking yourself with two full wings on your back," she laughed. "Get yourself changed and I'll see you downstairs."

"Why? What's so important?" Daniel groaned, sitting up in bed.

"We have a very special guest. So *please* get dressed," she said with a smile. She dabbed at her forehead with the cloth again before leaving Daniel to tend to the guest.

The floor was littered with feathers, and a t-shirt, tore in two, it was the third t-shirt within as many days. Daniel swung his legs around and faced himself in the wall mirror. "You've gotta get this under control," he spoke to his reflection

As he walked around his room getting changed, the feathers clung to him with a powerful magnetism, thinning into his skin. He needed most of the feathers back once he'd produced them as they were a product of his pure energy. Pure energy is produced naturally, but nobody can produce enough to be careless with it.

He dressed himself in a black t-shirt and a pair of dark blue exercise pants. He wasn't sure whether his mother had wanted him to dress smartly or comfortably. He combed a hand through his shaggy black hair and decided that it was smart enough.

His hand traced the cool rock face as he walked down the stairs. He paused as a fragment of his nightmare toured his mind. He shuddered and stumbled on the last step into the living room.

A man was sat on his father's chair, sipping tea out of one of the glass tea cups.

"Mum." A dark grey overcoat was hung on a peg beside the front door. *Expensive*, Daniel thought. He looked back at the man in his father's chair.

His mother made an appearance from the kitchen alcove with a teapot in hand. "Anymore tea?" she asked.

"That's okay," he said in his deep voice. "I take it, he's the son, Daniel?"

"Oh, Daniel," she said, placing the teapot on the table. She wiped her hands on her apron before gesturing for Daniel to meet their guest. "This is—"

"Where's dad?" Daniel asked. He looked back at the man in his black pinstripe suit as he tapped a finger on the cane his hand rested on. *Very expensive*, he mused.

"This is Reub—I mean, Mr. Croft," his mother said, "of the Croft Academy."

Daniel raised his eyebrows. *Sure enough from the Upperlands*, he smirked to himself.

Reuben placed the teacup on the table and stood. He pulled at the cuffs of his suit and patted his pants. He glanced back at Daniel, immediately realising that he was *too* casual for this guest. He approached Daniel and shook his hand. "Master Satoria," he said, "Daniel, is it? Well, it's a pleasure meeting you."

Daniel nodded as he pulled his hand from Reuben's grasp. "I'm fine, you know, I've already said that I don't want to go to school," he said as his mother sighed.

"Your mother thinks it's in your interests," he replied. "But I'll be the judge of whether or not you're Croft Academy material." Daniel turned to his mother as she glanced up at Reuben. "Shall we begin?"

Begin? Daniel shuffled on the spot and itched at a patch on his stomach. "I haven't transitioned yet."

Daniel's mother pushed a hand into the air. "But," she began.

"He's always been a late bloomer. Well, it's been ten years already."

Daniel's chest tightened. "I—I—I'm fine just doing what I do now, and then ma—maybe getting a job with my dad at the library in the Upperlands district."

Reuben tipped his head to Daniel. "You might end up doing just that," he said. "So, what can you do with the most skill?"

"Wings?" he said, turning to his mother. She nodded. "Yeah. I can grow wings, like seraph wings."

"Seraph? Like, angel?" He asked with curvature to his thin lips. "As long as you can prove it."

"Yeah." He hummed. "There's a book, I was obsessed with it when I was younger, and since then, I've been able to—"

"Perhaps, you should just show me."

Daniel's mother moved to Reuben's side. "He's good," she said. "And he reads all the time."

"Anyone can read," he replied, giving Daniel a once over. "If you're going to join *my* academy, I'll need a demonstration of *this* ability."

Daniel felt both obliged and compelled to do right by his mother's decision of inviting Reuben into their home. "We'll need to go outside then," he said.

His mother clapped. "I'll get you some fresh tea, Mr. Croft. Camomile? Chai? I even have some Hibiscus."

"Whatever is in the pot," Reuben said. "I don't want to be a burden."

"Okay, I'll be out with you in a moment."

Daniel led Reuben out the front door. He held his hand up to cover his eyes from the sun.

Templar Island is made up of three regions, the Lowerlands, the region closest to the sea with dirty beaches and a larger slum population to the Upperlands, the region closest to the sky, and legend says that it makes them closer to the Luminary. The Rockies is the central region, made up of dropping cliff faces with homes carved out inside those. Not every cliff face home had a landing ledge, some were doors that lead out to an almost certain death.

Daniel lived in the Rockies, on the third tier. The house was large in comparison to others, with a ledge and a tall tree. He took his spot, marked by a huge dent, and waited for his mother.

His mother handed Reuben a cup of tea, and he took a sip of it, keeping his gaze on Daniel.

"Watching?" he asked. He turned to face the forestry over the cliff. He pulled his t-shirt from over his head and threw it behind himself.

"Daniel, honey." He turned to see his mother swaying with a grin on her face and her hands pressed up against her neckline, holding her necklace. "Do me proud," she said.

Daniel closed his eyes and felt the warmth of the smile travel through his body. He puffed out his chest. *You can do this*. He rolled his head on his shoulders as they cracked. He arched his back and sucked in a deep breath before pushing himself up on his tiptoes.

A moment passed as Daniel held his breath and built the energy inside. He pushed the air out with one forced breath and dropped to his knees. Two thick bones shot up from his back. The skeleton of his wings formed, padding with muscle and sprouting ashy-white feathers.

In through the nose, out through the mouth, he told himself. Sweat glistened down his spine as he stood.

"But can you use them?"

Daniel nodded. His wings spanned open, casting a Daniel shaped shadow over his mother and Reuben.

He tilted his head at Daniel and took another sip of the tea. "This is really good," he said. "What did you say it was?"

Daniel's mother stopped chewing on a hangnail to look at Reuben. "Oolong," she said with a smile.

Daniel let his wings go limp on his back again. He flexed his shoulders and his wings curled to create two neat rolls on his back.

Reuben placed a hand in front of his eyes from the sun. A smile formed across his thin lips. "It will be a shame to see them go when he transitions," he said to Daniel's mother.

"They'll go?" Daniel asked.

"I assume so."

"I thought you knew," his mother said. "Or maybe they'll be bigger, stronger?"

"It's possible," Reuben said. "Usually though, people lose their childhood gifts."

"It's a part of me." He chewed on his bottom lip.

"Look at it this way," Reuben said, taking another sip. "Truly delicious. Um. Yeah, well, at my school, we have a special program for those who keep their animal abilities once they've transitioned, so it's within the realms of possibility that you keep your wings."

Daniel's mother sighed. "That would be my Daniel, he's always been a talent."

Daniel blushed before turning back. He listened to Reuben's words. "Can you use them?" And with a push of determination, Daniel edged closer to the cliff. He knelt down and closed his eyes.

One thrust from from his knees and he jumped into the air, catching the wind with his wings. He kept a steady height and pushed on higher.

"Maybe it'll transfer with him."

"I like the optimism," Reuben said.

"It's all we have down here," she said. "And he's been doing *that* jump since his first change."

"I'll happily admit that it's—" he paused and turned to Daniel's mother with a shifting glance. "You don't happen to keep a record of your bloodline to hand?"

Daniel hovered above with his wings flapping gently at the air. He watched from fifty feet above, not a clue how else to show his power.

"I don't, but his father keeps all the family books."

"Well you've raised quite the child. Quite the spirited one as well."

His mother nodded and smiled. "Oh, he is."

Daniel's wings flapped harder against the air until they turned into blurs on the ground. His wings batted harder and harder.

His mother raised a hand to guard her eyes from the sun as she looked up at Daniel.

"Struggling?" Reuben asked.

Blood broke from Daniel's skin. It coated a patch of feathers, and like an infection, each feather that it touched made its way to the ground.

"Is he okay up there?" Reuben asked.

"Yeah," his mother said. "Yeah."

Daniel wriggled around in the sky under the reign of his tempered wings. His body convulsed, from left to right, trying to tear him in half.

"Daniel," she gasped. "I think he's messing with us."

His blood feathers speckled the grey slate. His mother and Reuben watched, like the first droplet of rain hanging in the air, the anticipation washed over them.

Daniel's wings flapped harder until they slapped each other, demented and twisting, *whack*, *whack*. The left wing flopped by his side, swinging on a single ligament attached to his back. It twitched and dropped free to the ledge with a *womp*. Daniel bit at his teeth as the wound on his back cauterised itself. He spun in circles on the other wing.

A smirk pinched at the side of Reuben's cheeks. "Is that normal?" he asked.

"No," she croaked and swallowed at her dry throat.

Daniel dropped. The remaining wing battled up thrust. He flapped his arms and outstretched his fingers. *Snap*. He landed on his feet.

"Baby!" his mother screamed.

Daniel stood. Silent. Unmoving. First, he fell on his knees, and then he dropped to his chest and scratched up the side of his face. The wing on his back to twitched with a flap.

"Daniel," she gasped, rushing over to him. She knelt by his side and brushed back his wing to reveal a hole at the top, right through to the bone.

She hovered a hand above the large fleshy cut and sniffled. The heat resonated out, but he wasn't healing. "Hush, baby," she said. She wiped her eyes on an apron. "Hush." She sat and stroked his hair.

Reuben coughed from behind. He held out the teacup. "Well, this has been *interesting*," he said. "This must be him waiting for his ability to kick in. It's a shame that blood is being shed for it to happen."

She turned to him. "You can help. Right?"

"We cannot intervene, you know we can't. And if we try, it will only be rejected. I'm sorry, Mrs. Satoria."

"But my husband. He said he'd deal with this. He's trying to transition, isn't he?" She sniffled.

"Well, it looks that way." Reuben nodded. "If he pulls through you can tell him that he has an acceptance letter waiting. But if he dies, my condolences are with you and your husband."

"You—You—You're not staying?"

"I cannot. I have two more boys to see in the area," he said. The teacup vanished from his hands and his coat appeared over his arms. "I do wish you the best of luck."

"What–should–I–do?" she asked, her breaths now hooked at the back of her throat. "What should I do?"

"Be there for him. Everyone has a purpose. Some of us are born twice, while others are sacrificed." He gave her a crooked smile. "I wish you the best," he said. He bowed his head and disappeared.

She burrowed her head in her arms, sobbing. The wound on Daniel's back bled and coated his skin, even the smallest of cuts opened up to bleed.

She shook her head and covered her eyes, peeking through the spaces between her fingers. The wing on Daniel's back was propped up like a white flag. The top had rotted, feathers dropped from the muscle tissue, and the bones crumbled over his pale skin.

She wiped her eyes again. "You can do this," she told herself, combing a hand through her hair and tying it up into a ponytail. "You can do this," she said, taking a deep breath.

Daniel shivered. "Mum," his voice weighed heavy with phlegm. "It hurts."

"I can help," she choked, and picked up her son's t-shirt. She wrapped it around her hand and dabbed at the wound. "It's going to be fine. Everything is going to be fine. You'll go to school and live in the Upperlands. Everything is going to be fine."

"I got in?" he grumbled.

She opened her mouth to reply but smiled instead. She rubbed the back of her hand against his arm, touching the goose pimples on his skin. "I'll take you inside, get you comfortable."

She closed her eyes and placed her hand on his arm, but there wasn't enough energy in her to teleport them both. Her hands shook as she plied them from him. "But first you need to survive," she whispered. She pushed herself to her feet and threw her son's blood stained t-shirt to the ground. She rushed inside and scrambled up the staircase to her bedroom. As soon as she reached the room she pulled at her things with the energy she had left, letting the drawers in her dresser fly out across the floor, and the doors of the wardrobe swung on their hinges. She pulled and pulled until she found a small blue suitcase.

Small black bugs flew around him. She placed the suitcase beside her son's head, wafting the bugs away with the back of her hand.

"Hush, sweetie. Hush," she said, combing a hand through his hair. "I can patch you up, ease the pain, try and speed the healing." She glanced inside the case. There were bandages, vials, needles, sticky tape, and memorabilia of the people whose lives she'd saved.

"D—D—Dreaming. Is this–is this a–a dream?" he asked.

"You fell and hurt yourself, honey," she said and wiped her eyes again.

She wriggled a hand into a white glove and picked up a needle. With her other hand she sparked flames and sterilised the metal with it. She collapsed the fire in her palm and picked a vial of heavy sedative from her collection. She filled the needle and let it hover by her side as she tugged Daniel's arm free.

Daniel groaned at the pain. "Please.".

She hushed him, tapping his wrist with two fingers. She found a vein and plucked the needle from the air before injecting him with it.

"It'll all be over when you wake."

CHAPTER TWO

DANIEL'S mother pressed a warm cloth against his forehead. She hushed and cooed at him as he grew restless, wrapped tight in his blanket. He blinked dust and sleep from his eyes, watching the silhouette of his parents cradling over him.

The dim candle light hit his parents' faces, bringing them into focus as Daniel tried raising a hand. His arms pushed against his duvet, waking the splinters of pins and needles beneath his skin. He winced and called out through the coarse strain on his voice.

His mother dabbed the cloth. "He'll be okay now," she said, standing and moving to her husband's side. "He *still* needs to heal."

He found her hand and took a hold of it. "Thanks to you,"

he said, "our son's going to be okay." He gave his wife's hand a kiss.

"Well, it's how we met. Remember?" she grinned.

"I went with a bug bite," he said, "and found a wife."

She wrapped her arms around her husband and kissed his cheek. "It wasn't as fatal as I'd told you that day," she whispered in his ear. "All I wanted was to see you again." Roan pulled away from her husband as a smile filled the wrinkles on his face.

"Now you tell me," he chuckled. "For a week I thought I was going to die."

"Aren't you glad you didn't," she grinned.

Daniel's voice cracked as he tried speaking. His mother dipped to his side, hushing him. She removed the cloth from his forehead and rinsed it in the bowl of warm water on the bedside table.

"My mother told me that I would know when I met him. And I knew then." She wrung the cloth out and patted it back on Daniel's forehead. She watched her son for a long moment. "I shouldn't have pushed him, Erik."

"We can teach him here, honey. And you know Jac can help as well."

"But he was accepted into the school, and he'll live so much better out there."

"He needs to recover."

Daniel gasped through the small opening in his scratchy

throat. He dug his fingernails into the mattress and pushed his chin into his chest. The damp cloth slipped over his eyes. He gasped harder.

"Muh? Dah?" he called out from his aching throat.

Roan wrapped her arms around him. "Oh, baby," she said. He tssked and wriggled out of her grasp. She sighed, pulling the cloth from his face. "You're okay now."

"Just try not to move too much," his father added.

"We think it was the change."

Daniel's eyes opened wider. "Change?"

"Full power – adolescence." His parents spoke, one after the other.

A shiver rippled through him as he sighed. "Really?" he asked with a huge smile. He pushed at his elbows, trying to sit up. "Does that mean I can go out now?" he croaked.

His parents laughed. "Don't be silly. And where would you be going to at midnight?" his mother asked.

He pushed himself upright in bed. "To tell Jac."

His parents glanced at each other, and then back to him. His mother shook her head. "Just get some rest, darlin'," she said, kissing him on his forehead.

Daniel sighed as they said "goodnight" and left him.

He pulled his arms out of the duvet and settled back into bed, flipping the pillow over to get the cold side. He laid down and watched the candle flicker on the bedside table. *One, two, three, four…* he counted until his eyelids drooped and a heavy sleep washed across him.

"Stupid," he groaned, moving his hand to itch at a knee.

He pushed the duvet and sat upright against the cold rock. A throb jabbed at his jaw and another gnawed at his joints, hammering at his pain threshold.

He rubbed at the side of his face, it was partially swollen. "Great," he stammered. "Can't even remember *that*."

He climbed out of bed slowly, pressing the soles of his feet against the cold concrete floor. The cold soothed him, relieving the heated swell inside. He gestured to the small window above his bed and it opened up. "I guess it still works," he grinned.

The cool air touched his spine. He closed his eyes in relief, bearing a wide grin. He pushed and put pressure on his feet as he stood. He took his first step and stumbled over to his wardrobe. "Crap," he grumbled, holding himself up on the handle.

He put a dark hooded jacket on over his bare torso and grabbed a pair of exercise bottoms out of the washing basket.

"Honey," his mother shouted. "If you're still awake you might want to eat something."

Daniel froze with the bottoms tight in his grasp. His throat dried and ached like sandpaper had formed across his tongue. "I'm gonna sleep."

"There's stew on the stove if you do get hungry."

He sat back on his bed and examined the bottoms in his hands. They were torn at the knee and pitied with dry blood. "It must've been rough." He threw them to the side and grabbed a clean pair.

He blew at the candle on his bedside table and climbed on his bed, "ooing" and "aahing" at the tension in his bending knees. He glanced out of the small rectangle above his bed, grinding his teeth in frustration. If it was true, and he had gone through the change, then it was unlikely he'd be able to use *that side* of himself again.

A familiar feeling ran through Daniel's body. His muscles constricted and his throat tightened. He wriggled on the spot, and when he opened his eyes, he was no longer Daniel-the-human.

He perched in the form of an eagle on the window ledge and surveyed the area. *Blood.* He could smell it. He flew from the ledge and dropped to the ground out of the shifted form.

He stood in the middle of a large dark red mess. "That's mine. All of that is mine," he said. The blood was dry but there was still a cold wetness to it.

Feathers were scattered, stuck in the trees and clinging to crevices in rocks, squirming in the slight breeze. Daniel knelt to touch one, but it turned to dust and escaped in the wind.

He stood and swallowed hard, pushing at his abdomen. "What happened to me? I should've died." His eyes welled as he sniffled. The feathers on the ground had become a graveyard of lost energy.

He pulled his hood up and shook his head as he took a couple of steps back. The candle in the front of the window glimmered against the glass, it caught Daniel's eye. He ran and pushed himself headfirst over the cliff.

The gust ruffled his hair and choked him. He tried to force the tingling feeling of a shift through his skin. He covered his face with his hands and felt the air gliding with him. He swooped across the tree tops and found a clearing.

He dropped from the sky mid-shift; legs formed and dangling while the rest of his body elongated, absorbing feathers, and rippling out in his clothes.

Daniel stood in the clearing for a moment, adjusting himself. "Jac!" Daniel shouted, kicking at stones. He called out for his friend again before he headed out of the clearing with a map in his head to Jac's.

A snapping sound pulled Daniel to a standstill. He looked around as the sound of snapping and crunching continued. "Psst! Dan," Jac's voice filtered through from behind.

Daniel turned on a foot with a large grin on his face. "What are you doing back there?"

Jac cocked his head to the right as a rustling came from a bush. A soft purr escaped the darkness. Daniel stepped closer to Jac as he tried to turn his head. He caught a glimpse of it, a flash of green eyes, blinking in the bush.

Jac has a plan, he reassured himself. *He always has a plan.*

Jac gestured for him to come closer. "Stop turning," he whispered.

Daniel's feet trembled in the dirt as he stepped towards Jac. Sound pricked his ears as the soft purr became a loud growl, before a jaw snapping shut turned into a howl.

Jac jumped out of the bush. "Run!" he shouted and reached for Daniel's hand.

Daniel stumbled at the sight of the animal in the dark. A panther, digging its claws in the dirt and poising itself to pounce. He pushed himself along the ground until he backed up to the base of a tree.

Jac's jaw became slack as he looked at Daniel. "Dan?"

Daniel found his footing, but not in *his* feet. He was swollen inside something, thick and yellow with clumps of orange, all fur. On all fours, his hands and feet were thick paws. His voice pitched a light growl and flexed the claw feature of this animal. He noticed the panther above him mid-jump. It landed on his back and sank its teeth into him.

Jac watched in awe as the lion chomped the air in pain and bucked its hind legs. The panther lost tact and clung to Daniel with its claws. He shook some more and the panther went flying into a tree, landing on its back.

Jac cursed at the panther and enveloped his hands in fire. He pelted small bolts at the panther, but it only singed the fur.

Daniel roared, cutting them both off as he charged at the panther with his teeth bared, ready to snap. The panther tried to push itself up as Daniel sunk his teeth into the leg. Immediately, he let go and pulled away with blood on his tongue. The panther skittered away, yelping as fur eroded around the wound.

Jac stood with his hands jammed in his armpits, watching as the panther vanished and Daniel became human again. He spat and wiped at his tongue. "Uh! What was that?" Daniel groaned. He zipped up his jacket and wiped his lips on his sleeve. "Blood?"

Jac flailed his hands as he walked to Daniel. "And what was that about?" he asked.

Daniel pulled at his jacket and found large rips and fraying around the bottom of it. "Well, that's new." He looked at Jac with a grin. "Thought you'd tell me about *that*."

"I heard you," Jac said, "and then I heard somethin' else."

"You weren't hunting that then?"

"If I was stupid, then yeah," he laughed, wrapping an arm around Daniel in a hug. "Gonna tell me where *that other thing* came from then?"

The smile on Daniel's face faded. "What if it was hunting you? Have you been taking its food?"

Jac shook his head and rolled his eyes. "It wasn't a real panther, didn't you see it shift back after you bit it."

27

"Then someone wants *you* dead."

"That's not unheard of down here."

Jac had been living in the forests of the Lowerlands since he was fifteen, it was after running away from his parents. It had only been two years, but he'd known Daniel for several years, so he decided to make a *home* for himself close by, and he'd always regarded Daniel's family as his family for as long as he can remember.

"My dad said you should teach me," Daniel said, fanning himself in the heat with a large leaf.

"I told your dad that when he brought some books down," Jac laughed, patting tree trunks as he walked by. "I've learned a lot out here."

"Yeah, wouldn't it be great?" Daniel turned to see the darkness of the forest all around them. "Are we lost?"

The taller the trees, the thicker the forest you were in, and Jac had built his home in some tall trees. Although Jac knew where he lived, Daniel didn't have a clue, even after Jac had planted clues over the forest floor for when he got lost, or he had to venture out at night.

"It looks different," Daniel said as Jac patted tree trunks. "You sure you haven't moved."

"It always looks different at night. That's why I don't travel this late," he said. "So, why are you out here?" he asked, patting another tree.

"I went through the change! I now have my full power."

"Crap! No way. Really?" He patted another tree before pausing. "And you can still shift?"

"Looks like it."

Jac nodded. He turned to face a tree and rubbed the trunk with both hands. "This is it." He pulled away a few flakes of bark to reveal grooves in the trunk, several rectangle holes. He cracked his fingers and pulled himself up to the first groove, bouncing up the rest until he settled on a branch at the top.

Daniel pushed his fingers over the bark. "I can't see them," he said.

"You're a big boy now," Jac said. "You can use your instincts," he said before disappearing into the silhouette of branches.

Daniel found the first groove. He closed his eyes and pulled himself up. He pushed his other hand higher and clawed up the next, climbing until he reached the top branch. "Okay. Now where? I can't see."

"Along the branch until you reach the door," Jac called out.

Daniel centered himself and walked with a hand on a branch beside him. He walked face first into a slate of wood. "Great. Thanks, Jac." He took a step back and pushed at the door with his hand. It opened. "I kinda hoped you'd moved. But no. This is pretty much the same place," Daniel said.

"Pretty much?" Jac grinned, lighting a lantern. "I added those leaves over there."

"That's not your bed is it?"

Jac placed the lantern on a hook. "So what are your plans, y'know, with the change an' all?"

"I wanted to talk about that as well."

"If I know your mum, she's gonna push you into school. And your dad will follow."

Daniel glanced to the floor and nodded, he picked up his head and met Jac's gaze. "I am going to school."

Jac bit the inside of his lip. "Thought as much. Which one?"

"Croft's Aca—"

He shook his head. "No," he said. "You can't, maybe Aggie's School, just on the horizon near your dad's work, but Croft's?" He sucked in a deep swell of air.

"But—eh—mm, it's the best school."

"No!" Jac said. The lantern fell from the hook, smashing on the hut floor. "No, you can't."

"But I got in!" Daniel said. "Aren't you happy for me?"

"If you go to the Upperlands, you might as well sign your name in blood, and while you're at it, let them use you!" He knelt beside the broken glass, remodelling it with his energy. He glanced back at Daniel, standing in the doorway, his palms shaking by his side. "They're disgusting, Dan." He lit another flame inside the lantern.

"But—but, you've never been! My dad works up there."

"No, he works on the outskirts. Not the centre. One in ten people are persecuted there."

Daniel shook his head. "That's the inner city, Jac. I thought you'd be happy for me," he said, butting his lips. "Well, a *friend* would be."

Jac shrugged. "You'll change anyway."

"How can you say that? I kinda just saved your life."

Jac smirked. "And I've always been saving yours." He scratched at the back of his neck. "Look at that, your life is starting to become about what *you've* done. You might as well leave already." He turned away and wiped at the well in his eyes.

Daniel wavered on the spot. "Fine," he said. "I'm going."

He opened his hand to see the faint scar of a memory reflected back in his eyes; a night they spent camping, a night they'd cut their own hands, swearing to become *blood brothers*, to stick together for life.

CHAPTER THREE

ARYANA slept with one hand pushed up against the side of her face and the other twisted on her side. She laid, sound asleep in the bliss of her imagination, a hub of subconscious.

Aryana Bernstein of the south Australian coast had woke a couple times to utter terror in the pit of her stomach, growling and grabbing at her.

Her voice cracked in a whine as she wrapped her arms around herself and pushed her knees up to her chest. Her face flushed in the stuffy heat of the duvet. She opened her eyes, they flashed blue and green to orange before they faded back to brown.

"He—he—he's alive," she whispered to herself. The glassy seal across her eyes broke as tears glossed her cheeks.

Aryana stilled herself from shaking in her duvet. She pushed her head out to see the dewy orange light come in through the balcony as she inhaled the fresh cold air. She laid in her bed and glared up at the four-posts and the orange chiffon drapes slunk down and around.

She watched for a moment, scrunching her face up at the ache pushing down on her chest. The sticky tears cracked like a dry face mask. She finally sat upright and sat against the headboard. "*Yeah*. It's him," she whispered.

"Miss Bernstein, would you like breakfast now?" her housekeeper, Beatrice asked.

She clenched her stomach and shook her head. "I'm okay," she said. "I'm not that hungry."

"Let me know when you do," she said. "Lea's in the library, has been all night, would you like me to send for her?"

Aryana smiled at Beatrice. "That's okay. She's probably busy."

Beatrice nodded, leaving Aryana alone. She tipped a head to the roof of the four-poster bed, a seven-point star burnt into the wood. "I'll do right by you, mom," she said, pressing a hand to her chest. "Promise."

She smiled to herself and held out her hand. She fabricated a flannel, and with her other hand she ran a finger across it as it became damp. She dabbed the sticky tears from her face.

"It's coming," she said, climbing out of bed. She grabbed her blue silk nightgown and headed to the balcony. She pushed the jarred balcony door open and stood there, clenching on to her stomach. "Beautiful," she said.

Aryana's home was on the front of a private beach. She watched as the waves crashed on the shore and the soft glow from the sun came in. She took a grip of the balcony fence and closed her eyes.

She pushed herself up to her tiptoes, embracing a gust of wind. "I need to meet him," she said.

She looked down at her wrist to see a silvery scar embossed on her skin, the symbol of the Roman goddess Venus; Aryana's sign; the sign of a Luminary; one of seven beings to protect the belief and knowledge of all magical existence.

"I knew it," she giggled, tracing a finger over the symbol.

Daniel stayed in his room with a collection of books that his father had stockpiled for him from the library. He'd told Daniel that he needed to have an edge over those *entitled* kids, and continued to tell him that they'd most likely paid for a ticket, while Daniel would have to do some work.

Over a week had passed before Daniel found himself falling to sleep with excitement bubbling away in his stomach. He slept beside a large black tome with '*A Brief History*' etched on the side in gold ink.

He would wake up and stare at it, trace a finger over the letters and fall back to sleep with a smile on his face.

"Daniel," his mother called. "Are you awake?"

He shot up in bed and rubbed his eyes, whacking the book from his side in a stretch. He picked at the sleep in his eyes some more as his mother called out again. "I'm awake."

"Dan," his father said, knocking on the bedroom door. "Come on! The water's hot, grab a shower."

"Yeah. I'm up."

The cool air gave Daniel goose pimples as he leaned out of the duvet to grab some clothes from the floor; a pair of exercise bottoms and a black hooded jacket. He rubbed his arms and flicked the hood up over his eyes before making his way downstairs.

"Happy birthday!" his parents shouted.

He glared at them from beneath the hood. *Oh, that's today.* He half-rolled his eyes. "Thanks," he said, pushing a large smile. "You know it's freezing in here, right."

His mother gave him a hug and pinched at this cheeks. "Sixteen! Oh, you're still my baby," she said. "Your grandparents are coming later, so how about you grab that shower. You could do with a good scrub and don't forget to brush your teeth."

"We've already told them you're going to Croft's. So you

need to look the part now," he father said with a wink.

Daniel had turned sixteen, a big deal on Templar Island. Before that age, they were children, and now, they're classed as adults, getting jobs, supporting families and siblings. Even getting married. So sixteen was a big deal. Except, Daniel couldn't feel the excitement. So much in his life was already changing, he didn't want to think of all the other things that could change.

"And don't forget to smile either," his mother said. "They'll probably bring some expensive presents."

I don't even want to move out, he told himself. Daniel hadn't grown up like most children from either side of the Rockies. In the Upperlands they wore mostly tailored clothes and employed people from the Lowerlands, the scrawnier types, people who could go unseen within their large estates. While those still living in the Lowerlands coped with the numerous fights and the unstable day-to-day living.

He turned to walk back upstairs before glancing at his parents. "Do the Upperlands really hate the Lowerlands?" he asked.

"Well that's nothing to do with us, we're right down the middle," his father said. "They should be worried at that school because you have talent, and that talent does not stretch to wealth."

"Exactly," his mother chimed in. "We're far from wealthy."

She chuckled. "Go shower. You're aunt and uncle are coming as well, so make sure you're wearing something nice."

"You still have that black shirt?" his father asked.

Daniel rolled his eyes. "Can I open some presents now?"

"Oi, cheeky," his mother chortled. "Wait until *all* the family's here."

After his shower, Daniel found himself stood in front of the mirror in his bedroom. He eyed the scowl on his face, pulling funny expressions while looking at himself. He was scrawny like his father. That meant when he did look for a job he'd end up sweeping filings or undesirable meats off shop floors.

He flexed his muscles at himself. *Could probably pass for Upperlands*, he grinned. The men from the Lowerlands had always been notorious for their large muscles, something they'd told themselves about it meaning they had a lot of energy in them.

Daniel wore a pair of black jeans, a white vest top and a black shirt. He couldn't help but wriggle in the itchy fabric of the shirt. His mother's parents came from the Upperlands, and she liked to try and keep to their standards whenever they visited.

"Daniel, honey, we have guests," his mother called from the bottom of the stairs.

Daniel sighed. "Great." He itched at his armpits as the fabric clung to the heat spots around his body.

When he reached the living room, it was cramped. Pushed

up against the far wall there was a long table covered in a white cloth and several silver plates. On the plates there were sandwiches and baked confectionaries, and at the end of the table there was a jug of fresh fruit juice.

Across the room, his grandparents sat, and they'd sit there from the moment they got to the house to when they left. He only had one aunt, and she was married with three children: Fillipa, Tygan and Roma.

The youngest of the three, Roma, bobbed passed Daniel with her gaze glued to the ground. Her eyes flamed a faint yellow and her strawberry blonde hair stuck to the back of her head. "Get here!" she shouted as she shrunk into a small sandy lizard.

Her brother was a much paler lizard with a grey spot on his back. He was a few inches longer with a sharp tail, camouflaging into the slate ground.

Their grandparents laughed and encouraged them to chase each other between sips of their hot drinks and nibbles of their biscuits. Daniel's father watched, scared to the spot that one of them could be caught underfoot at any moment.

A mixture of 'happy birthday's' and 'congratulations' boomed as Daniel entered the living room. He thanked them all and smiled with his teeth; a large toothy smile. He shook his grandfather's hand. A strong firm handshake. He pulled away and eyed a small pile of wrapped gifts under the table.

"Later," his father said from his chair in the corner.

Daniel rolled his eyes and joined his mother in the kitchen. She busied herself and piped the cream on Daniel's cake before looking up at him with a smile and some powdered sugar on her forehead.

"Is Jac coming?"

Daniel shrugged.

"Hun," she said and stretched a hand around to Daniel's back. "Why not?" she asked, pulling her hand away from him and patting at the sugar and cream she'd accidentally wiped on her son.

"I told him I was going away to school. And I haven't seen him since."

"When did you tell him?" she asked.

"Last week."

"Oh. Guess he wasn't happy," she said. "You'll have to see him before you go. Or—or you'll regret it."

"I will," he snapped. He leaned against the counter and looked up at the stone work of the ceiling. "I'll probably see him last minute, because you know how Jac gets."

She nodded. "That, I do," she said and kissed her son on his forehead. "Go back in there and talk to your family, they came here for you." She shooed him as she resumed piping.

Daniel dragged a chair from the kitchen and placed it between the food table and his father's chair. He looked at the sandwiches and grabbed at a few with the honey-cured ham. He placed them in his lap and one by one he ate them all.

I'm not in the wrong. Jac's in the wrong. He needs to apologize first. Daniel grinned to himself.

"Daniel," his grandfather said in a gruff voice from the other side of the room. Daniel looked up and met his grandfather's gaze. "Don't let this *school* make you forget your roots. 'Cause you came from right here," he said, and prodded the air with a finger.

Daniel nodded and smiled. He glanced around the room and saw his father behind him shaking his head. He smiled, *best not be rude, or bring up the fact that he's actually from the Upperlands and lives on the same tier as us. Then again, he never lets anyone forget where he came from.* "I won't," he replied.

A knock at the front door roused his grandfather's gaze and Daniel jumped up from his seat. He brushed the crumbs from his lap and rushed to the door, almost treading on the tail of a cousin.

He opened the door to Jac, standing there with a thin smile on his face. "Still not talking to me?" he asked. "Well, happy birthday." He turned, but before he could rush off, Daniel objected.

"Come in," he said, and headed back into the living room.

Jac closed the door behind himself as Daniel slipped back into his seat at the food table. Jac stood and glanced around the room; he didn't know anyone, except Daniel's father.

Roma tugged on Jac's three-quarter khakis. "Can help me?" she asked. Jac looked down at the wide-eyed girl. "My brother'th hiding. He'th a lithard." Jac grinned at the little girl.

"Your grandfather doesn't like me much either," Daniel's father leaned over and spoke to him. "Not sure if he likes anyone."

"Then how come he let you marry my mum and have me?" Daniel asked.

"That's a long story." His father smiled.

Through the rest of the evening Daniel sat at the food table and ate to his heart's content. Jac had moved around from the living room of awkward stares and stood in the kitchen.

Daniel's mother brought the cake out with 16 candles on top. Daniel grinned and blew them all out. His grandfather whined about the practice of blowing candles out on a perfectly good cake.

The cake was cut and Daniel received the first slice, before his mother portioned it out into another eleven slices. All of the cake went, some of it wasn't ingested, but his cousins made sure that all the cake went.

"They really *really* love cake," Roan's sister said to her. "Especially the good cake."

She smiled at her sister and turned to Daniel. "Do you want to open your presents?"

"Um, yeah!" He watched as a larger than usual pile of

presents was pulled out from under the table.

"Open them then." His mother nudged.

An awkward nostalgia knocked him as his want to tear the paper from the gifts reminded him of the eager ferocity he used to have. But then he had to remind himself that he was no longer a child.

He opened them all, and thanked everyone for their gifts; three dark tan leather-bound writing books for school. His aunt handed him a small polished red stone in the shape of an eagle. "Something to remind you of your childhood," she said.

He received clothes from his parents. Almost a new wardrobe, but they told him that they were for him to take to the school.

"Well, at least I'll have more clothes than friends," he laughed, and glance over to Jac. Their gaze met before Jac turned away.

Dust fell from the ceiling. Thud. The ground shook. They wobbled on their legs. Another thud came as more dust cascaded from the ceiling, coating everything and sending them into darkness. The children paused and surrounded their parents with bulging eyes and bitten lips, trying not to cry in front of their grandparents.

"Is everyone okay?" Jac asked, coughing up dust.

Daniel's mother flicked her arms and dull orange flames burst out on candles and the few gas lamps they'd kept.

"You should move," Daniel's grandfather said, scrunching up his already wrinkled face.

Three blunt knocks struck the front door. Daniel looked around and found everyone shooing him to answer it. He smiled back at them and turned to the front door.

A tall pale man with a pair of shorts and no t-shirt stood in front of him. He pushed an envelope out and glared down at Daniel with his large jewel embossed green eyes. He nodded and grunted towards his hands.

Daniel took the envelope and the man fled. "Thanks," he said, watching as the man took a nosedive over the cliff. "It's only a letter."

His aunt pressed to her chest. "Did you see him?" she asked, rolling her eyes.

"Is it from the academy?" his mother burst. "Open it!"

Daniel turned the letter over in his hands. It had been sealed with a blue wax stamp and the Academy's emblem, a 'C'. He peeled the wax away and flicked it to the ground. His fingers fumbled around as he pulled the letter from the snug envelope. His heart thumped in his ears. He squinted at the letters in the dark. His mother approached him, but before she tried to read it over his shoulder, he moved and cornered a candle.

"I leave tomorrow," he whispered, and folded the yellow paper.

"When?" his father asked.

Daniel turned around to his family. "Tomorrow morning," he said. He opened it up again and scrolled with a finger, "It says, 'You will need to be ready for 9 a.m. on the 28th of August. Failure to meet this and you will forfeit your place at Croft's Academy.'" He glanced up to see the half-lit smiles on all the faces, even on Jac.

It wasn't long after that when everyone went back to their homes. Jac waited behind. He helped clean. He waited until he was alone with Daniel.

"Sorry," he said. "I'm sorry I flipped. But you're going up there. And that's a big deal."

"I'll miss you," Daniel said.

"I'll miss you too. You know, at first I thought your mum was forcing you to go."

"She *did*. But now I wanna go. And like you said, it's a big deal." Daniel smirked.

Jac pulled a coin from his pocket and flicked it into the air. "I found this a few years ago, and it's been *pretty* lucky for me," he said and handed Daniel the coin.

"What is it?"

"A Euro, something like that, nobody will accept it, but I've had it since I moved out and had to kill for myself," he said. "Some poor rabbit was choking on it."

"You sure you don't need it?"

"Ha! You're the one going to the Upperlands, that's more of

a jungle than down here will ever be," Jac snorted. "I guess I should go. I don't want to get lost in the dark. Especially since there's a panther still out there."

"I'm glad he didn't go back for you."

"You're glad?" Jac asked. "I'm trying to live every day just in case he does."

They both laughed and hugged, then Jac left. Daniel sighed to himself and fell into the soft cushions on the couch.

"Tomorrow," he said to himself.

CHAPTER FOUR

"LAST NIGHT. Last morning. Last time I'll smell breakfast being cooked as I wake up," Daniel reeled off to himself as he bunched the duvet up around his body. .

His mother knocked on his bedroom door. "Daniel, honey," she said.

"Yeah?" he croaked, before wetting the back of his throat with the stale water on his bedside table.

"Want me to make you anything special?"

"I only want a tiny bit to eat," he said. "I'm not that—" he paused as his stomach grumbled.

His mother barged in. She smiled and rest both her hands on her hips. "You're going to eat a lot," she said as Daniel buried his face beneath the duvet. "I don't want you to waste away while you're not at home. And I don't want you to faint or make a scene on your first day. So, breakfast will be ready in 5 minutes."

He pulled the duvet from his face and gave in to his mother's pandering. It would be the last time that it would happen in a while, so he figured that he'd best make some use of it. "Fine."

She chuckled to herself and patted his feet at the end of the bed. "Good! It's a big breakfast, you know, with the tasty meats from the market." She smacked her lips together and rolled her eyes in delight. "Can't you smell it?"

Daniel had been to the Upperlands market with his father once or twice when he was younger, and they hadn't shopped from their much at all, but when they did, it was always for a special occasion, whereas Daniel had been to the Lowerlands market a few times, and there was no sure way you knew what meat you bought until it was cooked and already in your mouth.

"Well, you get ready," his mother continued, eyeing the large suitcase in the corner. "And bring that down as well, we don't want any unexpected surprises." She left his room and he poured a little will into closing the door.

I suppose school could be fun. Playing with power every day, he thought to himself. *But they'll have more of it.*

He dressed himself in a pair of light blue jeans, something that didn't say he was close enough to the Lowerlands that he could touch the trees, but also not that close to the Upperlands that he could smell the arrogance. He stood in front of the full-length mirror, rolling his shoulders and adjusting his clothes.

"Breakfast is ready," his mother called.

Daniel grabbed the suitcase and hauled it down to the living room. His mother stood in the doorway of the kitchen. She planted a kiss on his forehead as he walked by.

"We've got cooked *piggy* bits," she said, "and some other animals from the Trident Mountains." She bit down on her lip and stared at Daniel. Her eyes welled. "I won't cry," she said.

It wasn't long after breakfast that it was time to leave, it came in a shockwave, hitting the house and waking the settled dust. It was followed by a loud knock at the front door.

His mother wrapped her arms around him. "Love you," she said.

"Love you too, mum." He pulled away and grabbed the handle of his suitcase.

His father stayed seated. "Do us proud, son," he said.

"I'll try." He nodded back.

Daniel opened the front door to two tall tanned men stood brooding. They looked like twins, or clones, both with their shiny bald heads, muscle bulked bodies, and they both wore a pair of beige coloured shorts.

Daniel took a step back. "Hi," he said, giving them both a once over. They were the tallest people he'd ever seen.

"Daniel Satoria?" the man to Daniel's right asked. "Is that you?" the other questioned.

"Yeah," he said with a huge grin on his face. They didn't smile back, although he wasn't sure whether they could smile. He looked into their eyes, set deep on their faces, and looked for some sign of life behind the burning coals.

"We'll take your suitcase," the man to Daniel's left said, grabbing at the case in his hand. "Go say your last goodbye," the other added.

Daniel nodded as he looked passed them to the grandiose carriage on the ledge. It was a mix of white, creams, and gold, with two reins limp at the front. *Surely they weren't going to pull it*, he pushed away a smile.

Daniel's mother rushed up behind him. She wrapped her arms around him and smothered his face in kisses. "One last thing," she said, handing him a small plastic box. "It's just some sandwiches. Something to eat on your way, or you know, just so you don't starve out there." She gave him another hug.

"Thanks," he said, looking down at the container in his hands. *Probably ham. Not sure if I like ham anymore.*

His father placed a hand on his shoulder and pulled him in a hug. "You're going to do well out there, Dan," he said. "I can feel it, I've always known you were special, and you're going to do *great* things."

"All thanks to you too," he said. "I mean, the books, the

49

support. I could've ended up living in the woods in the Jac, but no, I—I am going to school."

His mother pulled him in another hug and his father wrapped his arms around them both. "I told your dad I wouldn't cry," his mother sniffled. "These are just—just allergies. The seasons changing and all that."

Daniel's tear ducts wet his cheeks slightly. He pulled out of the hug. "I'll be home soon, it's not forever," he said, pulling at his sleeves. "And when I do come home, I expect a pot of tea to be boiling."

"Oh, always!"

Before they could exchange anymore words, Daniel was escorted to the carriage. The door was opened for him and three metal steps popped out. He climbed in and sat beside the window to look back at his parents as they watched him from the front door.

"Are you afraid of heights?" he was asked.

"Are you kidding? I love heights!"

The man smiled at Daniel as he secured the carriage door shut. "Make sure to buckle up." He walked off to the front of the carriage. "You hear that? Said he loves heights."

Daniel waved to his parents from the window. He watched as his mother buried her head in his father's arms. He couldn't hear her crying, but he could see her pushing a cloth to her cheeks.

He fastened himself into his seat and glanced out to see the men getting into position. They tied the reins around their waists and over their shoulders, leaving most of the thick leather reins slack. Daniel didn't look back at his parents. He watched the men at the front of the carriage. *Are they gonna fly? Like that?*

The men were on their knees when the shift rippled through. Their backs hunched and their spines elongated. Their skins became matted fur in an array of shimmering colours. And their arms transformed into two large wings.

Daniel's jaw dropped as he pushed his face to the window. His breath fogged the glass. "What are they?" he whispered, wiping away the condensation with a sleeve.

Their feet and hands were now talons. Their heads, their faces scrunched up into small balls with huge amber eyes and hooked beaks.

They raised their heads and squawked into the sky before beating down on their wings and leaping into the air.

The carriage jolted. Daniel gripped his seat and the safety harness strap around him. He sighed, looking down at his parents as they grew further away before disappearing behind the cliff.

They'd soon left the Rockies when Daniel recalled the stories his parents had told him as a child, the stories of the *big move* from the Lowerlands to the new tier inside the rock faces that had once separated Templar Island into two sections. He smiled to himself in recollection. He was getting a better life for himself, like they had done before he was born.

The carriage dropped and Daniel's lungs pushed his heart into his throat. He stared out of the window and watched as the clouds dissipated around the carriage. He noticed a small village of wooden houses, like a toy set he swore he once owned as a child.

Dumph. The carriage hit the ground and Daniel whacked the back of his head. "Ugh." His head wavered on his shoulders.

The house outside was a large black house of stone and wood with a barn attached. It was surrounded by a patch of thick forest.

The front door of the house whirled open as a boy ran out. He slammed the door behind him and headed toward the carriage with his two large suitcases flip-flopping behind him, collecting dirt.

"Get them then," he commanded the men as the suitcases did their final roll. He gripped the door handle and yanked on it.

Daniel could only watch, this was his first real encounter with someone his age from the Upperlands. The boy snarled and climbed in, sitting opposite Daniel.

"Applied three years on the trot. Only got in this year," he said.

"I only transitioned a week ago."

"Bet she bribed 'im didn't she?"

"I doubt my mum has that kind of money."

"Must 'av some talent. Eh."

Daniel nodded. "Something like that," he grinned.

The carriage jolted, harder this time. The boy opposite Daniel almost fell in his lap. Daniel held a hand out and pushed at the boy's shoulder while he steadied the container.

The boy sat back and glared at Daniel. "My name's Tanner by the way."

"Daniel," he said. "So how come you got in this year then?"

"I think my parents got fed up. Probably bribed 'im," Tanner chuckled.

"Won't they miss you?"

"Nah, they work all the time," he said. "Probably forget I'm even at school." They sat in a moment of silence while he fastened himself into his seat. "Wonder what we'll be taught."

Daniel shrugged.

"I bet your mum did bribe 'im, if not with money," he said and winked. "Then what?"

"She wouldn't give anyone her energy like that. Why? Would your mum?"

"If she was ever around," he chortled. "She's quite powerful, don't think a little energy would go amiss to her."

Daniel butted his lips and nodded. He zipped his jacket up and pulled the hood over his head.

Each time the carriage jerked, the movement was sharp and

painful. Eventually the carriage was full, each of them acted more like Tanner than the last, but Daniel kept out of their small talks and childish arguments.

He stared out of the window and pretended to be asleep. They'd say "hey you" and try and bring him into the conversation. He bored himself in thought, thinking about what Jac would say if he was with him.

The carriage slammed against the ground for the last time, jolting the people inside. Daniel listened to the men and pushed his face to the window as he watched them shift at the reins. They high-fived and laughed.

"Great job, twins. Now, let them out," a familiar voice said. Daniel peered out of the window to see Reuben, resting on his walking stick.

The carriage doors swung open as the two men jumped on the roof of the carriage. They untied and kicked off the suitcases, one by one.

Daniel watched as cases flew off the roof. He climbed out of the carriage with his sandwich box in hand and stared up at them.

One of the men climbed down with Daniel's suitcase in hand. He nodded and handed it to him. "Thank you so much."

Reuben smiled at Daniel. "I see you made it!" he said. "And you've won over these guys. They're not usually *that* nice."

"Really?" Daniel asked.

"Yeah, maybe because they're *like you*. I found them in the slums years ago, but they still hold a grudge to people like me," he said.

Daniel glanced over to the two men. They stood with their chests puffed out on top of the carriage, and watched as people picked their luggage up and hurl abuse their way.

Reuben turned to face the rowdy crowds of people across the field as they picked up their belongings. "The tour will start when *you've* all quite finished *faffing* about," his voice boomed.

CHAPTER FIVE

GREY stone slabs marked the pathways with perfect square hedges, they ran alongside the main path up to the main building. Daniel followed at half pace, pulling his suitcase at the handle and keeping hold of his sandwich box.

The main building was made of three visible floors, and decorated with four white marble pillars across the front. Daniel stopped in awe, fascinated by the shimmer as the sun passed by the windows.

A boy pushed Daniel into a hedge. "Move!" he said, running along the path.

Daniel pulled himself back to his feet and brushed himself off. A few people sniggered as they passed him, but Daniel was too engrossed in his new surroundings. He picked up the handle of his suitcase, switching hands to keep the strain off. He continued to follow the path, staring at the building—it was the tallest building he'd ever seen. He smiled as he saw the carving above the entrance doors, *The Croft Academy for Templar Island's most prestigious children.*

"Prestigious," he repeated to himself in a mumble.

Reuben limped passed and climbed the steps to the front door. He turned. "You see the vast land?" he said, and signaled to everything behind Daniel.

Daniel turned to see twelve or so people grouped behind him, all listening to Reuben.

"My grandfather sculpted this land with his bare hands, every seed, every brick, each piece of marble. All fused together with these," he said, holding his hands up. "You are all capable of greatness with these two very tools."

Daniel found himself nodding and looking down at his own hands. *Capable of greatness.*

"And if I see a soul step foot on my grass or touch any of the hedges, I will take it as a sign of disrespect." He turned to a tall boy and shooed him away, "No, no, I'll guide *this* tour."

Reuben led the group inside. The foyer was alive with action; parlour maids and butlers crossed paths without making eye contact or uttering a sound. Along with them, student pushed passed, some carrying things, some leading tours, but everyone was doing something. Everyone had a purpose here.

"They're well-trained, and no, *my* maids and butlers are not here for you, not like they have been in your manor houses. This is a school, and they serve me. The only thing that they do here for you, is wash your clothes, and that's only if your clothes are deposited at the correct times," Reuben explained, his eyes scanned the crowd of worried faces. "Manuals will be in your rooms." He smiled and turned to his right. "This room is the assembly room, where you'll be required to turn up every Monday morning for the weekly briefing."

"He's a jerk," Tanner, the boy who'd been sat opposite Daniel whispered to him.

There was a moment of a silence while Reuben glanced at him, but only Daniel had seemed to notice.

"And the room on the left," Reuben said, heading to the open door at the opposite side of the foyer. "That's the dining hall. You'll have three meals a day here, and they'll be at set times of the day," he said. "Now, if you'd leave you luggage here. We'll go upstairs to see the classrooms."

Everyone dropped their suitcases off in the middle of the foyer. Daniel quickly unzipped his back on the floor and squeezed the sandwich box inside. Reuben headed up the staircase and the group followed. The stairs were made of a black-silvery stone. It made their shoes clack and their voices echo, even the slightest whisper.

On the second floor there were five closed doors. Each door was dark mahogany with a brass handle and a silver plaque that had the name of the teacher etched into each.

Reuben went through the names of each teacher and what they taught, but Daniel couldn't focus. He remembered a few of the classes; life energy, offensive and defensive energies, he remembered those because he thought he'd need to prove himself there.

Before they left the second floor to the ground floor, a boy spoke up. At first he held his hand in hand in the air and waved it, and then he fought his way to the front of the crowd. It was Tanner.

"What about the third floor?" he asked.

Reuben grinned; the lines in his face sunk deeper to cast a sinister shadow across his face. "It's not a good thing if you're sent to the third floor. That's *my* floor, with *my* chambers and office. I suggest you think wisely before acting out." He gulped and rolled down his sleeves. "Now, if you'd go downstairs, you'll find your room keys."

They all rushed off again, except Daniel, Reuben grabbed his shoulder. "Hi," he said.

"I am *just* enthralled to see that you survived," he said. "Come. I need to speak with you." He headed for the stairs to the third floor.

Daniel hurried after him, trying to keep with Reuben's pacing

59

strides. Daniel kept quiet, even though his heart was now firmly lodged in his throat and ached at his Adam's apple.

Reuben stood in front of a door; a large black wooden door with his name scrawled in brass letters at the middle. "Don't worry." He grinned as Daniel forced a smile. Reuben pushed the door open to his office.

An icy draft rolled out of the dark room. Daniel watched as Reuben flicked his wrists. Thick pieces of rope tied the drapes back and let light flood the room. It revealed a large dark pine desk with a black leather chair behind it and two leather settees in front of it. The walls were white-washed and the floor was black stone.

A real smile formed on Daniel's face. "This is the nicest room I've ever seen." He wriggled his bare feet in his shoes. He could feel how cool the stone.

"It is a nice office. When I'm being nice," Reuben said with a grin on his face. He limped to the seat behind his desk and sat.

"You can take a seat if you like," he said swiveling in his chair.

Daniel shook his head. "I'm okay."

Reuben raised an eyebrow and shrugged. "I have some things for you. I know you're less fortune in the financial area. And all those kids downstairs are very *competitive*."

Daniel grinned as if 'competitive' was emphasised to mean arrogant. "I'm sure they'll all mature into their power."

"Ha! You're right. They'll all mature. Just like you'll mature further. That's why I brought you here, because there's something about you. There's promise. And I know you won't take this school for granted," Reuben said. He opened one of his desk drawers. "I have top of the range electronics from the city."

"Oh?"

"A laptop and a phone," he said. "They're easy enough to use. And they're already set up to the server. I've listed the members of staff on the phone, and once you start making friends your contact list will build itself. Not literally, though."

"Oh," he said.

"You'll get used to them." He pulled them out of his drawer. A slim silver laptop and a white touchscreen phone.

Daniel's eyes beamed. He squeezed between the two leather settees, almost stumbling to Reuben's desk. "Um, whoa, thank you," he said.

"Have you read about the advances we've been making on technology?" Reuben asked, handing Daniel the electronics.

"I have, a tiny bit, my father said that it was all since you stepped in on the main council and pushed for the advances."

Reuben's cheeks flushed and he threw a hand in gesture. "Nah, it wasn't all me," he chuckled. "I just want what's best for everyone, and I have the finances to help that happen."

"They do weigh a bit," Daniel said. "But thank you so much.

I thought people might have phones here, I've never even touched one, I didn't reckon I'd be given one." He smiled.

"You're welcome, Daniel, and I'm sure I don't have to say this, but don't be making friends with the wrong sort," he said. "I expect great things from you, Mr. Satoria."

Daniel butted his lips together and nodded. "My parents do as well," he said.

"As they should! Anyway, I will let you get off, your room key will be downstairs."

"Thank you so much, Mr. Croft," he said. Daniel bowed slightly as he left with the laptop and phone resting on his arms.

As soon as Daniel got his key he didn't know what to do next. He found a map of the campus in a frame in the foyer. There were three buildings hand drawn on the map with routes that would get you there. Two of the buildings were dorm rooms, and he was standing in the other.

Daniel set off on the path to the boys' dorms. He found a path that he didn't recall seeing on the map. He turned and clutched the laptop and phone against his chest and set off to see where it led. A few steps in and a large barn was in view.

"You lost?" a voice asked from behind.

Daniel clenched the items in his arms harder. He turned to see Tanner from the carriage he'd taken stood a few steps away. "Which way are the dorms?" he asked.

He signaled with a thumb over his shoulder. "Big buildin',

back there?"

"Oh," he said.

"That's a nice laptop."

"Thanks," Daniel said. He walked off to the dorm rooms.

"Remember me? Tanner." He walked after him.

"Yeah, I remember."

"Cool. So, what's your room number?" he asked.

"Not sure, key's in my pocket. Somewhere on the third floor." He rushed.

"Me too! How come you didn't say you came from money?" Tanner asked, keeping pace with Daniel.

Daniel stuttered. "Didn't know I had," he said.

"Well, you must have some *serious* money, this was my third try, and Reuben said I was lucky to get in."

Daniel froze outside the dorm building. He glared at the two large life-size panthers carved out of white marble with polished turquoise gems for eyes. Daniel knew one thing about panthers, how they looked up close.

"Apparently, Reuben hand carved them himself, without using any of his power. All of them," Tanner said.

"All?"

"Yeah, there are two here, two outside the girls room and I heard that there are loads of smaller ones, just sitting around."

Tanner followed Daniel up the flights of stairs to his room. Each room had a card reader by the door handle, and each door handle only had one plastic key card. Daniel stood for a moment with the card in hand.

"Don't you have these at home?" Tanner asked. "My dad has them all around the house, mainly for his work spaces."

Daniel jammed the card into the tiny slot and the door opened up. "Nope, first time I've ever used one of these," he said, pulling the card back out.

The room was larger than his room back home. The bed had been made and there was a vase with yellow flowers on the bedside table.

"Why doesn't he just get a switch-lock?" Daniel asked. He placed the technology on his bed beside his suitcase. He walked over to the large glass window pane and touched the frame.

"Because they're cheap and you can break into those," Tanner chortled.

"Oh, of course," he said and turned back to Tanner. "So, is every room like this?"

Tanner shrugged and looked around. "Pretty much, anyway, I best go, I still need to unpack and I don't have any maid service to help."

Daniel chuckled as Tanner rolled his eyes. "Right, it's laughable," Tanner said as he walked off.

Daniel close the door and took a deep breath. He ran his hands up the back of his neck and sighed. *He's nicer than before. But I come from money now.*

CHAPTER SIX

LUNCH and dinner had passed, and Daniel hadn't moved from his room. He'd snacked on the sandwiches his mother had prepared and he'd unpacked all his clothes just the way he liked them.

He flicked the light switch a couple times and played with the alarm on his bedside table. He also had a competition with himself to guess the flowers in the vase. He didn't know what flowers they were, but he was sure they were *roses*, no, *lilies*. "They're obviously daisies," he told himself.

He hadn't touched Reuben's gifts. They were now on the chest of drawers beside the sink. He was wary of technology because he couldn't understand how it would help him and his abilities. To Daniel, technology meant lights in the house, and if you were lucky, a tape player.

His stomach grumbled. "Dinner?" he opened the handbook. Dinner had been served at 17:30. He rolled over the bed to his suitcase and grabbed a second box. "Always trust her to pack extras," he grinned.

He walked around, taking deep breathes and forcing himself to smile. He looked at himself in the mirror. "Hi, my name is Daniel, I'm from the Rockies, and I'm not from any riches, but I hope we can still be friends," he said, holding his hand out and watching himself in the mirror. He repeated this, over and over, each time he shot himself a different look; shock, horror, amusement.

The book he'd been reading slapped him as he dropped it on his face. He shot up and blinked at the darkness of his bedroom. The alarm on the bedside table flashed *02:54* He groaned to and let the book fall as he wrapped himself up in the duvet.

Daniel woke to a loud bang at his door. "Mum?" he groaned, and wrapped the pillow around his head.

The banging continued as Daniel picked his head up and checked the clock. *08:02.* He pushed himself out of bed to see who it was, but there was nobody at the door. Daniel turned and closed it.

I guess they already know then, he thought, throwing himself on his bed. He hoped to get more sleep before the assembly at nine.

Another thud hammered against the door. Daniel ragged the door open. The hall was empty; he looked down both ends of the hall again, this time he noticed a tall boy coming out of a room.

Daniel stepped out of his room. "Hey."

The boy turned. He scowled at Daniel. Daniel tried to figure him out, but the longer he stared into the black ink of his eyes, all thought seemed to wash away.

"Yes?" he asked.

Daniel blinked as sounds knotted in his throat. His gaze fell as he brushed a hand through his hair. "Nothing," he said. He stumbled back in his room.

A bleep rang out in Daniel's ears, sending him to the bedroom floor. He pulled himself back up from the chest of drawers and swayed on the balls of his feet.

He glanced at the clock across the room. *08:47*. "Huh?" *Crap. I'm going to be late!* He rushed around as the dizziness wore off and fumbled around to get dressed. He almost forgot to put shoes on, and it hadn't crossed his mind until his feet touched the cold hallway. He'd never had to wear shoes at home before. At least not every day.

On his way down the stairs he slipped into his jacket and fell against the window at the bottom. He rubbed his arm and elbow as he adjusted the jacket properly.

He found himself on the path to the main building. He

reached a queue walking towards the entrance and joined it. It seemed that Tanner also had the same idea of being *almost* late.

Tanner grinned. "Over slept?" he asked.

Daniel nodded. "Just a little," he said quietly.

"Well, my stupid alarm clock doesn't even work."

"Mine does."

"Lucky you. I thought this school was supposed to be *prestigious*, it seems like a lot of it is about Reuben. I even heard his stuck up nephew comes here."

Daniel grinned and Tanner continued to reel off more issues he'd found with the school.

They reached the assembly hall. It was bigger than Daniel had imagined. He sat at the back and could see the front of the stage perfectly. There were over 20 rows in front of him, and at the front of the hall was a platform and a podium. Both were empty. To the side of the stage there were several teachers seated with their hands in their laps and smiles on their faces.

Reuben took to the sea of pale faces. "Good morning," he said. His voice echoed around the hall. "This term we welcome fifty *new* students, and welcome the hundred joining us from vacation."

"One hundred and *fifty* people?" Tanner whispered to Daniel, who nodded and continued to stare up at the stage.

"I would also like to welcome a new teacher, she's been an aide of mine for many years but I've offered her a permanent teaching role." Reuben turned to the teachers. "I would like you all to give a warm welcome, to Chey Coran, the new Life Energy and Skills teacher."

Everyone clapped as Chey stood. Her dark blonde hair was all scooped back into one long wispy ponytail. She smiled and gave a weak wave before sitting back down.

Reuben coughed his throat clear before speaking again. Daniel watched, while something else vied for his attention; at first he thought it was Tanner tugging at his jacket, but it wasn't physical. He cocked his head to the right and saw the boy from the hallway. He wasn't staring back, he was chuckling away to the person beside him.

"All new students must stay seated to collect their schedules. The rest of you may now leave for breakfast." Reuben turned and left the platform.

Daniel's schedule said that his first class was straight after breakfast, Life Energy and Skills with the new teacher. He had nothing on Tuesdays, and on Wednesdays he had Mythical Energies. Thursday he had Offensive and Defensive Energies. That was the only class he had with Tanner. Daniel grinned at the thought of jumping into practice straight away.

"Are you coming for breakfast?" Tanner asked.

"Yeah, sure."

The cafeteria was a large L-shaped room with counters connecting to a kitchen along the far wall. It reminded Daniel of the time he'd snuck into an old factory with Jac, the large metal tables and adjoining chairs, the huge conveyor belt counter where parts of metal and rock were fed through from different rooms.

"So what are you getting?" Tanner asked, handing Daniel a tray.

"I'm not that hungry," he lied, with one hand clutching his rumbling belly as he glanced down the aisle of food. "Probably some beans and toast."

Tanner snorted. "For a rich kid you sure don't have a rich appetite," he said.

Daniel raised his eyebrows and handed Tanner a wry all-knowing smile; *only hanging around with me because I have money, or fortunes, when I'm actually the poorest person here.* And Daniel couldn't understand what made for a *rich appetite.*

They plated their breakfasts and sat at an empty table. Daniel was all too quick to notice the boy from the hallway seated across from them. He stared for a moment, watching as a girl with blonde hair wrapped her arms around a boy with a small afro of curls. She was first to notice Daniel; she looked at him and winked. Daniel's gaze dropped, as he grinned to himself. He looked back up at them, and the two guys were glared back with their bewitched black eyes.

"I've got Mythic study today," Tanner said.

"Oh, I have that new teacher."

"Got her tomorrow. Thursday should be good though, get to learn some *tricks*," he said with a large smirk across his face. "I got told they make you fight first day. You know, learn as you do kinda thing."

Daniel glanced back up at the table and the people were gone. He butted his lips together as he replayed the image of the girl winking at him. It sent an electric charge through his stomach as he smiled.

"The blonde?" Tanner asked.

"Huh?"

He spooned beans in his mouth. "Well you're not exactly subtle," he said.

Daniel gulped. "Oh. Why? What do you know about her?"

"Same thing everyone else knows, she's a tease, and a bit of a leech."

"How do you know?"

"If you were here yesterday, then you would have been able to talk to people, nobody likes her much. They had some pretty harsh words to say."

Daniel looked down at his untouched food. He pushed the tray aside and gulped at the orange juice.

"You gotta eat," he said.

"Why?" Daniel asked.

"'Cause you need strength, power, will, y'know the sorta stuff that gets you ahead in a place like this," he replied in a matter-of-fact tone.

Daniel would've liked to introduce him to Jac, both stubborn, but different in how they became that way. Jac would've hated him, Tanner being rich *and* arrogant, and Tanner would hate Jac for being poor and strong-willed.

"You know I read a bit before I came here," Daniel said.

"Why would you do that?"

"Because I thought everyone would've been so far ahead of me."

"But you're parents are paying good money for you to be taught this," Tanner grinned.

Daniel hummed and nodded. That was right; Daniel was becoming 'friends' with Tanner because of the money. It was like he was somehow unwillingly infiltrating the inner circle of the rich people.

CHAPTER SEVEN

DANIEL made sure he was early to his first lesson. He marched up the stairs to see crowds of people all making their way into the rooms. Daniel stood at the door of Ms. Coran's room and looked for a free seat. There was one free on the front row, right in the middle. He smiled at the people at either side and took the seat.

The room was bare with white-washed walls and a maroon polished floor. No pictures, two windows, and several rows of chairs.

Chey wandered into the room with a smile on her face. "Well, good morning," she said. "First class, *ever*, for us all." She inhaled and took a look around the room.

Something caught Daniel's eye from the corner of the room. He was sure it hadn't been there when he came in; a small table with a teakettle, a cup and some cutlery. Beside it was a chair. He met Chey's gaze and pushed his eyes to his hands, fidgeting in his lap. She continued to look at him.

"You," she said, pointing at Daniel.

"Me?" he squeaked. He cleared his throat as his face flushed. "Me?"

She nodded. "Please stand." Daniel stood and tucked his hands in his pockets. Chey grinned. "Take your hands out, please. I have a little task for you. Don't worry, the rest of the class will be doing the same."

Daniel nodded and let his hands flop to his side.

"In fact, let's swap places, so that everyone can see," she said. She moved forward and gestured to him.

Daniel had now taken Chey's spot at the front of the room, while she sat in his seat, her legs crossed and arms folded.

"Outstretch your arms and cup your hands," she said. Daniel obeyed. "Now. Pool your power, your energy, *feel* it strong in your centre. It will be warm. When you feel this you need to pull your hands apart slowly," she said. "It should reveal *your* raw power." She had enticed the room into silence, and Daniel couldn't stop staring at her lips.

Daniel glanced down to his hands after he realised that Chey had stopped speaking. He tried to keep focus, but everyone in the room was staring.

"Take your time," she said. Her words washed over the class.

Daniel pressed his hands together. He closed his eyes. He felt a cool tingle zip down his chest and drizzle through his arms to his fingertips. He opened his eyes to peek at his hands and he noticed Chey's lips moving; to him they were just moving. "Pull," she repeated, "pull." Except this pull was imminent, it embraced him without order.

Like the flick of Reuben's wrist, and the moment had passed. However in that moment, seconds were filtered through as minutes. A fine vibration numbed his hand and rippled them apart. There was a crackle and a flash of gold.

Chey stood with her lips parted, ready to speak. She clapped instead. "Impressive. Not many can *master it* on their first try," she said. "Take a seat, Mr. Satoria."

Daniel stood with his hands in the air, shaking from the aftermath. He nodded and took his seat. People around him stared like he'd done something to offend them.

"I guess Daniel has set the bar," Chey said. "That is the task of today, I hoped, well I didn't hope that it would take you long to do this task, but normally people just need to settle into their environment first. Please don't be discouraged, awaking your raw potential is basic, after that I can teach manipulation of *that* raw energy," she continued, but to Daniel her voice had become a distant haze. "Two basic facts, if you're a boy, your flare will be blue-*ish* and if you're a girl, then your flare will border violet, light purple. A little bit of a gender stereotype there, but that's how it is."

The room woke with motion as people stacked chairs to the side of the room. Daniel stayed seated as heat gorged his muscles and flared up in his cheeks. He caught something, he knew something; his flare was neither blue nor purple, but the rest of the class had already realised that.

Daniel stood and someone pulled the chair from beneath him.

"Daniel?" Chey called from the front.

Daniel looked up to see Chey's face touched with concern. "What is it?"

"We should talk," she said, ushering him to the front of the room. She offered him a seat and forced another chair her way.

"Yeah?" he asked. He looked over his shoulder at the rest of the students trying out the task.

"That's some special flare you have, and I know someone else like that. You probably know him." She grinned, looking deep into his eyes.

He pulled away and frowned, something ached at the back of his throat and the nape of his neck. He rubbed at it with a hand. She reached out a hand and touched his. There it was. A taste, sweet, undoubtedly it was a fine energy, but it wasn't his. "Who?" he asked. He stared at her hand on his and pulled away.

"Reuben. He comes from a rich bloodline," she said, "not *finance* but substance."

Daniel looked up. "What colour is it?"

"He can change it," she said. Her smile spread. "A flare is energy in its rawest form. When you've got it, you'll know, because the next step is control. Truth being, I didn't think anyone could do that first time. In fact, I was counting on you burning out. It would've been a lesson on not being able to touch raw power without first building an immunity to it."

"Immunity?" he picked out.

"You felt the pain, right?"

Daniel nodded. Chey reached out her hand again.

"You build over the pain. And I figured a scrawny boy wouldn't be able to handle it," she said.

He ignored her remark. "Shouldn't you tell them?"

She smiled and patted his shoulder before standing and walking to the centre of the room. She held a hand high in hopes of getting their attention. They were too busy talking and forcing themselves to turn blue and purple in the face.

"Class!" She clicked her fingers. "Settle down, there is something I need to tell you all. Daniel has had training," she said. They all turned and stared and Daniel. "However, you guys need to try hard, you need to *tap* into yourself, and then *exert*."

Daniel stared. Of course she way lying, unless she knew about the books he'd been reading, and of course they touched on the topic of flares, but from what he'd read, flares took time to develop.

He heard their insults, strained beneath their breaths. Some of them would've found that this was a common ground with Daniel, having something that makes you less fortunate.

They haven't heard, he thought as Chey turned to walk back to him. *I'm practically from the Lowerlands.*

"I didn't mean to out you back there," she said with a sympathetic look in her eye and no smile. "But it's better they think you're a know-it-all instead of being *better.*"

"I came here to learn, not make friends," Daniel said.

"A good motto, because it's going to be hard for anyone, coming from the," she said, mouthing the word, "*Lowerlands.*"

Daniel couldn't process what she was trying to get at, and before he could start she'd moved away, apparently there had been a knock at the door, but nobody else seemed to have heard it. He turned to see Chey talking to another teacher, he poked his head into the room and glared at Daniel as they locked eyes. When Chey closed the door, she brushed the back of her hand against her rosy cheeks.

"Mr. Croft would like to see you," she said. "His office is the one with the big door on the *third* floor."

Daniel nodded and left the room without anyone noticing, but he could still hear their shallow whispers filter through the air about him. Daniel smiled; his parents had taught him how to control his shifts early on in life so that they wouldn't control him. It didn't work out that way, but it was one more thing people would be whispering about when they found out.

A tall pale man wearing only a pair of black shorts stood at the bottom of the stairwell. Daniel recognised him as the one who'd delivered the letter. "What's your business with Mr. Croft?"

"I've been told to go and see him," he said. He pointed at the room he came from. "The teacher in there sent me."

"Ahh, Daniel. Kid from the Lowerlands."

Daniel nodded at him. "Yeah, you delivered my letter."

"I did. I requested to. Y'know I came from the Lowerlands. Was an orphan, like many of us here," he said with a smile.

That was another thing he argued with himself about. What if people found out he could still shift? Would they *employ* him, or *enslave* him? One thing for sure was he wouldn't be scrawny any more.

He knocked twice on the office door and before going in for the third, the door swung open. Reuben stood over his desk pouring a dark amber liquid from a glass decanter into two square glasses. He looked up to see Daniel, and after wiping the lip of the glass his set it down and began clapping.

"A celebration, to that unique flare of yours," Reuben said, signaling for Daniel to come closer. The door slammed shut behind.

"You know about *that*?" he asked.

"Well, as soon as Chey had seen it, she *told* me," he said and tapped two fingers against his temple. Daniel caught the reference, telepathy; passing energy to another in the form of words.

"Cool, she also told me about your flare."

"Great. So, are we going to toast?" he asked.

Reuben handed Daniel one of the glasses. Reuben knocked the glasses together, he grinned with wide eyes.

"A toast to your power," he said, clinking the glasses again. "I knew there was something special about you." He brought the glass to his lips, but Daniel stared blankly. "Now we drink."

The glasses were clinked again for the last time, before they both knocked the liquids to the back of their throats. Daniel's face became taut with shock as the liquor touched his tongue and fired up at the back of his throat. Reuben chuckled as Daniel smacked his lips and tried to gulp the sensation away.

"It'll grow on you," he said, "oh, and don't go around telling people about this. Alcohol is only permitted out of school grounds."

Daniel gulped at his dry throat. It continued to ache with the lasting taste of the sour alcohol. "What does a different flare mean?"

"To some, it can mean nothing but a pretty colour. It isn't, it's all up here." Reuben grinned. "You can still shift, can't you?"

"Yeah," Daniel said, his mouth widened to a smile.

"Good, because I thought I was wrong for a second. We do hold a class here for the select few of you that do have that *power*, I shall enroll you. It's every Friday. There are about twenty students currently. Oh, it's in the barn, just around the back."

Daniel couldn't help but smile. "I didn't think it was normal."

"Perfectly. I'm guessing that it's given you grief. You have worry marred on your face," Reuben said. "But it's the jealous people you should be wary of; they're all out for their own ends," he said, "and the rich kids."

CHAPTER EIGHT

TANNER rushed up behind Daniel as he stood in the queue at the cafeteria. Daniel was wiping his fingers across his sweaty palm, touching the tiny bumps left behind. Tanner tapped him on the shoulder.

"Hello," he said and waved a hand in front of Daniel's face.

"H—hey!"

"I heard what happened. I mean, *we* all heard. You were sent to Mr. Croft's office," Tanner whispered. "What did he want you for?"

Daniel blinked. He closed his eyes tight and rubbed them. "I have a new class," he said, and opened his eyes. "Wasn't anything bad," he said with a grin.

"What? What is it?"

Daniel turned to Tanner. He wiped at his mouth and rubbed his tongue against the lingering taste. "I can still shift, so I'm being enrolled in a class for it, on Fridays," he said. He picked up a tray from the pile and worked his way along the aisle.

"How come I didn't know?" he asked as he kept with Daniel's pace.

"I've known you for..." he butted his teeth down against his lips. "For what? A couple of hours?"

"Oh, I s'pose, but it woulda been nice to know," Tanner said, "what about your flare then? I think *they*, all know." He tipped his head to the cafeteria of people. Daniel could feel all their eyes on him, even from those who were engrossed in conversations and eating their lunches.

"That's fine." Daniel picked up a cellophane wrapped sandwich from the counter. Tanner arched his brow as he eyed the sandwich. "It's to go."

"No. I have a table over there." Daniel wanted to object, but before he could say another word, Tanner had pulled him from the spot. There were a few other people sat around the table. "This is Daniel. Daniel, these three are from my Mythic's Class, Herik, Dena, and Lianne."

They exchanged awkward greetings, awkward because Daniel knew what they were thinking about him, just like he knew how the people in his first class were talking about him.

He set his tray on the table and sat, trying not to scowl down at his food.

"We heard you could shift," Herik said in a gruff voice.

"Well, can ya?" Lianne began, brushing her long fair hair from her face.

Daniel paused before he unwrapped his sandwich. *How do they know? I've only just told Tanner. Was I being loud?* He couldn't remember.

"So?" Lianne continued.

"Um. Yeah," he replied, "I can grow wings on my back, and I can shift into these birds sometime. Well, just the one bird actually. Can any of you?"

"No, but my older brother could. He was killed though," Lianne said. She shrugged, "well he wasn't that nice anyway. A complete waste if you ask me."

"Nobody should be killed. Nobody *deserves* to die," Daniel said.

Lianne's face contorted with disgust. "You didn't even know him," she said, gritting her teeth. "Eh. Actually, I'm going, are you guys coming?" She didn't glance at Daniel before leaving the table with Herik and Dena.

"Nobody," Daniel said quietly.

"She knows her stuff. Try not to annoy her," Tanner said.

"What do you mean?"

"I think she said her parents are ambassadors or something,

close to *royalty* anyway." Tanner shook his head and sniggered, "and she's in our Offense Class as well, so let's hope you're not paired."

"You mean, like, Luminary royalty?" Daniel asked.

"Exactly."

"Great," Daniel said with a thin grin as he unwrapped his sandwiches.

Tanner left Daniel to eat, he spoke another word of warning about Lianne's heritage and it reminded Daniel why they were friends; they all thought he came from some kind of heritage, or money at least.

Daniel took a bite of his sandwich before looking up to see a blonde-haired girl jump into the seat opposite. She smiled and gazed into his eyes while she played with her hair and giggled.

He looked around to see if the guy she was with earlier was around. "Can I help you?" he asked.

"Do you *want* to help me?" she asked and winked.

Daniel coughed into his hands. "It depends."

"You're real strong you know. I can feel your heat, inside that core of yours. That warm centre," she said, closing the space between them.

Daniel jumped to his feet. He grabbed at his tray and she slammed her fist down on it. The tray broke in two and everybody stared, but nobody had witnessed the event, and those who did wouldn't speak up.

"Oops," she giggled.

He put the pieces of plastic into one hand and picked up his sandwich. "Sorry, what's your name?" he asked.

She bit down on her glossed lip. "Carlie."

Daniel butted down his lips and tried to stand still. She continued to glare from beneath her hooded eyes, trying to make them meet. Daniel clenched his jaw as he watched her bite her lip harder.

She took a hold of his hand. "So what's your name cutie?"

Daniel's heart pounded. He dropped the plastic pieces and she dropped his hand. Everyone stared. He blinked at a dizziness in his head and took a deep breath.

He turned around to look for her. But she was gone.

"Looking for someone?" a light voice asked, and Daniel turned to face him.

"Nope," he replied. He turned to walk away before stopping. Stunned with a crucifying pain in his shoulder. He winced and almost fell, but the pain vanished as he touched it.

"You're a bit of a teacher's pet aren't ya?" the boy asked over the loud cafeteria.

Daniel swore he knew who it was, but he didn't turn. Instead, he walked, he paced until he reached the main door. He didn't look back, his body jolted, and he kept on walking. Before he could stop—he was lost.

He looked around. He was heading into a forest. He'd

approached the barn he'd seen yesterday. The door swung open, he fell in shock as he glared out into the darkness. He gathered himself and rushed back to his room.

He stopped at the entrance and leant against the wall beside the marble carving. He took a deep breath and looked at the handiwork as he calmed his nerves and the acid swishing in his stomach. His eyes traced the curved spine of the panther until he found their paws, tied to their pedestals with vines of ivy. With a hand over his chest he could feel the thick pumping beneath tingle his sweaty palm. He rubbed his hands on his t-shirt before heading into the building.

He was soon stood outside the door to his room. He fumbled around in his pockets for his room key, but it wasn't there. He double checked to be sure.

"Is this it?" a person to his right asked.

There was nobody there. He turned to his left, and nothing. He did a full circle, watching as a fist pulled back and then whacked him in the side of his face. The pain was a soft pulsation at first, until it drained colour and fogged up his right eye. Black. White. Blue. Red. It flashed harder and pulsed deeper. Daniel wobbled on his feet while his head wobbled on his shoulders.

"Again—Jasper?" someone asked between snickers.

They cracked their knuckles. "No, let's see what he can do. See what he's made of," they replied.

Daniel couldn't hear, or speak, and his sight fell heavy and blurry. He stumbled into the wall and pushed himself up as he caught a glimpse of the two guys. One of them he'd seen before; the guy from that morning.

"Should I?" he asked.

"Mark, I said no."

Daniel gasped as his eyes watered and burned at the side of his bruised face. Jasper and Mark chuckled while Daniel wavered to keep still on his feet. The swelling on his face had turned into a light fleshy pink and his eyes were bloodshot.

"What can *you* do?" Jasper spat.

Daniel opened his mouth to reply, and instead he sucked in air like he was about to drown.

"Looks like a fish," Mark chuckled.

"Because he is out of water, aren't ya? People like you should go to schools down there, with the other *scum*." Jasper joined Mark in laughter. "Now you can hit him, use some of that ice stuff, the one Rik said was *too* advanced."

"Oh, or some water," he said.

Daniel tried to control his wobbling and focus his eyes. He made out the dorm key in Jasper's hand, and then something convulsed in his knees and ate the balls of his feet; an infectious cramp. He bent his knee and clenched his teeth, biting the inside of his cheeks until they bled. He tried to make his hands into fists, but they wouldn't tense up.

"Fight back then," Mark said with a huge grin on his face. He closed his eyes and poised himself with his hands to his side and palms facing Daniel.

"Summon and simmer," Jasper chanted in a whisper.

Mark's fingertips turned white, and slowly the white made his skin thick. He wriggled his fingers and the ice spread to his wrists. Mark glared at Daniel's swollen face, he didn't have a clue if Daniel was looking at him or not, and although it was Daniel's plan to undermine Mark and dodge the attack. He couldn't. .

Mark thrust his hand towards Daniel's chest, the ice spread and clung to his t-shirt and latched to his skin. Daniel collapsed to his knees, coughing and tearing at his t-shirt. *Why?* He screamed at himself.

Mark and Jasper high-fived, their mixed energies cancelled each other out. They stared. Jasper drew his leg back and laughed as Daniel flinched.

Daniel's fingers trembled closer to his chest as the cold burn disappeared and the ice melted away. "W—W—Why?"

"You're not welcome. And I bet that Tanner, I bet that you lied to him didn't ya," Jasper said.

A heat rose inside Daniel and his temperature evened out. He pat his chest to find his clothes were dry.

"You learnt a little Lowerlands trick." Jasper scowled.

Daniel jumped up from his knees, it reminded him how flexible he had to be, coming from the Lowerlands where you were taught to climb trees and fend for yourself. He stood up and puffed out his chest. *I'm not weak!* He clenched his hands into fists. "You should probably work on that *ice* thing,"

Mark charged forward as Daniel planted his feet. He swallowed hard and swung his fist. He hit him on the bridge of his nose. A steady flow of blood left him stunned and Jasper bewildered. Daniel went on to try and hit Jasper, only to have his hand whacked away.

"Mark's not stupid, he'll get you back. And I'm not stupid enough to make the mistake in the first place," Jasper said. He grinned in Daniel's half-swollen face. "Take your card, and stay in your room." He flicked it from his fingers to Daniel's feet, and then walked away with Mark in tow and a trail of blood dotting the floor.

Daniel opened the door and threw himself to his bed. His face was cushioned by his pillow, but it still hurt. *Did that just happen?*

CHAPTER NINE

DANIEL stayed in his room. He stood in front of the mirror and touched the swollen side of his face. The lump beneath his eye discoloured from fleshy pink to a dark purple. It spread into a thick blue. He cursed at his reflection and touched the lump for the last time.

He shut the curtains and turned all the lights off. "What would she say?" he said, throwing himself to his bed. "Sleep it off, it'll heal, or *you've been through much worse*." The pillows were cold as he shoved his face in them. "She was right, she? She?" he laughed to himself. *I've gone mad. Crazy. Insane. I'm speaking to myself.* It hurt in his cheeks as grinned to himself.

The alarm clock sounded. He grabbed his pillow and

rammed his face against it. "This—is—not—happening," he said. "I've only just gone to sleep." He'd slept for ten hours. He whacked the top of the alarm clock. The morning alarm sounded again fifteen minutes later, and then several knocks pounded down on his bedroom door.

"You okay? I heard your alarm. You up?" Tanner asked, his voice was muffled behind the door.

Daniel slammed his hand on the snooze button again and grit his teeth. He touched the throb beneath his eye and noticed the swell twitching at his vision.

"Gonna have a lie-in and a wander around," he said. "Take the whole school thing in."

"Um. See you at lunch then," Tanner replied.

The crease in his smile caught his eye and turned his smile into a wince. Daniel knew what he had to do; go see Jac, but he couldn't go home with his face like that. Jac would know, Jac grew up defending himself. Daniel only wished he'd learned how to defend himself properly beforehand.

He pushed his ear to the door; there was no sure way of knowing if Tanner had gone. He paced across the room and occasionally stopped by the window. He sighed and opened the window up to its fullest. "Three floors up," he said to himself, poking his head out. *Need to turn into a bird! I can't just grow wings, they'd notice. I need to be something people wouldn't take a second look at. I need to be a bird.*

Daniel took several steps back. He closed his eyes and exhaled slowly. He took his t-shirt off and put a jacket on, zipping it up to the top. He wasn't risking another t-shirt being ripped.

He couldn't take a huge run-up; the room wasn't that big. He took his run-up and leapt out of the window, his body curved in a downward swoop. He fell half a floor before his swift shift and the wind stopped hitting his face and instead, aided him. He opened his now pale blue eyes to see a tall metal fence ahead with an intrinsic ivy pattern crawling it.

He flew over the gate in the smallest of bird forms he could think of. His golden feathers would go undetected beneath the sun. He homed in on the Lowerlands. A unique beacon of light broke inside his head and steered him.

His wings grew restless as he reached the halfway point. The Trident Mountains were the middle, and he was too late to pull out and go around, he was heading for a dip in between two of the hills. He continued full throttle.

It was once said that small people with small thick arms and legs wondered that part of Templar, *small folk*, and Daniel was hit with the realisation that these people could exist.

His wings quaked on his small bony bird back. He ducked and dipped, trying to stay low, but not too low that he was able to see beneath the treetops. There was something hot and sticky following him; his feathers stuck to the air and slowed him down. But he continued with force, craning his neck and pushing his wings out further each flap. He'd pushed, and pushed, finding himself hit with cold air as he made it out.

He squawked. This side of the mountains was lower. He strained his neck to stop the decline and swooped closer to the ground. His feathers flayed from his skin and drifted off behind him. He looked back, and gave in, collapsing into a rolling heap at the bottom of a grassy mound.

Back in his human form, Daniel lay in his grass-stained clothes, concealed in the long grass. He broke from the fetal position; arms twitched and legs kicked from the cocoon of his body. He coughed until his face turned red and his eyes puffed. "Never—again!" he thumped at his chest.

He stood and coughed a final time before throwing his arms down by his side and pushing himself up to his tiptoes. "Ah," he sighed. He relaxed his body and rubbed at the dirt on his knees. He turned and looked up; the three mountains cast their shadow over him, famed for looking like a trident. He rolled his head down and scanned the dip he broke through. He noticed his feathers scattered up the hill. "I should go back."

Daniel looked the mountains over again. *I need to go.* His body snapped back into the bird. He forced himself into the air, pushing himself higher and higher, debating where to go. *See Jac. Go see Jac.*

He flapped his wings furiously and crossed the grey stone

flats of the Rockies. He fought with himself to go home, but he soon reached the canopy of trees in the Lowerlands.

He found a clearing, and soon enough he bowed his head and aimed for it, manoeuvring a land mid-shift, only falling slightly once the wings were gone.

The cold dirt of the forest floor sent ripples of excitement through Daniel's body. The feeling was natural to the calluses that gave him an immunity to thorns and sharp stones.

"Daniel?" Jac said, pushing his way through a bush with a large stick in hand. His forehead creased with question. "But—what?"

"Jac! How'd you—"

"Weird, I know. Except I don't *really* know," he said, itching at his arm as he stumbled closer to Daniel. "What's that?" he nodded.

Daniel turned slightly to see if there was something behind him. He glanced back to see anger and sympathy in Jac's eyes.

"Your eye," he said, tipping his chin.

Daniel touched the swelling and opened his mouth to speak. He stuttered before biting the inside of his lip. "Some. Um." He coughed into his fist. "Well you were right."

"I didn't think they'd do that. At least annoy them first."

"I don't even think I did that," Daniel replied, "but I did put up a fight."

"I can imagine. And honestly, I thought you'd be able to

handle it, especially after you handled that panther."

That was the worst part—he thought he could handle himself as well; he went away thinking he knew more because he'd been reading about it since he was young. Yet nothing he learnt could match a punch or the pain of ice breaking his skin.

"So, what are they teaching you?" Jac asked.

"Only had one lesson so far, I learnt that I had a *weird* flare," Daniel replied. He watched Jac stretch until his bones clicked.

"What kind of weird?" he asked. "How weird?"

"It's gold," Daniel said. "I think that's why they beat me." His face contorted.

"*They*? I thought it was a fair fight!" Jac twirled the stick in his hand.

Daniel grinned and took a step back. "Well, it was more of an ambush. But I did get a few fair shots in."

Jac rolled his eyes. "Gee, I thought the people in the Lowerlands being violent to their gifted was something, but I thought it would've more civilized up there, you wo-"

Daniel butted in. "Well apparently not, in fact it's like the higher your status, the more people can hate on you."

"Status?"

"Oh, yeah. Someone thinks I'm really rich, he thinks I bought my place in the school."

"Why?" Jac laughed.

"I was given some electronics. This laptop and a phone."

"What?"

"Erm. Well they're these electr—"

Jac butted in. "I know what they are. We make them down here. Who gave you them? I know how much they're sold for, and you can't afford them."

"Reuben, he said it was to even the playing field."

"Don't go changing on us," he said as he drew circles in the dirt with his stick.

Daniel grinned. "I don't think I could, if you could see them, you'd know I wouldn't change."

"So you came here to be taught some tricks, ay. Let's face it, you'd rather play dirty than follow the rules of your school," Jac looked up at Daniel with a grimace. "You could always try something forbidden."

"Forbidden?" Daniel laughed. "Let's not jump to extremes!"

"You're right, I mean, mixing energies is probably too advanced for you."

"Mixing?"

"So you're interested?"

"If you give me something real, then maybe."

"Real," Jac laughed, slamming his stick into the dirt with a thud. A small vibration buzzed through the ground. "People can usually only use one at a time." He rested his arm on his stick and counted on a hand. "There's fire, earth, air, water, and then pure energy."

"And we can only summon one at a time?" Daniel said. "Anymore, and you'd kill yourself.'

Jac chuckled. "No, anymore, and you'll scare the crap out of anyone who tries punching you."

"And get thrown out of school in the process."

"It's not the worst that could happen."

"Killing myself would be the worst."

Jac resumed drawing circles in the dirt and humming to himself. "Don't be dramatic, Daniel. This isn't something you'll learn in school, *this* is something you'll learn defending yourself."

"So what would happen?" Daniel asked.

"Remember when I was really ill last year?"

Daniel nodded.

"I tried it, and it kinda sucks life out of you, you know, saps at your energy," he said, "but it doesn't kill you."

"It doesn't kill you, but you just said *sucks the life*."

"And that's what using your energy does, it takes your energy, but you regain it," he said. "I've been practising."

"Why didn't you tell me before?"

"You'd end up telling your parents," Jac said. "Besides, you weren't strong enough to try it for yourself."

Daniel waved a hand at Jac. "Right, right, whatever, c'mon then, how do I do it?"

"It's simple, summon two or more energies at the same time."

"Fire and water? They'll just cancel each other out."

He grinned. "You summon fire in one palm and counter it with water in the other. Pound your hands together once," Jac said. He demonstrated with a thud of the stick. "That's a basic way of connecting the two. Put together with some of your flare, and then fire it at whoever, whatever, and it's supposed to do something," he said, "never got that far."

"Then that's a *no*, what else have you got?"

Jac rolled his eyes. "You were accepted into Croft's Academy, I think you'll have the will to see it through. And I don't know what it does, it might *paralyze* them. But if he—*they* beat on you again, I'll find my way up there," he said, his smile faded and his face heated with anger, "Upperlands scum."

"There's this girl there as well, I think she's his girlfriend."

Jac grimaced. "You know how to get back at him."

"How?"

"Steal his girlfriend."

A smirk washed across Daniel's face. He massaged the prickly hairs on the back of his neck and stared out into the treetops. "If only."

"So what's this about your flare anyway?" Jac asked. "Mine's blue." He glanced out into the opening in the trees where Daniel had been looking. "What's up?"

Daniel flinched out of the trance. "Um—No—Nothing."

"C'mon." Jac ushered Daniel into the forestry. "People have

been seeing that panther around, he, she, it's definitely a shifter. There's also a raven that's been seen hanging around. I think it's a warning."

Daniel eyed Jac. "You sound scared."

"Well, it's gotta be after something. You don't think it's me, do you?" Jac asked, staring at his bare feet pitied heavy in dirt.

"Stay with my mum and dad, or *just* don't go out at dark. But if you honestly think there's someone after you, go stay at my parents," Daniel said, cocking his head in the direction he'd flown in.

"Yeah," he mumbled.

CHAPTER TEN

DANIEL stumbled in through the bedroom window, whacking a leg on the ledge as he shifted forms. He fell into bed and slept until a bleep rang down his ears.

A patter of knocks chimed through the bedroom. Daniel's hand found its way to the bedside table, whacking around until his hand slapped the top of the alarm. "Great," he mumbled to himself, stifling a yawn.

"Daniel," Tanner called from the bedroom door. "Oi, are you even in there?"

He rubbed the sleep from his eyes. "Okay, okay!" he shouted and the knocking ceased.

"Are you *okay*? You haven't been out of your room."

Daniel watched as the door handle dropped and flung back up seconds later. "The door's locked," he said.

"No one's seen you since yesterday."

Daniel kicked his legs out of his duvet to reveal several small purple welts up his skin. He ran his fingers down them and sighed, recalling the *training* he'd done with Jac, fighting with sticks. Tanner knocked again, rousing Daniel from thought.

He climbed out of bed and limped around as he tried to get dressed. He had to make an effort for the class he had.

"You're coming, right? Thought you were dead the way Jasper and Mark kept going on," Tanner said. The words sent a shiver through Daniel as he remembered what happened.

Daniel caught a glimpse of his eye in the mirror and paused. He pulled up his jeans and continued to eye himself. His eyes looked better; the violet had faded to a light blue. He touched the swelling beneath his eye, but it didn't hurt.

"Is it bad?" Tanner asked.

"Just getting dressed," he said, kicking the dirty clothes to a corner.

He opened the wardrobe in the wall and pulled out a white t-shirt and grey jacket.

"We'll miss breakfast," Tanner said.

He opened the front door and slipped into his jacket. Tanner was stood in front of him, he took a step back to get a better look at Daniel.

"Ah, shoes," Daniel said, grabbing a pair of plimsolls by his door and shoved his dirty feet into them.

"Don't know what the big deal is, there's not even a scratch," he laughed.

"Just a little swelling."

They found their way to the cafeteria and ate their breakfasts. Neither of them spoke about the incident, even though Tanner began, often with *"well"* before Daniel would change the subject.

"I have a—Mythic's class this morning," Daniel said, interrupting Tanner.

Tanner nodded to the table behind Daniel. *"Look,* they're over there," he said.

Daniel shrugged and took a bite out of his toast. Tanner watched Jasper and Mark glare holes in the back of Daniel's head.

Daniel turned and looked at them. "I—I should be going to class." He pushed his chair out and stood. "I'll see you later," he said, nodding to himself before hurrying out of the double doors.

Daniel was on his way up to the second floor by the time Tanner had cleared away the trays. He took a deep breath and closed his eyes for a moment, when he opened them he caught the tail of a group walking straight for the classroom he was in. He wriggled his way through and took a seat at the back.

"Oh," a girl said, noticing Daniel sat beside her. She bit the inside of her lip and took a different seat.

What? Daniel laughed to himself.

A woman found her footing at the front of the classroom. She cleared her throat. "Good morning," she called out. "I am Marianne van Hectar, and I am your teacher. I will teach you the mythology and history of Templar Island. You will learn about the founding figures, and how you can so graciously wield energy, as well as explaining the myths and the laws of the land," she explained, gesturing with her hands.

Daniel nodded to her words. He relayed the information back and told himself that he needed to make notes in the journals his grandparents had given him. He looked up at her, black curly hair flowing down her chest and back, he peered over the heads in front of him to see her hair fall by her waist.

"Master Satoria, do you have a question?" she asked, and Daniel snapped back in his seat.

"No," he said with a tremble to his tongue. *Great, I sit at the back, and I'm still at the centre.*

She smiled and nodded. "Let's continue then. Everyone should know the principle theory—the seven luminaries, the seven pillars of light and without them we would not exist, *that* is what we believe," she said. "Now I know that most of you don't send prayers to them, but I so desperately encourage you to, I don't know if they're real, but there's hope in praying, instead of leaving it all to chance." She grinned.

The crowd of pupils nodded to her words.

"We no longer know their original names as they are said to have changed over time. So we send prayers to their planet or star." She perched on a stool and smiled out into the crowd.

Daniel knew it was going to be a long haul talk when she took her seat. He itched at the palms of his hands. "All theory?" he mumbled and pulled up his hood.

"Yeah," someone said from in front of him. "How can you practice this?" The girl turned to him, the one who was going to sit next to him. She snarled. "Ugh. It's disgusting that they allow people like *you* in."

Daniel rolled his eyes as he tuned in to what Marianne was saying. "There's the Sun, the Moon, Mars, Mercury, Jupiter, Venus and Saturn. They are the seven who we pray to and in turn they bless us with abilities that are capable of doing both good and evil," she said and stood. "The Sun is not a planet, I know, so whatever qualms you have with calling them planetary beings, take it up with them," she laughed. "None of them have more power than the other. They are each weighted equally in power, but the Sun is regarded the centre," she said to the room of wandering eyes. "Who knows what *this* is? You might have seen your parents with one. Or you may have seen pictures of them." She pulled at something around her neck.

Daniel peered over the crowd again; small hairs cowered on the nape of his neck. He fell back into his seat and massaged his shoulders. The mere touch of his skin made it feel like a layer of something else. He swallowed and nibbled on his lips, his tongue was tainted by the numbing in his skin.

Marianne pulled something shiny that she'd concealed inside her shirt. She held it up high so everyone could see. Daniel caught a glimpse of it. It was a silver star with seven spokes, he'd seen it before, for as long as he could remember, his mother had always worn one around her neck.

A light refracted and hit Daniel in his eyes. He shunned his head down into his hands and pulled his legs up to his chest.

"You okay?" the boy beside Daniel asked.

Daniel glanced up and held a hand to his mouth. He turned to see the boy mixing and meshing from one into ten and then back again, falling out of focus and then back in. The one thing that stayed in focus was the star in his teacher's hand.

He wiped the drool collecting in the corner of his mouth and held his hand there.

"Marianne," the boy beside Daniel said.

Daniel stood. His free hand trembled over the back of the chairs as he tried to support himself. He barged through, knocking over chairs and pushing people out of the way. He walked from side-to-side, swaying as he rushed towards the door.

"Excuse me, are you okay?" she asked.

He ended up face first on the floor. He turned his head to

her. His lips tensed together to hold the bile back. His eyes clocked her pendant again, swinging back on forth around on her neck.

"Oh, Mercury, bless him better," she said, clasping the pendant in her hands.

Daniel squeezed his eyes shut. He wanted to plug his nose to keep the smell of peppermint on his teacher's breath. He pulled and slipped away. Pulled and slipped. Pulled and—*fell*.

White and black blotches flashed before Daniel's eyes. His legs and arms jolted. He pinched himself, and it stung. He was standing, shuffling around on his feet. Darkness everywhere. Blinding.

"Hello. H—he—hello. What's going on!" he cried out. He waved a hand in front of his face, clear before his eyes. He sighed and caught the smell of his own breath, warm and stale.

"Shhhh," a soft voice cooed, it rasped against the hairs on his neck.

Daniel rolled his shoulders and turned. The only thing behind was the same black backdrop.

"Shhhh," the voice came again.

He turned again, and again, circling himself as if trying to cover each part of the darkness. A figure stepped forward, a man, he blended in with the black.

Daniel squinted, and while he couldn't see the man walking,

he was sure that he was getting closer. Until only a couple of metres separated them. The man wore a black shirt and a pair of white linen pants. He had olive skin and puffed out his chest.

"Daniel?" he asked. Daniel nodded. "I feel a lot of things from you. *Fear*. Hatred. Pain. All quite negative." He tutted. "It's not good for you."

Daniel took a step back, but it didn't change the distance between them. He shook his head. His lips trembled as he voiced a weak, "no."

"I don't believe you," he said. Daniel glared into his eyes and noticed his pupils eating into his irises, turning them black. "I know *who* you want dead," he said, humming a gruff laugh until his lips pursed a grin.

"I don't want anyone killed," Daniel said.

A groan ran throughout the darkness, rumbling like a fading thunder. And from the corner of Daniel's eyes, he watched as another stumbled in and fell to his knees before the man.

"Him," the man said, and forced Daniel to look down.

The boy had a mess of dark blond curls wrapped around his head. He looked up to see Daniel, and behind his off-white skin, it was Jasper. Jasper's head collapsed back into the light, and Daniel noticed the glossy tear-stained face and a thin layer of grey sticky tape covering his mouth. Muted hums and screams came.

"I don't," Daniel said.

The man grinned, flashing his white teeth. "He's the one who gave you that." He pointed toward Daniel's eye.

Daniel's eye swelled and throbbed once again as he touched it. "No, I don't want it."

"You want them *both* gone then?" he laughed.

Daniel's teeth ached in his jaw. He stared at Jasper in a lump at the man's feet. Daniel shut his eyes and shook his head. *It's a dream, it's a dream.*

"Oh, but. Oh. How it's not a dream," the man said.

"It is. It is!"

Another whimper came from Jasper before he broke out in tears. Daniel opened his eyes to see the man had grabbed a handful of Jasper's hair. He teased at the corner of the tape against Jasper's lips. He gripped it and ripped it straight from his skin. Jasper tried to cower but his head was held up by his hair wrapped around the man's fingers.

"You want him dead. Don't act like this doesn't make you happy. It's who you are, like you should think any more of *scum*, their only purpose is to serve you," he laughed.

"Kill him. Do it," Daniel said as every muscle in his body felt a tight rip as if it had all been a test and he would be killed for even thinking of doing it.

The man pulled a small ridged blade from a concealed holder on his belt. Daniel kept eye contact with him, and the man stared back. He toyed with the blade in one hand, and Jasper's knotted hair in the other.

Jasper groaned as Daniel took a look at him. One look did it all, the man let go of Jasper's hair and thrust the knife into his back. Blood squirted and splashed the man in his face. Slowly, the blood soaked Jasper's white clothes.

Daniel shut his eyes and gulped at the trapped air inside his mouth. It lasted a moment of what forever would taste like; *a nightmare*. He replayed the visuals as he fell to his hands and knees. "No," Daniel voiced. A dazed sensation rushed through his body.

"Fine" the man said. "Welcome, brother."

Daniel opened his eyes and shot up. He was in bed, but none the less startled. His breathing slowed and he closed his eyes again, scarred by the emptiness in the black of his room and the camouflage of the man's eyes. He laid back on the pillow and tried to keep his eyes open.

He shivered in his duvet and cuddled up in his arms with his eyes closed. The warmth around him vanished.

He was far from his bed, far from his room. He stared ahead to see a girl standing on a ledge, her wispy night-dress flapped against her legs. She sniffled and rubbed at her nose.

"H—hey," Daniel called out.

Her legs trembled and her knees knocked.

CHAPTER ELEVEN

SHE stood on the ledge watching Daniel wrap his arms around himself. He stared at her as her nightdress billowed and she wiped her eyes.

"What do you want?" she asked.

Daniel hunched his back. "W—where am I?"

She jumped from the ledge to the roof. "You're on the Lexar Hotel, where else would you think?" she said, walking out of the floodlights.

"Where's—"

"New York," she said with a smile.

"Where?"

"Exactly," she chuckled. "So, what's your name?"

"Daniel, what's—"

"Hi, Daniel. I'm Mia," she said, pushing her hand.

She was a few of inches shorter, but not so much that Daniel had to look down. He shook her hand and glanced around. For all he knew it was another dream; it was dark, but he knew where he was, he was on the roof of the Lexar Hotel in New York.

"So, where are you *really* from?" he asked. "Rockies? Lower? Upper?"

"London, but my dad got a job here and we had to move. I hate it, I woulda jumped y'know. He doesn't think about anyone else, I mean, he didn't even ask me if I wanted to go, I would *not* have agreed. And my stepmom wouldn't even let me speak up, she's all *but your dad's been workin' towards this for ages, you knew it could've happened, so don't look at me like that*," she said and gasped for air. She rolled her eyes and looked as though she was about to begin another short rant.

"Oh," Daniel said in confusion, "I moved to the Upperlands."

Mia grinned and chuckled. "Oh, well, you're funny."

"Yeah," he said, with an unsure sigh. "Is *The City* nice? I always hear people from the Lower areas of Templar Island talk about it."

"It's gorgeous, sometimes," she said as Daniel stood shivering. "Oh my god, you're freezing."

"Just a little."

"You know, I was going to wear my dad's overcoat—take something sentimental with me," she said.

"Hmm," Daniel nodded.

"So, where's Templar Island?" she asked.

"What do you mean?" And then he realised that for whatever reason, he was no longer on the island, and of course it made sense, he'd known since he was little that there must be more to life than the island. It brought something else to mind, people who tried to sail away from the island or teleport, were often found dead the next day, there was something about keeping the island a secret that he'd read in a book from the library. "Oh, it's just a small place like there's a chain of them, just, around."

She raised an eyebrow. "Like Hawaii?"

"Hawaii."

She pursed her lips and eyed him through a squint. "How come you're so pale?"

Daniel shrugged. He glanced from his feet to her. He looked into her eyes; soft, powder blue. His mouth was half-opened to speak, but he stared in awe. "W—well, what are you doing up here?" he asked breaking their quiet bond.

"To jump," she said, stern with a smile.

"Would you?" he asked.

She grinned as their gaze met. Daniel didn't know what to do, he couldn't smile at the thought of someone taking their own life, it wasn't the Templar way; nature took life. She then shook her head, and sniffled back a sob.

"Don't cry," he said. He fumbled with his hands, half-wanting to pat her back and the other half not wanting to do wrong.

"I'm not," she snapped, shooting him a sharp look. She had black smudges around her eyes and black mascara tears running down her cheeks. "I know, I should get waterproof mascara, right, another thing wrong in my life," she said, breaking off into a small fit of laughter.

"Do you ever dream about free-falling off a tall building?" Daniel asked.

"You mean skyscraper, a tall building just wouldn't do. You'd *splat*," she said clapping her hands together once in emphasis. Daniel grinned. "Come see the drop." She grabbed a hold of his hand and pulled him.

The Lexar Hotel was 40 floors high, and still it would've only taken them seconds to hit the ground. Daniel leaned over to see the street below; illuminated with incandescent yellow street lights.

"What are they?" he asked, nodding to the speeding cars.

"Traffic. Appalling, I know," she said.

"No, not that. Those?"

She turned and wrinkled her face. "Cars, taxis?" she asked.

Daniel met her expression and sucked in a deep breath. "Oh." *Of course, I'm not in Templar anymore. And those things, I'd only ever seen them in books.* "I'm just a little tired."

Mia grinned. "You're strange, you know that."

"I've seen some heights."

She bit her lip. "As big as this?" she asked.

"Well."

Mia gripped hold of Daniel's hand and peered over the edge. Daniel choked back soft breathes as their palms clammed up. He let his arm go limp in her hand.

He turned his head to cough before he spoke, and when he glanced back, her sapphire eyes, glittered against the black night. "H—how often do you come up here?"

"Every day," she said. She turned her head and glanced up at the sky. "I usually come up here to watch the sunset. I know, it's not the best view, but I pretend I can see it over the buildings." She pulled her hand out of Daniel's and wrapped them around herself.

"I'm surprised you can see it with the all the light."

She shot him a sly glance. "Yeah well, I preferred the view in London, it was amazing." She broke out in a short abrupt giggle, "I actually get my friends to message me pictures. But, like now, when my friends are in bed, and I'm the only one awake. That's when I don't want to be here. I'd just end it." She turned, and looked up to him, her eyes glossing over with tears.

Daniel could only let himself smile. He prayed she would not cry. Although he knew how she felt, he just couldn't sympathise—she wanted to take her own life because she wasn't someplace else, but he could go anywhere, he could take *her* anywhere.

"I have to show you something," Daniel said. He stood with a large smile on his face.

"I'm not that sort of person," she snickered.

Daniel couldn't begin to break down what she'd eluded to, but apparently it had been funny. She was laughing and he smiled with her.

He grinned. "Close your eyes," he said in a whisper.

She raised an eyebrow and repressed her lips from smiling. "Okay." She closed her eyes.

Daniel walked behind her. He turned and glanced down at his bare chest pricking in the cold with goose pimples. *Just show her already*, he thought. He rolled his shoulders and his back cracked. He closed his eyes, and felt a blanket of heat break over him.

Daniel opened his eyes again. He was cocooned deep within his duvet. He struggled at first as he fumbled his way out, and then he fell into a heap at the side of his bed. *Another dream*, he gritted his teeth and butted his lips white.

"She was just a dream," he sighed. *I want more.*

He stood and threw himself on his bed. It felt more like home without the duvet, colder, but the air was still different. He fell to sleep, pushing scenarios of greatness for his first Attack and Defence class to the forefront of his mind.

CHAPTER TWELVE

THE NEXT morning Daniel went for a run. He showered and dressed, and all before Tanner could knock at his door or let the caffeine spike the bodies of those who were comfortable with the Upperlands' amenities.

They were in the canteen before Tanner spoke. "Are you going to tell me what happened then?" he asked. He handed Daniel a tray at the canteen and took one for himself.

"I just fainted. There isn't that much to say. I'm not up for breakfast," Daniel replied. He tried to hand the tray back.

"You have to eat. *Or* you'll faint again, and it's our first *real* class on how to use energy, like *really* use it. You need that energy!"

"And this class is the only one where you can *test* your power, and show the rest of the school what *you* can do," Daniel said. He took his tray back and moved down the serving aisle. "Y'know, people like Jasper, that's how they get their reputation."

"Yeah, and –"

"No, they showed people what they could do. Hell, I felt it first hand, didn't I?" Daniel grinned. He picked up a plate with a toasted bun, some sausages and bacon.

"S'pose so, and I heard that the class is integrated with second and third years, and they even match us up against 'em," Tanner said, moving along the food conveyor towards an empty table.

"Really? What for?"

"Power classes. You, from what's been going around will be at the top end. You know you don't get a flare like that for nothing."

Everyone knows. I bet it's gone around that I fainted as well and it will only be too soon before people start talking about where I'm from. Then I'll have nobody to talk to. His stomach grumbled as he buttered his toast.

Daniel raised the toast to his lips. He looked straight ahead and saw her. The blonde girl who'd spoke to him yesterday, she was alone and only sat a few tables back. He lowered his toast and a knock of nausea made him contemplate waving her over before two others joined her; Jasper and Mark.

"Hey," Jasper said. He kissed her on the lips. She glanced straight ahead at Daniel and winked.

"Who you lookin' at?" Tanner asked. He turned his head. "Carlie's bad news, she's Jasper's girlfriend."

"She's not like him though. She looks like the only nice one there. She's probably only in it for the power trip. I mean, she could have anyone, right, and chooses the guy who just happens to be a *leader*," Daniel said, staring off into space.

"Daniel," Tanner interrupted.

"Huh?" Daniel noticed a lanky boy stood at the end of the table. "Yeah?"

The boy coughed several times. "Mr. Croft would like to speak with you immediately," he said before leaving.

Daniel turned to the heated stares on him. Their ears were strained to listen to the boy, but nobody could hear over the clatter of pots and pans.

"Why?" Tanner asked.

Daniel shrugged. "Probably how I feel, I did *faint*."

"Yeah. You said you were feeling better though."

"Maybe he cares."

"Yeah, sure. He's probs just covering his back, insuring his own safety an' all." Tanner grinned; the whiff of a scandal seemed enough to make him forget about warning him against Carlie.

"I'll see you in class then."

Daniel walked up to Reuben's office. He noticed a boy quivering with his hands clutched as he rushed down the stairs passed him. Daniel knocked twice on the huge door, and each knock echoed in the small hallway of the third floor.

"Come in!" a voice boomed. It shook Daniel, almost to rap his knuckles on the door once again.

Daniel twisted the brass handle and the door carried him in. Reuben was seated; his elbows on his desk and his reading glasses perched on the end of his nose. He glanced over them briefly to make eye contact.

"You wanted to see me," Daniel said. He approached the sofa.

Reuben immediately flicked his wrist and the sofas popped; they became thick, hard wooden chairs. "Take a seat." Daniel took the offer. He wiped his hands on his pants and tried to smile patiently. "So, Daniel. Why do you think I've *summoned* you here today?"

"I fainted yesterday?" he asked.

Reuben grinned; he took his glasses off and stared into Daniel's eyes. "People faint all the time." He glanced away to his fingers toying with the frame. He shook his head slowly, "I'm a little disappointed in you actually."

"Me?" Daniel's face flushed. He bit his lip to stop himself from panting.

"You broke a fundamental rule. Not once, but twice now. You've been leaving the compound, the campus. The first was Tuesday, and then I'm *woken* late last night to a call of another breach."

"Last night?" Daniel voiced from a gasp. *It was real? I met Mia last night? I knew it!* He smiled haphazardly, and then looked back up at Reuben.

"This is not a *grinning* matter, Mr. Satoria," Reuben growled. He grasped a hold of his glasses frame harder.

"No, sir."

"Good. Are you going to tell me where you were then?"

"Yes, sir," he said, and held a hand up to his mouth to cough. "On Tuesday I went home, I went to see a friend."

"And did you receive any permission to leave the grounds?" he asked as Daniel shook his head. "And what about last night?" and Daniel shook his head again. "Your whereabouts last night?"

Daniel shrugged. "On a skyscr—I woke from this nightmare and then, and then I was there. I thought it was still part of my dream. But you just said—you just said that it wasn't." Daniel looked up to see a lax expression across Reuben's face, before he smiled.

"Ah that would've been The City, an awfully cramped and busy place. You may leave," Reuben said. He smiled again as he pushed his glasses back on.

Daniel rushed off to his class on the second floor. The class had already begun and the door was closed. He took a couple of deep breaths and wiped the sweat from his palms. *Be confident*, he told himself as he opened the door. There was a loud squeak and everyone turned to see him walk in.

"Our first challenger," the teacher said, throwing his hands in Daniel's direction. "What is your name?"

Challenger? Daniel grit his teeth. "Daniel." He glanced around the room in search of Tanner.

"Let's welcome Daniel to the stage, guys!" the teacher, Rik parted the crowd to a large white square in the middle of the room. "Mark, make your way over."

Daniel took one look at Mark and realised just who he was; Jasper's friend. Mark stood in one corner, his chest puffed out as the class cheered him on. Daniel was yet to receive any words of encouragement.

Rik pushed through to the white stage. "The aim of this game," he started.

Game? Daniel thought, rolling his eyes. *This is one funny game.*

"You have to affect your opponent physically, without touching them. Although you may use techniques which value motion and allow you to manipulate your energies much easier.

You may quit, but you will lose. If you step out off the stage, you lose. And if you come into contact with your opponent, then you lose," Rik explained. "You both got that?" They both nodded.

Daniel scanned the stage, his first thought had been the only trick Jac had taught him, but he couldn't do that here. He couldn't *mix*, he didn't even know what it did, it could kill him, and get him thrown out of school. *Play it cool*, he told himself.

"He can go first, he's a first year," Mark said.

"Okay, Daniel, you will start, you get one move, then it's Mark's go. Don't forget to block, this class is about being able to defend against an attack as well. Start when you're ready," he said, "and guys, try not to scuff the floor we've only just had it repainted."

Daniel inhaled and looked out across the crowd again. Behind Mark was Jasper and Carlie, he looked out further and could just about see Tanner's head popping up. Daniel shivered at the faintest echo of laughter.

Mark glared into Daniel's eyes as he cracked his knuckles. Daniel took a slow deep breath. He flicked both of his wrists at once; a thread of gold shot free from his hands. There was a crackle and grey smoke appeared at the bottom of Mark's pants with the smallest of flames. The class gasped, and then huffed in disappoint as Mark put the flames out with a stomp.

"Really? That's weak," Mark grinned, rubbing his palms together.

Daniel didn't see it coming, until his clattering teeth hurt his jaw. The group laughed. He was grounded by a small bump of ice over his feet. It was his turn again.

"C'mon!" Mark groaned, his voice muffled in Daniel's ears.

He stroked his goose-pimpled arms as he tried to keep from shivering. He closed his eyes and tried to string together something warm, something that would burn Mark. The more he thought about it the warmer he got. The hair on his body matted and thickened in record time, with the ice crumbling at the long talons of his feet. Without realising it, he had taken the form of one of the carriage men, and he squawked in Mark's face.

Mark fell to his knees and cupped hands over his ears. The rest of the group followed suit; taking steps back and curling their heads into their abdomens.

Jasper stood still. His eyes glazed over as he stared at Mark.

"Stop!" Rik shouted. The room went quiet.

Daniel wriggled back into his human form, inhaling the process away. Mark was the last to stand, his legs quaked at the balls of his feet.

"Cheating," Rik said, and glanced from Mark to Daniel and then to Jasper.

Mark started to snigger, "knew there was a rule against *that*."

"No, not that. You, you cheated. Jasper fed some of his energy into you, that's why the noise couldn't pass his ears. Not until you took too much, trying to retaliate I suppose," Rik explained. He left them clinging to his every word and searching for answers.

Daniel couldn't help smile, although it wasn't one of the ideals he'd planned out for the lesson. It was better. Jasper and Mark were being laughed at while Daniel was praised for turning into a bird and then breaking from a double energy bound ice bond. It was a good first impression, if you discounted the weak fire summoning.

Jasper and Mark were sent out and Rik gathered the rest of the group around in a circle.

"I despise cheating, of any kind," he said. "What Daniel did is a talent, and you *are* allowed to use those, if you have an affinity to something, please, bring it along to a session, show us all what you have to give."

"I've always fancied myself as a strong earth creator, y'know, like flowers and plants," a girl in the front spoke. "But, I don't know how to use that to protect myself."

"*That*, oh that is the kind of questions we want here," Rik said and with a fist he pounded against his chest. "I feel *that here*," he said. "So strongly, so patiently for *this*."

"H—how do you think I could do it?"

"There is *always* a way to turn what you think is quite harmless into a strength," he said. "Earth is powerful, earth is around us, earth is moving, yet it's quite still." He took a deep breath. "With practice, you can create any number of plants and control those with a whim. Ivy, the kind that crawls, weaves its way into everything, that's where you start."

"And what about if you don't want to hurt anyone?" Another asked. A boy made his way through to Rik. "I'm not saying that I'm a wimp, I want to protect myself, but I don't want to hurt anyone."

"Demonstrate your power without any ill intentions," Rik said. "The thought of being hurt is stronger than anything you could do to them physically."

CHAPTER THIRTEEN

DANIEL found his way back to his room without Tanner in tow. It remained the same state as he'd left it in; duvet on the floor, the sheet halfway up his mattress.

He stood at the door for a while, reeling in the high from his class, and with wonder in his eyes he caught himself in thought, thinking the ways he could clean his room without the littlest effort possible.

He flicked his wrists and managed to pull at the sheet slightly. He tried again before frustrating himself and doing it manually. He made his bed up and sat, staring up at his ceiling, but nothing could match the stars he saw. They were different to those above Templar Island, but equally beautiful.

"Mia," her name trickled off his tongue. He closed his eyes and tried to create her face from behind his lids.

Daniel's door swung open. He opened an eye to see his door open, and then a girl walked in, Carlie. She slammed the door shut with the heel of her foot. "You," she said, biting her lip.

He pushed himself back against his wall. "Uh, what are you doing?" The pitch in his voice went higher.

"Don't act so surprised." She grinned. "This can be a secret." She winked. "I'm good at keeping secrets."

"No," he said. "N—n—no."

She laughed. "You want to kiss me, *Dan*. Everyone wants to." She ruffled a hand through her hair.

"Carlie?"

"What is?" she asked, pouting.

"I—I—I don't want any trouble," he said, waving a hand and closing his eyes.

She climbed on his bed and crawled to him. "You're strong, I can feel it. Please, just one kiss."

Daniel opened his eyes again and watched as she pawed at his duvet, each time getting closer to a leg. He pulled away, pushing his body closer to the wall.

"You're teasing!" She jumped on him. "I don't like to be teased," she whispered in his ear and kissed him on the cheek.

Daniel pushed harder against his bed as in hopes of escaping Carlie through the stone wall. He opened his eyes and they were

129

inches apart. Face-to-face. There was a shared mix of shallow breaths as Daniel's hands relieved the strain on his body, easing up against the wall.

"See," she whispered, and kissed him on the lips.

He pulled back but she pressed harder. He tried to pull away again, but he couldn't, his head was against the wall. She grabbed his hands and wrapped them around her waist. She kissed him harder, holding his face and kissing him. Daniel finally moved his hands and pushed her off by her shoulders.

He wiped his mouth. "No, no," he said. But there was something that wanted to continue, the thought that kissing her could hurt Jasper.

"You're nicer than he is. He's so demanding," she said, sulking her body across the bed.

"So why are you with him?"

"Don't you like me?"

Daniel sighed, he didn't even know her and it was harmless up until now. He'd read it in the books his father had brought home, if you told a girl you didn't like her, she'd think it was about her looks and then break down in a fit of hysteria. If you told her you liked her, then she'd expect more kissing and hand holding.

Carlie flicked her hair back and grinned. "Oh, it doesn't matter anyway," she said and kissed him on the lips again.

She kept on kissing him, and Daniel didn't pull back; he kissed her and then one after the other they kept on kissing. The contrast in the pale skin tones became blurred as Carlie's glow shone.

Daniel stopped and took a deep breath. He pushed at Carlie's shoulder to make her stop.

"Oh, it's okay. I was thinking of leaving, I have an early morning an' all." She waved at him. "See ya."

Daniel spat random words. At first he didn't realise, his blinks became longer and his vision blurred. The last thing was Carlie blowing a kiss as she left. His eyelids collapsed and his head rolled to the side.

Black swirls crawled up his skin. It woke him, coughing on the surreal canvas around him. He waved a hand in front of his face to see his skin, dull in the unknown light source. There was nothing. Just black all around.

"Again?" A familiar voice asked.

Nostalgia took Daniel by the throat as he dipped and spun around on his foot.

"That's something you can't do so easily, is it?" the voice asked.

"What isn't?"

"Watch your own back. Although someone has been. Yeah, and that someone is *me*."

"What? It's my dream! Show yourself!" There was a dryness in Daniel's voice, he'd read a book, among the many books that he'd read, one he wasn't supposed to. It was about people who were mentally weak being controlled or killed from inside their own minds. *No. I am strong!*

Daniel turned once more, and he found the man. He was lightly tanned with a prominent jawline and he was still wearing the same clothes that Daniel remembered him in.

"You're right, you are strong, and people *can* and *do* intrude on other people's thoughts, sometimes taking bits out, or pushing stuff around, like a lobotomy," he said. He was stood several feet away with his hands tucked in his pockets.

"A lobotomy?" Daniel stuttered, glaring at the man.

"It's when you get this steel pick," he said and a sharp-edged stick of steel materialised between his fingers, "and then you open the eye and right beneath the eyeball you put it in, and *knock* it, with a hammer." His face twisted into a smile as he thrust the pick into the air.

Daniel took a step back and watched as the man's theatrics wore away. He looked at Daniel and his smile grew.

"Don't look so worried. It's not like I want to *kill* you." he grinned as a dim light touched his cheeks and cast half his face into darkness.

"What do you want then?" Daniel asked.

"Nothing. I'm part of your dream, willed to do as you want. After all, it was you who summoned *me*," he said, taking a step towards Daniel. In one fluid motion the man was stood inches away. "Have you killed him yet?" he whispered into Daniel's ear.

"I don't want to kill him," Daniel said. He looked into the man's eyes, one eye was green, and the other was blue. Daniel took a couple of steps back.

"Let's not start this headache again. Be careful of who you trust, Daniel. Or they'll be picking your spine from their teeth." He moved closer once more.

"What?"

He huffed. "They are going to eat you alive."

"Who's going to eat me alive?"

They both stared. Daniel drew a deep breath, as one single understanding of something pure and innate pulled itself to a balance. Exhaling, he wavered on the balls of his feet as his muscles and skin became heavy on his bones.

"Trust me, okay," he said, and gripped Daniel's arm before he toppled over.

Daniel shook and pulled from the man. "Who wants to hurt me?"

"You're from the Lowerlands," he said with a wry smile and a shrug. "You were born out of place here."

Daniel took a moment, he repeated it to himself. He glanced back but he was gone.

"Hello!" he called out. His voice echoed. "Hello!" he shouted. He took another breath to call again, and found that he was sucking himself in. The black vacuum around him shrunk, smaller and smaller.

You can wake up. It's your dream! He panicked inside himself.

The absent light chewed at his vision and reduced him to a pile on his bedroom floor, twisting and convulsing. His arms were gnarled, upturned and out of place. He let go.

CHAPTER FOURTEEN

PAIN was a fixture inside Daniel's dreams; a darkness etched with precision that slept while he was awake and woke while he slept. All good memories could be turned with an incident, a misplaced foot, a *what if* scenario.

Daniel's lips were dry as he came to. He was laid with an arm bunched up against his stomach and another clenched up at his clavicle.

A spasm broke in his arms and fought to wake him. The small energized surge sufficed in his fingertips, turning them gold. He rolled over to his back as a stream of air gushed into his throat. The gold on his fingertips popped, rippling energy through the air as the mirror above the sink smashed.

Daniel jumped to his feet. "What," he gasped. He glanced at his tingling fingers and rubbed them against his clammy palms. He yawned and rubbed the sleep from is eyes.

The alarm clock behind him bleeped. *09:17*. He stared for a moment before rushing. Today was his first Animal lesson.

He tugged his cold sweaty clothes from his body, falling over himself to get his pants off. He changed, and before blindly shoving his hands into the sink to wash his face, he noticed the thick pieces of glass reflect him; his skin was sickly and his eyes were puffy. He poured the cold water over his fingers and splashed them up at his face.

He jumped whole flights of stairs, and as he landed his legs trembled. He burst out of the large glass door and fell into Jasper.

Jasper pushed him up against the wall. "I'm not going to let you put me in a bad mood!" he growled. He let go of Daniel and pushed him. "First Animal class this year. Nobody is going to ruin a great start to the day."

Daniel brushed himself off and opened his mouth to ask Jasper where the class was, even though he had to think about it for a second, had he heard correctly; Jasper could shift. By the time Daniel thought it was a bad idea to ask, Jasper was already gone. He made his way down a path in search of a sign, something that would lead him to the class. A group of people walked off behind the main building.

He shouted after them and bit his tongue, even though Jasper turned to look. Daniel hurried up to join them.

He'd seen this place before. On his first day when he'd taken the detour. *So this must be the stables then.* He followed the lightly worn path to the large barn. The people he'd been following entered, but that's where Daniel stopped. He loitered outside for a moment.

He listened to the sound of their brash voices from within the huge barn. He walked around and pushed up a slate of wood. He peered through to see several people standing around in a group.

"Spying?" someone chimed in. Their voice was louder than all the others.

The people inside the barn turned to the gap.

He gulped and let the slate fall back into place. A patter of feet came closer from inside. Jasper was the first out to see Daniel's red face.

"Go back inside," a man said, shooing them.

"Is this the Animal, shifting class?" Daniel asked. He glanced up.

"I guess you're Daniel," he said with a grin. "They're very cautious in this class, a nervous of sorts. People often call them out on being *freakish* for continuing on in their shifting. Well, I'm Enek." He offered his hand and Daniel shook it. "It's very rare chance that all the teachers are talking about one student."

137

"Oh," Daniel said, letting go of Enek's hand.

"It isn't bad, honestly. I've been waiting to meet you, and I'm sure the rest of the class will be *thrilled*. But you are the only first year, so far," he said. He nodded and brushed his hand against Daniel's back, ushering him into the barn.

They smirked at him as he noticed a few familiar faces from his class yesterday and from the looks on their faces, they all remembered the showing. The group felt huge to Daniel, all eyes on him, all 12 sets. Daniel flinched as the stable doors slammed shut and a loud clang latched the locks.

"This is Daniel," Enek said.

Jasper made his way to the front of the group. "We know," he said.

"He's the first year that beat Mark," A girl sniggered from the back.

"I know. I heard, and that's where we're kicking the semester off; controlling your animal form to defend as well as to attack. So can you control yourself, Daniel?" Enek asked, and tipped his head to him.

"Yes!" Daniel said in defence.

"Looked more like rage to me," Jasper said, sparking a coo of laughter.

"How would you know? You were caught cheating!" Daniel grinned as the laughter got louder.

Enek's cold expressions silenced everyone, including Jasper who had opened his mouth to spit another witty retort. "What animal are you affined with?" Enek asked.

"So far, *just* bird types," Daniel replied.

"*So far?*" Enek laughed.

Daniel looked around at all the grins settling on people's faces. It was the kind of smile you gave a person who was downright stupid or naïve, Daniel had seen it too many times on Jac.

"We only have a connection with *one* animal," Jasper said what no one else could say from laughter. It ached Daniel's face red.

"Jasper!" Enek snapped. "It is rare that a person is gifted with more than one animal, but some cases have been documented, like the greats, the Luminary! The woman of Jupiter, *Juperae*, very fond of cats, big cats, small cats, house cats, and she could also turn into a mouse."

"Exactly, she was a Luminary. We were taught that last year, she's *mythical*, bloodlines with that power cannot live without consequence, it defies nature," Jasper said. He rolled his eyes at Enek, "it's better if you don't think you're special, even if the rumours say that this *golden* flare is something to be in *awe* of."

"Jasper, a flare is a personal thing, and it's a shame to show so much jealously. You said that he lacks control, how about you show us some," Enek barked back.

"What?"

"If you can shift and everything goes off without a hitch, then I'll presume you're okay, but if not, then you'll have to sit the lesson out."

"This is stupid," Jasper said. He turned to see the encouraging faces of the group behind him. "And what about *him*? Don't we get to test his little, *I can turn into different animals*, speech." But the truth was, nobody wanted to ask Daniel to prove it, not since Jasper had taken the full force of Enek's attention.

Jasper formed a wide circle, leaving enough room for Daniel and Enek to join. He shooed people back as he marked his space with a foot. Daniel wondered just how big Jasper was going to get. He stood in the middle and turned his body to face Daniel before bowing his head. Jasper's shaggy blond hair became thicker. It sprouted out down his neck and under his chin, framing his face.

Jasper glared with his beady jaundice eyes. In a sudden movement, he fell to all fours and his back cracked.

The torso and head of a man shimmered in the light above Jasper. It was the man who had been in Daniel's dream. Time slowed as Daniel watched the winking man, right before he plunged a jagged slate of steel into Jasper's back. Jasper collapsed to his abdomen as a thin electric plasma covered his body.

Everyone clapped and Daniel blinked. The man hadn't been there, and Jasper was perfectly fine.

A growl shook Daniel. He was in the form of a lion. He walked around the circle like he was perfectly trained to do so.

"I see you haven't shifted in a while, Jasper. Anyway, that there, is rage!" Enek called. He took a deep breath and turned to Daniel. "You're still calm and collected. I think you should fight?" he whispered.

Daniel shook his head. "No. I'm not fighting."

"Why not? You both seem to have issues with each other. You can both shift, which means you'll both heal faster. It makes sense to cut the tension under a teacher's supervision."

Jasper growled, cutting their talk short. He lifted a paw up above Daniel, and took a swipe. He missed and tried again.

"No!" Daniel said. He watched as Jasper took another swipe, this time with claws. Daniel backed away, but the swipes came faster and closer.

"He's got a weak spot on the centre of his paw. Hit that and he'll cower away. It may also make him shift back." Daniel turned, the voice was familiar, but he wasn't there, nobody was. He turned again and Jasper swiped. He clawed at Daniel's ankle and dragged him to the ground.

"Shift!" Enek shouted. Daniel couldn't hear him, his heartbeat throbbed in his ears.

Daniel held his hands to his face as Jasper's lion paw took another swipe. The circle moved around them, shoving Daniel into Jasper. A slow chant of "*get him*" and clapping ensued. Enek was speechless as he watched; Daniel still wouldn't shift.

He stood. "The paw. His paw," he whispered to himself.

Jasper swung again, and Daniel batted the paw away with the back of his hand. He persisted to push himself back into the crowd.

Someone kicked at the back of Daniel's knee and knocked him to the ground. "Hit the damn thing!" a roar shook Daniel from his insides. He threw a fist into the air and stuck the soft spot on Jasper's paw.

Jasper roared and pulled his paw away. He clawed at the ground and his jaw snapped shut.

"He's the flaw in nature. He's the weak spot," the voice chimed in to the rhythm of Daniel's heart.

The chanting died as all eyes turned to Jasper.

The fur from Jasper's form deteriorated and dripped from his skin like excess fat; he slipped right out of it. He choked and flopped around on the floor. They made a new circle around him. And from the gaps in the circle Daniel continued to watch, gnawing at the inside of his cheek.

A figure in the darkness stood on the balcony. He pressed a finger to his lips and shushed.

"Is he okay?" they called out to their teacher, but all Enek could do was watch. It looked like all the animal was being sucked out of him, and the consequences seemed dire.

"He's going to be *really* annoyed now. And it will all seem like your fault. He doesn't know it, but he's temporary disabled in *that* department," the man snickered.

Enek glanced over at Daniel, his face pained with remorse.

"You wouldn't know who did this, would you?" Enek asked as the circle disbanded and tended to Jasper.

"No, I thought he was going to kill me," Daniel said.

"He probably would've, but it also looked like you tried to kill him. What is it again that you can change into?"

"Just birds. Really! But once, I—I turned into a lion," Daniel glanced around.

"Really?" Enek asked. His eyes widened with intrigue.

He nodded. "Would that have anything to do with it?"

"I'm not sure. It could just be that Jasper has a reset button," Enek smiled, "but it could be that you have an untapped reserve of energy, many families have them, these *wells*. I'm not that into history, so you best ask one of your other teachers about that."

"I don't know what I did though. Am I going to get in trouble?"

"No! This life is a learning curve, trust me, Jasper will learn a lesson or two from what happened today. For now though, I think you should go, I'll break here, but you should probably come back next week. It's been very eventful. I'm giving you the heads up because I know that Jasper will treat this as a threat. I only hope you're not after a title from what you did today."

Daniel nodded as Enek pointed to a side door where he could leave without being spotted.

CHAPTER FIFTEEN

DANIEL sat on his bed and stared at the remnants of glass still stuck to the wall. He didn't care for clearing the shards up from around the sink. He stared at them like they'd glue back together any minute. He asked himself how it happened; did *he* do it; the man who was so firmly planted in his head?

"Daniel! Are you in there? You missed lunch." Tanner knocked at the door. "It's almost time for dinner."

"How can you miss something you didn't want?" Daniel mumbled to himself as he stared at the ceiling.

"You're lucky actually, you missed Jasper and Mark shouting off about something that happened," Tanner said, "I don't know what though."

"I think, I know," Daniel said, catching the look on his face in the broken mirror.

"What then? Was it you? He did say he was gonna to go all *lion* on the guy," Tanner sniggered. "Let us in."

It could have been two things, kissing his girlfriend or whatever it was that had happened in their class. Daniel favoured the latter. He itched at his palms and scrunched his face.

"Jasper got a little wound up in our class this morning. He tried to kill me," Daniel said, sucking a breath.

"Whoa, you must have *really* wound him up!"

"And I wish I knew how," he said to himself. He swung his legs over his bed and stood. He pushed his window wide open, and sucked in another deep breath. The cold air tingled at the back of his throat until he coughed. "But you wouldn't understand."

Tanner's voice was muffled behind the door as Daniel wandered around in his head.

"Tanner, we'll talk later, yeah?" Daniel said, without waiting for a response, but the silence was assuring.

I need to talk to someone, I need to share this. Someone has to know how to deal with this! Daniel stared up as the stars in the evening light twinkled. They spoke a language, like Morse code and he pretended that he understood. "I want to go home," he said and closed the window.

He fed his arms into a clean jacket and put a pair of plimsolls on, careful not to tread on any glass. He had a tingle in his fingers, ready for someone to get in his way. He pulled his hood up over his head and rushed off out of the dormitory building.

Daniel watched as the main building glowed with lights and activity. He glanced over his shoulder, making sure Jasper wasn't behind. He replayed scenarios in his head of Jasper being in Reuben's office waiting for him to turn up. *What could he get me done for, really? I didn't do anything wrong, I didn't do anything.* He climbed the steps and stroked a hand against one of the marble pillars.

"If it defies, kill it," a soft voice said, it sounded like something he would hear coming from the dark. He paused, and kept a cool grasp of the pillar. *You defy me. Should I kill you?* Daniel entertained the voice. There was no reply, but as he looked up into the sky several stars twinkled back at him; he felt like they understood.

He shook his head and made his way into the main building, alive with busy bodies. He peered into a hall and noticed they were setting up for something.

"Oh good, there's more," a girl said and grabbed Daniel's arm. Daniel pulled back, and she let go. She stared, her eyebrows furrowed and fused together. "You're here to help set up, right?"

"I study here," Daniel said.

"Sorry. I thought you were from the Lowerlands, you just look *so* familiar. Sorry sir. It won't happen again," she said and rushed off into the hall.

Daniel stayed in a rouse of shock. "It's fine," he said, and rushed off again; up the two flights of stairs to Reuben's office. He wiped his sweaty hands on his pants and up his jacket, trying to cool down before his heart exploded in his ears.

He knocked on Reuben's door just once, he agreed that if he didn't answer it meant he wasn't in, and a part of him hoped that he wouldn't hear it at all even if he was in. He turned his back to walk away when he did a full spin on his foot and knocked again. The door opened.

"I thought that were you, although I saw it happening," he said and glanced up from his paperwork.

"What?"

"You mean, pardon."

"Yeah, pardon. How did you see me?"

Reuben pushed his glasses up to see Daniel properly. "It's only natural considering your previous breach*es*. So yes, you may go see your parents tomorrow, but you need to be back before the afternoon. An assembly is being held, compulsory for all first years. And you being a first year, it's compulsory," Reuben explained with a smile on his face.

That was easier than planned, Daniel sighed. "How did you know I wanted to go home?"

"It's a first year thing, and you're from the Rockies. Your parents are dear to you. Y'know I'd half expected you to ask me on your first day," he said. "There is a list for carriages, but considering your unique ability you don't need one of those."

Daniel wiped his hands on his pants again and sighed, smiling. "How long is the list?"

"Long. People do errands on their days off for me and go up the list, or receive special treatment. But that won't apply to you, so I'll have to think of some different boundaries," he grinned, "I won't go into technicalities just yet."

Daniel nodded and smiled. "Thank you, sir."

"Before I forget, Enek came to me and told me that your first class went slightly sour."

"I'm not surprised. All my classes this week have been full of *drama*."

"I've heard. You're getting to be quite the act, aren't you? How has your first week been?"

"Oh, I don't mean to be at the centre of it," Daniel said, averting his glance from Reuben.

"Just keep a low profile. There are quite a few people here who will challenge you if you get *popular*. And you don't have the greatest background do you," Reuben chuckled, and then settled himself. "How are you finding the technology?"

"I haven't really touched it."

"Oh, but it was meant to help. There's an entire backlog of information stored on that computer."

"Really?"

"Yes, I figured it would be an edge, well, that's why I thought you'd been causing so much concern."

"I never really grew up with technology."

Reuben chuckled to himself. "Nobody really has. They're very new advances within The City."

Daniel nodded. "Thank you."

"Let's keep this between us, okay? You may leave. I have lots of paperwork for this assembly tomorrow."

Before Daniel went back to his dorm, he checked the shower rooms on the ground floor to make sure there were no unexpected surprises. The best times to shower were either really early in the morning, or really late at night. The shower room was huge; five stone and steel welded shower cubicles against both walls with grooves in the ground to move the water to the drains.

Daniel fiddled with the controls and the head of the shower above him. It was much more technical than it had been at home. He turned the numbered dials and pressed buttons with weird symbols beneath them until something came out of the head. "Ack!" he yelled and flinched out of the freezing water. He held a hand under as the water went from one extreme to the other. It happened to him each time he used the showers, but he never learnt his lesson.

"I don't know what he did, but he'll pay," Jasper shouted.

"Maybe we underestimated him," Mark said.

"We'll get him though. *I* am affined with the lion."

Daniel turned his shower off to listen, but they'd stopped speaking. His skin pimpled in the cool air. He turned his shower on and strained to listen; he'd have to get out after them, or before. The thought of timing plagued his mind, and he could barely rinse the soap from his hair with his fingers trembling.

He heard their showers start. He washed the suds of his body and turned his shower off. He put some underwear on and wrapped a towel around his waist. He piled all his clothes into his arms and took a deep breath. He unlatched the cubicle and the door swung open, slamming against the brick.

"Did you bring towels?" Jasper shouted over his cubicle wall.

"Yeah. Oh, crap. I left them hooked up," Mark shouted back, his shower went off and the clang of his latch drummed through Daniel.

Daniel ran through the water. His feet splashed around, and although the room had steamed up, he knew that if he was noticed something would happen.

"It's okay, I have one!" Jasper shouted. And in the same instance, "he's out here! Jasper, he's out here!"

"Who?" Jasper unlatched his cubicle and peered out.

Daniel rushed towards the doors at the bottom, clutching the towel around his waist and clinging to the bundle of clothes in his arms. He could see Jasper stepping out and tying a towel around his waist.

Jasper grinned. He was stood between Daniel and the way out. While Mark was stood behind him. "What was that stunt?" Jasper asked. "Oh, you're quiet now." He glared.

"I wonder what would happen if I froze him in this steam," Mark giggled. "Do you want me to?"

Daniel dropped his clothes on the wet floor as something trickled down the back of his throat. He scrunched his hand up into a fist and as he flicked his fingers an electricity caught the steam and bolted through the vapour. It singed the edges of their towels. Smoke and steam filled the rest of the room. They panicked and put out the fires on their towels while Daniel grabbed his clothes and slipped out.

They shouted and cursed after him. Their voices faded as Daniel headed for the stairs. He dressed on his way up, hooking his arms into his t-shirt, and limping into his pajama bottoms. He managed to bundle his towel and dirty clothes into his arms as he slowed down. He turned and saw them, clutching at their charred towels and slipping along the floor.

It became a race to the third floor. Daniel reached it first. He slammed the door and conjured all the will inside himself to lock it. A *click*.

He made his way down to his room, and glanced back to see Jasper and Mark's faces twist as they banged on the glass.

The door opened. "Oi, we'll get you back!" Jasper shouted.

"Gotta catch me first," he said over his shoulder and then sprinted for his room. He dug his hand into his pocket for his card, but it wasn't there. He felt around in his dirty clothes, but nothing. They were metres away. He tugged on the door handle and it dragged him inside. He slammed the door shut and flicked the lock. He sighed and leant against it.

"It's a door, we can break it!" Mark rapped his knuckles against the wood.

"We can't," Jasper said in a whisper but Daniel heard, "people listen to him, he'll just tell and then we'll get shouted at or something. We need to get him off timetable, and *off* campus."

CHAPTER SIXTEEN

EXCITEMENT quaked in Daniel's stomach, waking him before his alarm. He relaying thoughts of what he was going to tell Jac and his parents and how he was going to show them some of the new stuff that he'd learnt, even though he didn't *really* know what he'd learnt. It was all a new understanding.

He scrambled around and dressed. Checking his reflection in the remaining mirror before he rushed out of the building. He raced with himself down the long path to the towering iron clad front gates. There was a small booth integrated into the cladding where a man sat up to a control board. There was another man; he was shirtless and he stood beside the booth. He glared down the path, eyeing Daniel.

154

The guard flared his nostrils and sucked in a deep breath. "Your name?"

"Daniel," he replied.

"Last name?" his face eased up.

"S-Satoria."

The guard picked up a clipboard from inside the booth, and scrolled his finger down the side. "Oh." he smiled. "You're the kid from the Lowerlands," he said. Daniel nodded. "The flying one. Well we don't get many Lowerlands here, in fact unless you work here, you're probably the first."

"Can I—can I go?" Daniel asked.

"Oh, yeah. You're on the list. I guess there's no waiting around for carriages."

Daniel smiled back at him and took a step back to face the looming gates as they screeched open. His heart raced at the sound of iron being pulled against stone, meshing against his eardrums.

"Have a good day, Mr. Satoria," he said, and waved Daniel off as he left through the gates.

Daniel walked for a minute or so until he was alone and standing in the midst of the dense forest. He sighed and placed a hand on the trunk of a thick tree. The tree thumped beneath his touch. He gasped.

"Hey," he said. He stroked the trunk again. It was a pulse. He smiled. "Beautiful."

He grinned to himself and sat on the grass, taking his shoes and odd socks off to be placed beneath the tree. "Can you watch these for me?" he grinned. He wriggled his toes around in the cool air before pressing them against the spongy grass. He took his jacket and t-shirt off, throwing them besides his shoes. He flexed his chest and bent backwards to crack the tension in his body.

A new tension prickled his shoulder blades and numbed him. He shivered and straightened his back, revealing two pieces of bone. They were thick at the top and massed golden feathers. He closed his eyes and pushed himself up on his tiptoes to embrace the air. His wings took one powerful slash through the air and pushed him up two feet above the ground.

Something unsettled him and he dropped back to the ground. He couldn't wash the feeling of being watched away. He turned and glanced in each direction before he laughed to himself. *Insects are always watching, and trees have pulses*, he told himself.

He brought the ends of his wings around his waist. "Long time," he said, stroking them as they tickled the sides of his abdomen. "If only you guys were permanent," he grinned.

He picked his t-shirt up and tucked it into the front of his pants before tying the jacket around his waist. He hunched his body low and controlled his breath. He jumped with little effort, bouncing off the balls of his feet. His wings spread and caught him with a gentle flap.

He hovered above the trees and through a few low clouds that disbanded when he wafted his wings.

"It's so beautiful," he mumbled as he looked ahead to the next town, *Mirau*, he guessed.

There was a house in the centre; a huge house made from white square-cut bricks, the only building of its kind to Daniel. There were other houses, hundreds of them, surrounding it. They were smaller, but bigger than any building from the Lowerlands. By the white house was a grey stone fountain and on the grass families were sat playing games and eating from wooden hampers.

Daniel pushed his stomach and watched the families as they sat on the greenest of grasses. He could hear their laughter echo up.

It wasn't long before he reached the Rockies, most notably the only part of Templar Island that was lifeless; grey, drab, dull, except for the tree that had grown beside Daniel's house, as well as moss and the different ivies that grew up the rock face.

Daniel almost passed his home until a cinch in his throat stopped him, and his wings batted backward. He found his regular landing spot and let himself free fall as he aimed for it.

The gush hit his face and rushed down his throat. He landed and a wave of pain touched his feet. He looked down to see the dried blood still in the dust.

The front door whooshed open. "Daniel!" his father shouted.

"Dad!" Daniel shouted as his wings pulled back into his body. He grabbed his t-shirt from his waistband.

"You've been gone a week. In fact less than a week, why are you back?" his father chuckled softly.

"If you don't wanna know how it's going I'll just talk to mum, or go see Jac."

His father opened his arms to embrace him

"Getting stronger as well," his father said, letting go.

"Where's mum? Thought she'd be out already," he said.

"She's working again. She's been working since you left. She needed something to fill her time, especially after all the special looking after you've needed," they both shared a laugh.

They both walked into the house and his father closed the door behind them. Daniel sat on the settee, he felt a little awkward. He didn't know how to handle himself. His father sat in his chair. The house was dusty and streams of it could be seen in the light.

"So. Have you seen Jac?" Daniel asked as he shared an uncomfortable stare with his father.

"Not lately, but your mother saw him the other day, and he said you'd been to see him. Oh, well, she did say that he's gone on some chase for a panther," he snickered, "who'd have thought he'd lose his mind already. Guess that's what the Lowerlands does though."

Daniel smiled, but he couldn't imagine Jac going after the panther, more like hiding from it, or trying to find out its identity. "School's good," he said, "although they made a big deal about my flare."

His father's face straightened and he pushed forward, hunching his back with unease. "What do you mean?"

"It's gold," Daniel said.

His father's eyes widened and he sat back. "Oh, the Satoria bloodline has always been *prophesied* for good things," he boasted, "my grandfather told me a story about his father who gave it all up for a girl, she was from the Lowerlands, but he used to change the story every time he told it me." He grinned, and stared straight ahead, his eyes glazing over in recollection.

That was the first time Daniel had ever heard any stories about his great-grandfather and he wanted to hear more, and ask more, but the upset look on his father's face told him to do otherwise.

"When's mum gonna be back?"

"Late, I think. If you'd have sent us a letter, then we could've made you something to take back with you," his father said, "well your mum would've."

They both fell silent. "Dad?"

"Yeah."

"Is there anything *off* the Island?" he asked and saw the question send shivers inside his father.

"The outside world was another one of my grandfather's stories, he often told me how he didn't come from this island, but another, a huge other, one where we're a dot in comparison," his father said. He fidgeted in his lap. "They can't harness or have any energy off the island. And apparently, Satoria is the namesake of Saturn, one of the seven who unleashed our capabilities all those generations ago. Or that's what I was told."

Daniel took that into account as another reason Jasper hated him. "So why don't people just come and go from Templar if we're the only ones who can use these energies?"

"Hidden, perhaps. And rumours say that if you go off to some other land then you'd die, or be killed by the guards, but they're just rumours. Our existence to them is fairytale."

Yeah, rumours. Daniel strictly remembered the fury on Reuben's face when he'd confronted him about being off campus that night when he met Mia, something he still couldn't remember much about.

"Can we teleport *off* the island?" Daniel asked.

His father grinned. "This sure is some serious talk. I suppose so. Have they taught you that yet?"

Daniel shook his head. "But I did it once by accident. I'm a little confused."

"That's because it's instinct, I was never taught at a school like yours, in fact it was all a learning curve for me. I am glad that you're there though," he said.

"I don't like it," Daniel mumbled.

His father laughed. "It's for a better life. And by the sound of it, you're getting along okay. Reuben is a very famous man; he doesn't just admit anyone to his school."

"Oh, he does," Daniel laughed, thinking about Tanner and how he behaved when they'd first met. And then *with* a punch to his stomach the thought of Carlie, but it wasn't a savoured thought. "And the food there isn't the best."

"I'll make you something then," his father said to Daniel's grinning face.

CHAPTER SEVENTEEN

DANIEL couldn't get Mia out of his mind. He knew now that she wasn't from his island, but he'd known that at the time. She was real and she was from *somewhere*. He knew where, it was finding that on a map he didn't possess that was proving difficult.

"Lexar Hotel. New York," he repeated to himself as if he would forget it any moment now.

As soon as he got back to his room, he grabbed the laptop from the chest of drawers. His father had explained that it was just like a computer he'd used in the library. It took a while to load. But when it did he could load the servers and search the net.

I'm sorry, the page you are looking for is out of bounds. Please redirect your search. He read the words, over and over. He then typed 'skyscraper' into the search bar and waited. He drummed his fingers on the plastic. Over 50 million results came in; he clenched his teeth. *There aren't even that many people alive*, he told himself.

He clicked on *'images'* to see if one of them could spark the image. "C'mon, c'mon," he said, scrolling. One huge glass tower after another, some of them twisted against grey skies while others reflected sunsets.

Ten minutes of clicking and manipulating the images on the screen to fit what he'd seen, and he'd almost lost the image in his head. He closed his eyes, *it's all intuitive,* he repeated to himself. He tried to recreate her face, small and oval, and her brown hair and the stray bit at the side which she stroked behind her ears, and how she smelled of coconut. His eyelids flickered as he tried to remember. *What a weird thing to smell like, coconut,* he smiled.

Mia watched pink and orange marshmallow clouds shift across the dark skyline. They trailed past the small crescent moon anchored in the sky. A crackle caught her ears; she gasped and hooked her hand around the handle of the closed picnic basket.

She stifled a shriek with a hand as she watched Daniel materialise. Stress creased her face, mixed with her disbelief and blinking.

"Mia?" Daniel said.

She glared as her knuckles turned white from the grasp she had on her basket. "What the hell are you?"

"I don't know. What do you mean?"

"Well you weren't here a second ago, and now you are! You just *appeared!*" she said and gasped for breath. Her grip tightened around the handle.

They both fell silent together as neither knew what to say next. Daniel smiled and Mia couldn't look away. She shot him a quizzical look and her lips parted, ready to question him, instead she patted a free spot on the blanket for him to sit. Daniel knelt on the corner, apprehensive of the quirk in her eye.

"Do you want a drink?" she asked and opened the basket.

"Yeah," he replied in a squeak.

She grinned and handed him a carton of orange juice, stabbing it with a straw.

"How long have you been up here for?" he asked.

"Every night since we met, I did my homework up here the other night," she said. "It's stupid."

"Why?"

"The same reason why I'm not trying to stick a stake through your chest, because you're—"

"I'm not harmful," he butted in. "I'd never harm a beetle, well, *there was that—*"

"Oh, god, I know you're not *dangerous*, but now I'm worrying," she smirked, sucking on the straw in her carton. "You're different, that's what I was going to say. You're not from around here, and I like that."

"No, in fact, I'm still not all too sure where *here* is."

"Me either. I hate it." She rolled her eyes. "Can I give you my phone number?" she asked and glanced at Daniel's unsure look, "you do have a phone right?"

Daniel pulled the phone from his pocket, he hadn't bothered with it. "I don't really get technology. It's still new."

"It's fine, I'll put my number in," she said taking the phone from his hand. "It's a touchscreen, and you're *new* to technology. I can't say I've seen this model before either."

Daniel shrugged. "It was a gift."

"Whoever gave you this must be some person," she said, "I mean, like amazing, it looks like it came straight from the manufacturer."

"The same person admitted me to his prestigious school, it's a great school, he says that I'm really talented, although I don't think that's a good thing," he grinned.

"I can see you're talented, and I suppose people would get jealous," Mia said, "but surely if everyone knew about you then there'd be a worldwide search for the guy who can appear wherever he wants. You're a national threat," she giggled.

"I hope it's nothing too serious," he grinned.

Mia settled. She looked from her phone to Daniel's. "Why's your time different?" she asked, pushing the screen up to his face.

"Why, what time do you make it?"

"Nearly seven," she said, "and you make it almost one."

Daniel took his phone back off her and pushed it into his pocket. He touched her hand, and she smiled at him. He pulled his hand away as he felt tiny throbs in the end of his fingertips and nothing good ever came of those.

"Do you ever just sit *here* and watch the sunset?" he asked.

"That was the plan," she sniggered.

"Plan?" he asked, catching a glimpse of her eye.

"Picnic and sunset," she said, "I did it all the time when I was at home. With family."

"You *can* still picnic together."

She shook her head and shunned her eyes. "It's awkward, she's like twenty-three or something, and he's nearly thirty-six. She would have been seven when I was born," she said and crinkled her nose.

"On Templar Island, we don't marry. We exchange something far greater than that of, what is it?" He furrowed his brow. "Ah, words, although there are words involved in the ceremony," he explained. "There's just *more* to it."

"What? Go on, tell me. What is it?" she asked, perking and sitting on her knees.

"I don't know, that's all I've been told," he replied. "My parents wouldn't tell me, and it's not a big deal really, I'm only sixteen."

"I don't want to marry full stop, but I bet yours is so special. Special enough not to cheat," she laughed.

Daniel nodded. "That's another thing, whatever it is that's shared keeps the two of them together forever, there's just no arguing. My mum told me that sometimes she has the same dreams as my dad."

"You're gonna have to take me there. In fact, I'll just look it up online."

"I don't think you'd find it. I'm rather lucky to be there in the first place," he grinned.

She pulled the basket closer. "Hungry?" she asked, showing him the plastic boxes of food.

"What have you got?"

Mia picked through the plastic boxes and placed them in a row for him to see. There were grapes, labeled '*grapes: seedless*' and two boxes with sandwiches labeled '*Ham*' and the other '*Cheese*', and beside them were two apples wrapped inside a plastic film.

"I have chocolate for dessert," she said.

They ate, Daniel was more nervous than hungry, but he ate. He performed little tricks like throwing grapes into the air and catching them in his mouth. Mia couldn't do it for some reason, although Daniel knew exactly why, because he kept pushing them away.

"Stop it—whatever you're doing," she said and playfully hit his shoulder. She moved down and gripped his arm, "oh, you're so muscly," she giggled.

Daniel blushed, it was the first comment he'd ever received from a girl, the exception being his mother, but then again, that had never been about the shape he was in, or how strong he was. He smiled, and she went in closer, he watched her close her eyes and pucker her lips. But he couldn't. He pulled away and stood.

His heart vibrated in his ears. "Um. I best be going. I have this thing that I need to get to at school. So phone me," he said with a pant in his breath. He closed his eyes and turned. He wanted to take one last look but before he could blink and *snap* the photo. There was a cold explosion inside. It rendered him to his hands and knees on the floor in his room.

Several loud thumps accompanied the ache in his head, and again, louder this time. "You in there?" Tanner shouted from the other side of the door.

Daniel glanced up, confused by Tanner's tone. Unless Jasper had done something. "Yeah," Daniel replied. He pushed to his feet.

"I've been knocking for like ten minutes," he said.

Daniel unlocked his door and Tanner stood glaring into his eyes, his cheeks puffed red.

"Are you okay?" Daniel asked.

"No. You lied, Lowerlands scum!"

"Scum? Scum!" Daniel bridged the gap between them, he was a little taller than Tanner. "I'm scum?" he asked and stared. He clenched his hands into fists for an opportunity to hit him.

Tanner stuttered. "Yeah." He continued, "and a liar. You said you were rich. I bet you stole those things, didn't ya!"

"Shut up, and go away. Who are you trying to intimidate?" Daniel asked, his fingers urged to prod Tanner in his puffed out chest and then laugh at how he'd followed him around like a lost puppy. He didn't want Tanner to reply, if he did, he wouldn't contain himself, he promised that, something touched a nerve, not only did he disapprove of Tanner's actions to the carriage staff, but he brought Lowerlands into it and he was from the Rockies.

Tanner stuttered again before he could string any sentences together. Daniel pushed passed him and shut his door. He hurried to the end of the hall, his hands still clenched into fists and his teeth grit together. He listened to the slow footsteps follow behind.

He unclenched his hands and walked out of the doors at the end of the hall. He glanced through the glass and noticed Tanner's red face getting closer. Daniel shivered as he summoned two strands of delicately weaved energy from his fingertips. He tied them around them handles and grinned.

"You're going to be late for the assembly," he laughed as Tanner pushed himself up against the doors. He rattled them slightly and shouted something that was muffled behind glass.

Daniel was early for the assembly. He sat in the middle and watched as people filled the seats around him. He kept an eye on the door and puffed at his cheeks when he saw Tanner. He walked in with Jasper, Mark, and Carlie. Jasper glanced right at him with a smug grin on his face and a curl to his lip. Daniel turned his head and kept his eyes forward.

Reuben took to the stage. He cleared his throat and everyone hushed. "The first week of the semester has passed, and quite frankly you've all passed that all important first test, so well done. Unlike previous years no students have been sent home, well there are a few who've asked to go home for a visit but nobody has thought of quitting altogether. Probably because this year's *hand*-selected students are the most special by far," Reuben said. He grasped a hold of the podium as his right leg wobbled. He stumbled slightly as he left his post. He tapped Chey on the shoulder to take the stand.

She walked on the stage with a few cards in hand. She placed them on the podium and wiped a hand through her hair. "As many of you know, this school also offers other lessons and activities to aide and develop current skills, such as learning about the different faculties of your being, and how to use them to your own advantage. How to call on the seven Luminary presences, and even which ones you should prayer to. Perhaps you're an altruist and want to learn about medicines to help people, or learn about plants, gardening and *that stuff*," she said, flicking through the cars. She glanced at Reuben as he smiled and nodded. "I don't think there's anything else that anyone wants to discuss. There will be several piles of leaflets in the foyer, return any slips, forms et cetera to the teacher who is offering the activity as it is first come, first serve." She turned to leave the stand, but the assembly hall was still quiet. She grinned, "you may leave. But all first years must take their first year pin, these must be worn at *all times*."

Daniel noticed Reuben stand and take a hard grip of his walking stick. He eyed him suspiciously as he dragged his limping leg.

Daniel pushed through people and chairs to get to him. "Are you okay, sir?" he asked.

"Oh, it's nothing. Well I broke my leg a while ago and sometimes it plays up and splinters," he replied, and waved a hand at the matter.

"I bet that hurts."

Reuben shook his head. He paused. "I have a favour to ask," he said, and Daniel perked up, trying to listen over the stampede of feet and screeching of chairs.

"Yeah. Sure."

"There have been a few breaches from the campus to *lands* outside the island. Have you heard anything about it?" he asked.

Yes "No," *it was me*, Daniel said, gulping and shaking his head.

"If you hear anything about it, come and tell me. I'm on the board for island safety, and part of my responsibility is to keep all *threats* detained."

"Threats?"

Reuben smiled. "Not to us, but to the people on the outside. People have started families off the island and all of them have been killed within moments of us knowing about it. This is serious, and I trust you. Lowerlands people like *you* never lie. So if you hear anything, just knock on my door, I'm always happy to listen to their *pathetic* excuses," he snarled.

Daniel forced a dazed smile and nodded. "Sure thing." He blinked to focus himself and Reuben had gone. In his hands, Daniel held his first year pin, the golden letters '*year one*' engraved on it glittered in the light. He sighed and dropped against a wall. He brought a hand to his neck and felt his pulse kick from beneath his skin.

"I can do this," he said. A rush hit him as he fought to teleport back to his room.

That's going to come in handy. Being able to go wherever I want and not being caught by Jasper, he thought and fell back on his bed.

He moved around the room to the window. The sun was high in the sky, and to think that not so long ago he was watching that same sun as it set, it just sounded bizarre, like thinking, or knowing that he was the one breaching the law. *Maybe I should plead my case? It can't be that pathetic; a girl, if she wanted she could learn, right? But then there was that man, he had a family off the island. And they were all slaughtered.* He pressed the palms of his hands against his forehead and pushed.

"I'm glad I didn't kiss her, in fact she's probably being hunted down. My fault. All my fault," he forced out from beneath his gritted teeth. "It's gotta be easier than just—trying to force it all away. Can I even make it right? They'll figure out soon enough!"

He picked his clothes up from the floor and made a small pile of laundry. He looked at his alarm clock; it was *16:00*. He wanted to get away again. He stayed in his room and after making his bed, he dressed in his pyjamas and climbed inside.

CHAPTER EIGHTEEN

THE BLACK backdrop of Daniel's dreamscapes washed over him in his bed. He tried to push at it, painting the sunset he'd watched with Mia.

He failed. "You found me," the voice spoke. "Oh, well she's very pretty. How did you come by her again?" he asked, standing tall in front of Daniel. A smile touched the side of his lips. "More importantly. How did you find *me* this time?"

A grumble voiced from inside Daniel's throat. "What are you doing here?" He threw his hand up to his face. "And who's pretty?"

"Who?" the man mimicked, "Mia Crosgrove, 16. She's originally from London, but moved to New York when her father found a higher paying job. You know this girl, right? Brown hair, blue eyes, and the odd freckle."

"You only know that because you're a part of my imagination," Daniel said. He sniggered and looked on.

"Oh, kid, you might just be part of me."

"I don't know you! Who are you?" Daniel shouted. His voice echoed in the slick black fields around them.

"*Karsar*, Karsar Hanley, but of course you already knew that," he said, his laughter filling the dark void. "You're in *my* dream tonight."

Daniel closed his eyes and for the first time the darkness was comforting. He felt the air in his face, and at that point he opened his eyes. But he wished he'd kept them closed. He was standing on the ledge of the hotel where Mia lived. He gasped and panicked, looking over. Karsar grabbed his arm from behind and steadied him.

"You wouldn't die anyway, probably just be in a lot of pain when you woke up," he said and let go of Daniel's arm.

"Of course, it's a dream," Daniel chuckled. He stepped down from the ledge and walked through the floodlights.

"You could've put some clothes on, but it's fine. We're going indoors anyway. Let's see who it is you *adore* so much. Heck, I feel like one of those ghosts from *A Christmas Carol*," he grinned.

"What's that?" Daniel hunched his shoulders and pulled at his t-shirt.

"A book, also a film."

"Never read it, and I watched television once when I was little. That's about it though."

Karsar stared. "Not living like a *king* at all then. We're going to take a look at Mia, I've studied where she sleeps," he winked.

"Eh."

"I'm looking out for you," he said and walked away in a flicker.

Daniel shook his head. "C'mon, Karsar," he said. And again, the surroundings changed, everything was unusual except one thing; Mia, she was asleep in bed.

"I told you this was my dream tonight, I don't want you to know too much about dreams, they're not that useful *really*," he snickered. He snooped around Mia's room, touching her belongings.

"What are you doing?"

"I'm not allowed to look? Although we can interact with our surrounding, nothing will really move. And you're not really *breaching* any rules," he grinned.

"How'd you—" Karsar lifted his hand to pause Daniel. "So what is it you wanted to show me?"

"Her. Asleep. They've not taken her or imprisoned her or *hung* her."

"What?"

"You overwhelmed me. You induced yourself into a nightmare whilst I was asleep, and it was your worst nightmare apparently," Karsar said. "Strong emotions can dictate what we do."

"It's not like I even know who you are," Daniel said. "You're some weird *nightmare*, and you're not even that scary anymore."

Karsar rolled his eyes as he picked up Mia's book bag. "I had this *dream* of yours without even yawning or *needing* sleep, in fact I fell down like a narcoleptic in a bar somewhere, and your head is still god damn clear."

Daniel yawned. "I'm sorry."

"She's reading the classics, *Robinson Crusoe*, *Gulliver's Travels*, you'd think she hated it here with this type of escapism."

"Never heard of them."

Karsar dropped the back and grit his teeth. "You're annoying me," he said. "Now leave, I need to wake up."

"But I have questions now."

Karsar raised an eyebrow and grinned. "Not my problem," he hissed. He swung his arm around and punched Daniel square in the face. Daniel shuffled back on his feet and fell, disappearing in a flash of light.

Daniel woke coughing, one hand on his chest and another blotting the pain on his face. He groaned, and turned in his bed. He opened one eye to see Carlie. She was laying on her side at his side with a hand on her hip, and the other playing with her hair.

"So," she began, stroking the side of his face. Daniel didn't try and wriggle out of her touch, at first; he didn't understand where he was or what was going on. He'd locked his door, he was sure of that, and he'd tied a knot of energy to keep it bolted. He glanced over, and it was still intact. "Mr. Sleepy."

"Carlie?" he said. He tried to blink away the sleep from his eyes.

"Shush," she said softly and kissed him on his lips.

He pushed her back, but she didn't budge. He shuffled out of his duvet and off his bed. He stared down at her. She brought herself up to her knees, and they were at the same height. She kissed him again and pushed her head against his.

"Go away," he said, holding his hands up to protest. "Stop."

"You don't say stop. Nobody ever says stop," she giggled and pursed her lips.

"I don't want you here, and you're the reason that Jasper's been at me!"

"No, he just hates you. Besides that, he doesn't even know about this, *yet*. You're all anyone needs," she said puffing her chest out and biting her bottom lip.

Three bangs shook the bedroom door from its foundation. Daniel eyed Carlie's grin as she stood before skipping over to the door. She flipped the lock and broke the seal of energy, letting the door roll open. Jasper stood in the doorway.

"I'm glad you're here. He *tried*—he tried to kiss me," she said, pretending to sob into her hands. She threw herself into Jasper's arms.

Jasper gently pushed her away. She rushed off down the hall whimpering. Jasper glared, the colour of his eyes glazed yellow and rivets of fur broke his skin.

"I didn't. She was in here when I woke up!" Daniel said.

"To be honest I don't care. This was going to happen anyway, and there's no teacher here!" he roared and pounced at Daniel as he shifted into the lion form.

Daniel dodged the attacked and jumped on his bed. Jasper growled and snapped his jaw at Daniel. He climbed up on the bed with two of the paws and let out another roar.

Daniel held himself back. He tried to push his way to the corner of the room to reach the door. Jasper shredded the duvet, tearing into it with his claws. Daniel stopped, he was shaking, he tried to shift, he tried to teleport, but nothing.

"I want you dead!" Jasper shouted.

"Why?"

Jasper forced himself forward for Daniel. Daniel made fists of his hands, ready to fight, and he did. He swung and the lion collided with his fist, Jasper sat on top, digging his claws into Daniel, piercing his skin with three fresh cuts down his arm.

"Get off!" he shouted.

Jasper lifted his paw to take another hit, but he couldn't force it back down. Daniel turned under him and grabbed his arms tightly, his grip slipped as he pulled fur from the lion. Jasper fell; his fur molted and littered Daniel with dark blond clumps, until all that was left was Jasper, twitching in a slump on top of him.

Daniel pushed Jasper away. "You weigh a ton!" he said, "get up!" He nudged with a foot, but Jasper didn't move.

Thrangs of pain ran down Daniel's arm. He looked once, and the cuts were only faint marks of where there was open wounds. He rubbed his fingers over it and the already dry blood crumbled. It looked as though the cuts had never been there.

Jasper groaned and mumbled something as he tried to push himself up. "Think—think again! You should never. Ever!" he shouted. He stood, balancing himself against the wall before rushing out of the door.

Daniel watched as the door slam behind. He felt somewhat empowered, without knowing exactly why, or what he'd done.

CHAPTER NINETEEN

KARSAR couldn't find comfort. He kicked the silk sheets off his restless legs and climbed out of bed. The room was dark. He fumbled his way to the bathroom and the lights popped on overhead.

He ran the cold tap in the sink and watched his reflection in the mirror as the hum of pipes carrying water chugged around the bathroom. He splashed water in his face and looked back at himself.

What will I tell them? He thought. *It was a simple task*, he repeated to himself.

"And what is troubling you?" a deep voice rumbled from behind.

"*Richard*," Karsar said. He turned the taps off and picked a towel from the handrail.

"Hmm. So what is it?"

Karsar dried his face and hands. "Nothing. Just a little tired."

"I hope Elisa isn't working you too hard," he said, walking out into the fluorescents of the bathroom. He wore a shiny black suit and toyed with his cufflinks.

"No. No, I'm working myself too hard," he chuckled. "I've been watching him a lot, in fact I think he's watching me as well, that, or he's stronger than *we* thought."

"What do you expect, we all thought that line was gone, but we felt the shift, we know he's real," Richard said. He walked around the bathroom and admired the use of glass and mirrors in the tiling.

"I'm still young. I can't read them like you can, any of you." Karsar sighed. He glared at his bare feet on the cold rock tiles. "I'm trying to learn. I'm trying."

"Daniel is as well. Daniel is younger in fact, the more you have in common with him, the more trust you'll instill in him. We *need* that trust."

"And if not, then what? I tried to go there, *like I am*, but I felt something, a trigger."

Richard shook his head. "I explained, and I did so perfectly, with the barrier still *up*, nobody can enter or leave."

"How come he—"

"Figure—*it*—out."

Karsar took a deep breath and nodded to Richard. "I'm trying, but I'll try harder."

"Does he *even* know yet?"

Karsar bowed his head and stared at his feet once more. "I just don't know what to do. Can *I* tell him? Elisa keeps on telling me to wait, but he's getting restless. I feel it, and the more I tell him, the more I worry he'll become strong on his own."

Richard burst into a hum of laughter. "The more we tell him, the more he'll trust us, and the more he'll tell us. But hold up on telling him anything that could make him spiral, it's for the guardian to tell him *that*."

"My father ruined that for me," Karsar said. He lifted his arm to show a scar, a horned circle with an upside down Catholic cross; the astrological symbol of Mercury. He scowled at it.

"That's natural. You must *bleed*. We've been through this, stop fretting. You're a Luminary. A pillar of existence, and when we have another, the world will know our names."

"You always know what to tell me."

"And you always need to be told what to do," Richard said, "I know you're a little upset, but I have to leave. I can't keep a lady waiting," he winked, and disappeared.

Karsar sighed. He held himself up on the basin with one hand, and with the other he rubbed his eyes. He stood and studied his body, and then lifted his arm to himself in the mirror.

He looked at the red symbol scabbed over across the left side of his ribcage. His fingers lingered across it as fragmented pieces of his past tickled him.

Daniel watched the steady downpour clatter on the single-pane window. He listened to the drum rolls of thunder entertain the sky and break even in the centre, spreading their electric charges through the thick clouds outside. It was mesmerizing. Daniel had never watched it rain before, he didn't get the sights back home because there was always some cliff covering the view.

The screen on his phone flashed. He turned to see it flash again. He picked it up to see a missed call from Mia. "I don't think I can talk to you, Mia," he said and threw his phone to the end of his bed. "It's not fair. To either of us," he whined and closed his eyes. He hadn't hoped for anyone to answer him, but hearing his own voice was a gift.

*Life—is—it's—*each word ended with a loud crackle inside his ears. He pushed a finger in his ear and itched. He winced at the sounds, but it wasn't Karsar, the voice didn't feel ominous or cold. *Never—not—really—fair—is it,* the voice finished with loud static flooding his ear drums. He plugged his fingers harder in his ears. But that didn't satisfy the pain.

"You can hear me?" The voice asked as Daniel pushed his head into his new duvet. *"Get some cold water on it."* Daniel gritted his teeth and told himself that he wasn't going crazy.

184

He pushed himself from his bed and rinsed a cloth by the sink with cold water, hoping not to cut himself on the discarded mirror. He slapped it across his face. The cold sent relief through his fingertips and as it dripped down his neck he rolled his eyes.

"I've been better," he said to himself.

"So you can hear me, I knew it!" The voice broke again in his head.

"What?" Daniel said.

"It's me," the voice replied, *"Jac."*

"How? How is this even possible? I'm asleep aren't I?"

"It is possible! And no you're not asleep, you're fine! I woke from this dream the other night, and everything seemed to slot into place."

"But how is *this* possible."

"I met with a woman from Carster. She reads dreams. She read mine, and found something, well she sparked something really."

"And at what part did you realise you could do *this?*"

"Actually, she said it isn't uncommon, and it's not just us. It's natural; the woman told me that this is something twins can do, but also friends, especially if they've got a connection like twins."

"So we have a connection. And I'm paying for it," Daniel chuckled.

"Yeah, wait, no. What do you mean?"

"My head is throbbing, like I fell from a tree into a pile of rocks."

"She said that would happen, in fact I had that same feeling, just drink lots of water. And watch the rain, I mean, you were watching the rain, right?"

Daniel reached for his cup full of water and chugged it. He wiped his mouth and felt the cold spread in his chest to his stomach where he tensed and clenched. "So, what was this dream then?"

"You were killed. He was going at you, his claws full and everything. He was going for your throat, and then…and then, you weren't there, and I was…and I was standing at your grave."

Daniel's eyes glossed over as he blinked away tears. He thought he was content with death and dying, considering he faced it in almost every situation. But when his best friend had dreamt it, standing at his graves and being witness. It was almost a truth, it sounded like something that could happen, yet anything seemed possible lately.

"Are you okay? Do you want to know more?"

"Yeah. Dreams are dreams," Daniel tried to reassure himself.

"It was a lion, he was huge! And there was a girl on her knees in tears watching, but she couldn't see me. In fact I don't think I could see me. She was at your funeral as well. Her name—her name—her name was Mia. But it was just a dream."

"Mia," he said, sucking in a sob.

"Why? Who's Mia? Are you crying?"

"She's not from the island, and *no*!" he said, "I'm just ill, sniffles and everything, that water did nothing but make me cold."

"Wait. What! You've been off the island?"

"It was accidental, but they know that someone breached the island. That was *me*! You know what happens to them? They're killed along with everyone they bump into along the way and everyone that they've ever known!"

"That's some serious stuff you got going on there. But really, how would they know who you talked to, do people you touch start to form large black ulcers on their skin?" Jac asked, and Daniel could feel his smirk.

The phone at the bottom of Daniel's bed buzzed, and the screen flashed. He picked it up, it was Mia.

"How do you stop this?" he asked, gesturing his hands to his head.

"Well she only told me how to start it. And even then she said that it might not have been possible."

"I just need it to stop."

"Why? What's more important than catching up?"

"That girl, *Mia*, she's phoning me."

"Phone? Well, haven't you gone up in the world," Jac laughed. *"I'll just try and do the opposite of what she said then, and pull away."*

Daniel didn't speak back. He felt the phone vibrate several times in his hand before it finished, and start up again.

"Hey," he said, answering the phone.

"Daniel, come back. I need to see you," she said.

"What's up?"

"It's my dad. He woke me up shouting, and rambling about how I needed to adapt to the city or he'd send me away—to—to one of them homes where parents send their children if they don't like them," she sniffled.

"He wouldn't. That would be stupid. Does he drink?"

"I don't know. I pushed him away. And I was crying. And he told me how much of a disappointment I was," she said between sobs.

"He did? I'd come over but—"

"Will you?"

"But I can't. These people are strict, and they know that someone has been off the island. You know I can be killed for that, right? And you will as well. I don't want that," he said.

"Me either. Keep safe. I don't want you to die."

"Just avoid him and finish school. And when I finish school I'll know so much about what I can do that we can go somewhere they can't find us," he said, smiling to himself.

"You know, I'd like that," she sniffled.

"And if anyone asks you if you know me, you have to say no."

"I will do. I should really be asleep, my dad will be extra mad if he comes back in, unless he wants to apologize for acting like that," she said.

"Okay. Phone tomorrow, even if I'm asleep, I'll answer." he chuckled, "just don't let him get to you. But if he acts like that again, I'll come visit."

Daniel hung up and pulled the phone from his ear. He didn't know what to do. He was stuck. She was stuck. He contemplated on trying to talk to Jac again but what he wanted more than that was to see Mia and make sure she was okay.

He bit the side of his lip and winced as blood touched his tongue. "Ow," he moaned, prodding the cut with his tongue.

He turned to face the window, but the storm was quieter now. He sat and trudged the duvet up around him as he settled in them for the night with the cold cloth over his face.

A soothing voice swept by as he bordered the edge of sleep. *"Hush. Don't let it get to you. She needs saving, and of course you could just go there now and take her in your arms, take her and bring her here. But then you'll both be hung by the peak of the Trident Mountains. Wait it out, and you'll both be saved, but don't wait too long, Saturn,"* the voice was soft and serpentine, spinning a web of sleep.

CHAPTER TWENTY

THE CAMPUS had been quiet for a little over a month. No dramas, or scuffles, or midnight breakins, at least none that involved Daniel. He was restricted to his room and his classes. It was in his best interest.

He woke to his phone buzzing in his hand; he pushed it up to his face and winced at the bright white screen. "Hey," he answered. He wiped at the sleep in his eyes.

"Good morning," Mia said with a pinch of cheer.

"I don't even need an alarm clock," he chuckled, flicking the rest of the sleep from his eyes.

"It's the afternoon, well nearly 3 p.m. I thought you'd be up already."

"Wait. What. Three?" he asked and leapt from his bed.

"Yeah, why?"

"I have a meeting with Reuben at nine," he said. He grabbed clothes from his closet and threw them on his bed.

"Are you in a rush?"

He hummed and grit his teeth. "Yeah, but I'll phone you right back when I can," he said with his phone resting on his shoulder as he pushed it up to his ear. He climbed into a pair of smart pants

"Okay," she said and hung up.

Daniel dropped the phone on his bed and hurried into his clothes. He shoved the phone into his pocket and flipped the hood of his jacket up before leaving.

He'd become lazy, but more active at the same time. He was trying to master the art of teleporting, probably why there had been less trouble around the school, yet people still knew who he was, and his family roots were definitely still being talked about. Reuben insisted that Daniel stay at the school and learn, although he could've benefited from one-on-one teaching and not being shoved to the back of the room where he still had to endure the people in front of him calling him names in sly coughs.

He appeared outside Reuben's office door and took a deep breath. He didn't know what Reuben thought of him, everyone else had made it clear that they hated him, and sometimes he could see it behind Reuben's eyes and beneath the intent in his voice. He worried when Reuben requested him to visit.

Daniel knocked twice on the office door, the sounds bounced around while he waited. A different door jarred open, to Reuben's personal quarters, the door opened fully and Reuben ambled out. He straightened his tie with one hand and clutched his walking aide with the other.

The office door swung open with a wave of Reuben's hand. "Go on in then," he said and ushered Daniel. "Just running a little late today." He passed Daniel and pushed his office chair with his stick to sit down; he comforted himself and pulled up to his desk.

"You wanted to see me?" he asked, holding his hands behind his back to refrain from fidgeting or staring down at them.

"Nervous?" Reuben grinned.

"Ask if I can visit?" Jac asked, popping Daniel's ears and wobbling him.

"No," he said. He held his nose and popped his ears.

"Good, there is no need to be nervous here. I have a few questions," he said.

"Well I'm going to come visit anyway. I just wanted you to ask," Jac said.

Daniel nodded and Reuben continued. "How's your first month been? Good?"

"I'd be lying if I said so. I'm—I'm *scum* to these people," he said, taking a deep breath.

"Ah, I know about this, and I'm sorry that it's happening. You're a threat to these people because they don't understand the concept of power, it doesn't come from wealth or where you've lived or studied. It comes from the pure of heart."

"Pure heart? What's he been drinking? Is that what the water does to you up there?" Jac laughed.

Daniel nodded again. "I think the people around here are jealous that you are a late bloomer, and when you bloomed, everything about you *burst*, unlike some people who have yet to learn how to teleport or even dabble with the different facets of their being, let alone learn about them," Reuben explained. "I know that you can teleport, and I know that you can create and tamper with the fine bonds of the elements. You should really be in advanced classes. Which brings me to my next point; you didn't join any clubs, why not?"

"You join clubs to make friends, and *I* can't make friends. They said that my mum was unfaithful, and—and," he gulped and took another deep breath, "and it's stupid that they say stuff like that."

"Who? You never told me! Well I did teach you that invocation stint, just use that, you might be able to frighten them," Jac snapped, causing Daniel to stand abnormally straight.

193

"That's their jealousy, but I propose that it will all end, like I know it will. I'm setting up a group. A select group. There's not going to be a list out in the hall for people to join. Only the best and brightest students, including my nephew, Jasper," he said, leaving Jasper's name to ring through his mind, of course that's why he thought he owned the place, because his uncle did. "It's going to be held on a Tuesday morning, and of course you don't have a lesson, because you didn't pick up any extra-curriculars."

"So it's his nephew then. That psychopath, the one who wanted to kill you, bet you're glad you didn't out him when he tried to then, aren't ya," Jac said.

Daniel hummed, thinking over what they'd both said. "Okay. What's the class about?"

"Natural energies and stones," he said. He glanced up from the paper on his desk. "You're the only first year attending, so best not brag, or that could earn you some more unwelcome attention."

It was easy for Daniel not to brag, because he had no one to brag to, except for Jac, but everything Daniel heard and sometimes saw was relayed to him ad vice versa.

"So, what do you say?" Reuben asked.

"Sounds great."

"Lies! I don't know what you're thinking, but I can feel it!" Jac shouted.

"It starts this Tuesday?"

"Yeah. Do you have any personal matters that you'd like to discuss?"

Daniel hesitated, his heart throbbed in his throat as he contemplated saying anything that could offend him about his nephew or equally anger him to ask him if he could go and see Mia, in fact bringing up anywhere off the island could spark something far worse than anger, but that was only a theory.

"Don't do it! But if you're going to do anything, ask if I can visit," Jac said, his voice bounced around inside Daniel's head.

"Sometimes I just can't control it. And I went somewhere once. And I'm sorry," Daniel blurted. He bit his lip to stop it quivering.

"I'm not following," Reuben said, wrinkling his face at him.

"I was the one. I went off the island that time. I went to a skyscraper somewhere and it was amazing, and then I woke up here again," he said.

Reuben smiled, or grimaced, Daniel waited on his lips to move and push something other than the anticipated angry shouting. "I thought so. You seem like the type to have the means of teleporting that far. I think congratulations are in order for progressing faster than any other student here, and even faster than I had," he said. "I'm a little shocked that you just came out with it, people have been killed, like I told you. So why are you telling me?"

"Honestly. I don't know. It felt right and—and I thought you might understand."

"Well now I can cover for you, instead of setting up a man hunt for someone who's heard rumours of the outside world and touched the outskirts of it because that's as far as they could get," Reuben grinned, but it could have been a snarl.

"Did I hear that? He's talking about pulling some serious stuff to let you get away with that. You could have just been killed. Don't you think? Don't you consult me anymore?" Jac ranted and ached at Daniel's brain. *"Now ask him if I can come visit."*

"Power is stronger off the island, there isn't a *blanket* over there." He gestured to the ceiling, "that's how they know when someone goes, because a foreign blimp appears, I can erase that blimp though, but then nobody would know if you're in or out."

"We're being followed?"

"Not followed, watched. And it isn't just *us*, it's the blanket, if you try to take too much then you suffocate, and that's why people die when changing. It is a miracle that you can handle it," he said.

"But who watches the blanket?"

"There's a counsel," he said. "I'm sure of which you've heard. I belong to that very counsel, and I have a feeling that one day you will too."

"Well that actually makes sense. Why didn't you read a book with that in? That would be good stuff to sell in the Lowerlands," Jac laughed,

although his voice was quieter as Daniel pushed him to the back of his head.

"So what do you have to do?"

"Just take you off the map. Like you've been deleted, but only on the surface of things."

"Delete me?" Daniel asked, "and why just me?"

"I take it that you can still do that wing trick."

"*Trick*? Well, yeah."

"Don't do that over there, if you expose yourself in any nature, then that's as good as asking to be killed."

"Can I have a pass as well? Ask him? Go on," Jac's mind prodded Daniel, but he continued in ignorance.

Daniel nodded obediently. His hands loosened to his sides, he wanted to bow to Reuben. The mere thought of calling Mia and telling her that he'd get to see her again sent phantom vibrations from the phone in his pocket.

"May I leave?" Daniel asked.

"Of course, but remember, your power is much more powerful there because of the boundaries. I should know, I've lived there, but I'll tell you that some other time," he chuckled and gestured for Daniel to leave. "Have a great day."

CHAPTER TWENTY-ONE

DANIEL left Reuben's office and walked straight into his room. He sat on the end of his bed and fell back, staring at the ceiling. He stared for several moments, grinning to himself. He wondered where Jac had gone for a moment, but figured he'd take the opportunity where possible. He pulled his phone out and dialled Mia's number.

"Was it bad? Did you get told off?" she asked in a low sympathetic voice.

"No, no, no. I have some good news, some *really* great news in fact," he said, hushing his excitement

"What is it?"

"I can visit you. I—I am allowed to visit," he said, giggling over the phone.

"Oh my god, really? How?"

"I don't know. I told him, like it was the most natural thing in the world, and he supported it!"

"When can we meet?"

"Now?" Daniel asked, biting his lip. He hadn't forgotten what she looked like, but he was unsure if he could picture her perfectly.

"Yes! There's this coffee shop across the road. So meet me on the roof and we'll go there. They make *really* nice coffee and muffins and cakes and, oh my gosh, just meet me okay," she rambled.

"Okay."

"Wear something warm, it's kinda cold. When you get there, just wait for me, I'll be a few minutes."

"I will," he said in an excited whisper and hung up. He slipped the phone back in his pocket and bunched up the duvet in his exited fists.

He routed around in the mess of clothes on floor of his wardrobe to find the only jumper that he owned. He put it on and a larger jacket over that. He wore his cushioned shoes; they always kept his feet warm but were surprising loose.

He stood and looked in the piece of the mirror still attached to the wall. He looked into his eyes before closing them, and in his mind he pieced together Mia's face. The butterflies of recollection rolled in and his skin quivered as electric tendrils reached out of him. His heart flipped, over and over until a cold bit at his face.

"Mia?" he said, opening his eyes. The sky was bright and blue without the imperfection of clouds. He stood there for a moment and looked over the ledge where they'd first met.

Mia burst out of the security door. "You made it," she said.

They smiled as they ran to hug each other. Mia squeezed her arms tight around Daniel. She pulled away and smiled, wiping the fringe from her eyes. "I'm glad you're here."

"It's been a while."

"And yet you're all I've thought about. And since you told me about being *you* I can't stop. You're really special," she said.

Daniel's white cheeks blushed pink as he suppressed a smile. "I think you're pretty special as well."

Mia slipped her hand into his. "Are we going to the coffee shop?" she said.

Daniel nodded. He blushed a deeper shade of pink. Mia guided him out of the security door to climb down narrow steps until they reached another door. She opened it and stuck her head out. "All clear," she said. The corridor was deserted. They rushed out to the end of the hall where there were two elevators.

"We could just teleport," he grinned.

"That would be risky, wouldn't it?"

"Well, yeah," he said as they stopped at the elevator. "They could probably use one of these where I'm from." He squeezed her hand lightly, and turned to see her staring into his eyes.

They were face to face and staring into each other's eyes and before they kissed the elevator dinged and the doors opened. Their lips touched, but only just. Mia backed away and pulled him into the elevator.

"I've never—I've never *really* kissed a girl before," he said, taking his hand out of hers and wiping it on his jeans. *Well not one that I liked*, he thought.

Mia grinned at his honesty and opened her mouth to speak, but instead smiled. They stayed in comfortable silence, glancing to and from each other until the elevator stopped. They reached the ground floor where they had a clear view of the entrance doors and the cars whooshing in all blurs of colour.

Daniel pushed the front door wide open and remained in a state of shock. "These are cars?" he asked.

"Yeah," she laughed.

"They're so loud," he said with a smile. "And fast!" His head went from one side to the other as he watched.

"Still don't have cars?" she asked and raised her eyes.

"No. But I guess we don't need them. Besides, they turn the air black."

Mia laughed. "Yup. Good ol' pollution." Daniel continued to stare at them in wonder. "C'mon, traffic lights are up ahead," she said and grabbed his hand.

He followed her and watched the cars and the drivers who slammed fists to their horns. He witnessed the light above him change from green to red.

"Traffic lights. To control the traffic," she explained.

"So why are they angry?"

"Because it's nearly rush hour, well it's always rush hour. Everyone tries to get ahead of it but no matter what, everyone else has that same thought, and then some people think that they're wise not to, and it just makes every hour rush hour," she sniggered. "A vicious circle."

"Yeah. We don't have anything like that. But you do get a lot of angry people in the markets."

"You're going to have to take me to wherever you live one day. No cars or traffic, it sounds like my kind of heaven at the minute," she said as she led Daniel down the street.

They stopped outside a tall building with steps leading to a huge green door with green glass panes, and a silver metal sign hung inside, *Berlucci's Café* written in fancy calligraphy.

A bell chimed as they entered, and the sound of soft jazz welcomed them. A woman jumped out. "Hi. Table or booth?"

"Booth," Mia said.

"Okay, right this way," she said and led them to a free booth. She pulled a menu out from under her arm and handed it them to share.

"I normally just get the cappuccino," she said and noted the puzzled look on Daniel's face, "It's coffee, but with frothy goodness. Sometimes I put chocolate dust on top."

"Where's the band," he said, glancing around.

"Band? Oh, you mean the music," she giggled. "It's played on a CD, through the speakers."

"But where's the music coming from? There are no instruments."

"It's recorded on a CD and that's played through a CD player and then the speakers," she explained, grinning at his innocence.

"That sounds complicated. I've seen tape players, but this system looks complicated, and it sounds so clear."

"No more complicated than you having *all that magic*," she said. "So what do you want to order? I'll pay, but then you have to show me something."

"We usually refer to it was energy or will, or ability, even power," he said, "only a few times have I heard magic before."

"That's what it is though," she said. "Anyway, whatcha having?"

"I'll have a—one of them, cappa—cuppa—cappuccinos," he said.

Mia flicked her hand up in the air to signal one of the waitresses. The woman rushed back to their table and Mia placed the order. She came back minutes later with a rack of condiments; white sugar, brown sugar, cocoa shaker and an icing sugar shaker. And then minutes later she came back balancing a metal circle tray on the palm of her hand with two small thick cups of cappuccino, a third of each made up of froth.

"Don't drink it straight away," Mia said as Daniel picked up a cup. "It's hot. And, you haven't shown me your *power* yet."

"I'm not supposed to use it in public," he whispered.

"C'mon, how will they know? Really? They let you off the island didn't they? They'll probably just slap you on your wrists or something," she laughed.

"Yeah, probably." He laughed along, although he knew that wasn't at all true. "Okay, I know what I can do," he said eyeing the pots in the spinning rack.

"Go on then," she whispered.

Daniel took the cocoa shaker from the stand and dropped it. He left a vine of energy around the pot, it kept it suspended in the air. He sucked in and his head began a course of fuzzing and crackling. For a moment he thought Jac was trying to talk to him, but his throat dried and his tongue throbbed in his mouth.

Glasses on tables around them clacked together and drowned out the music. The people in booths and around tables shouted "*earthquake*" and "*tornado*" as they climbed out of their seats and headed for the exit. Mia and Daniel stayed seated.

"Is that you?" she asked.

Daniel couldn't reply. It was intoxicating, and he kept on taking from it. The cups rattled with an air of impatience until one tapped its way to the edge of the table and dropped to the floor, with a crisp clear break.

The noise broke his concentration and the café stopped shaking. He turned to hear an excited mumble from Mia, but something else distracted him. A girl, sat at a table with her hood up. Her brown and blonde hair flicked around her face. She sat, unstirred, dipping a finger into the foam of her drink. Daniel couldn't help but feel compelled to watch, she glanced up, and looked at him.

"*You're him,*" a cool voice spoke. He took a hard gulp and glared into her eyes. It was her voice speaking to him. He clenched his jaw and blinked. He glanced back over to her, but it was empty.

"Was it?" Mia asked. She tapped on Daniel's arm. "It was, wasn't it?"

Daniel turned to Mia as she waited for an answer. "Mm, I think so," he said. He glanced back over to where the girl had been.

Mia grinned and dipped her finger in the froth. She wiped it on his nose. "You're super powerful, aren't you?"

"I really don't think I should've done that. I should go," he said. He rubbed at his nose with his sleeve and smiled.

"Oh." She pouted.

"I'm sorry. I wish I could stay and show you more."

"You can."

"No, I really do need to go," he said. "I'm sorry."

Mia lifted one of the cups to him. "Drink all of this and I'll let you go."

Daniel grinned. "That sounds fair, I guess." He grabbed the warm cup and emptied it in his mouth. The froth dribbled down his chin and made a thin moustache above his top lip.

CHAPTER TWENTY-TWO

HER VOICE played on a loop in his head. He'd gone looking for her, but she'd gone. He found himself standing around with his eyes glazed over as he repeated *"you're him,"* to himself in her delicate voice.

Chey clicked her fingers in front of Daniel's face. "Daniel," she said. "I'm sorry," she repeated.

A shiver ran through him as he looked around to find himself standing in the hall for his class. "What for?"

"You can no longer attend this class. I don't have anything to teach you. Not until the rest of the class has reached your level anyway," she replied with a wry smile.

He nodded for several seconds and turned. The door slammed shut behind her. He blinked the daze out of his face and when looked up. Reuben stood at the top of the stairs with a hand on his walking aide.

"Daniel," he said.

"Hi, Mr. Croft," Daniel nodded.

"It was my idea that you'd be withdrawn from that lesson. And now that you have, would you mind doing me a favour?" he asked.

Daniel smiled. "Sure. What do you need?"

"It's prep for tomorrow's lesson. All I need you to do is go out by the woods and collect some wood and stones, at random, or where you feel the most power coming from."

"Okay," he said, and Reuben turned to walk back up the stairs to his office. "Is there anything else?"

"Nope. That's it," his voice echoed down.

"And you mean the woods by the barn?"

Reuben nodded. "Exactly."

Daniel stood in the hallway for a moment. He'd listened to Reuben's request, but he couldn't help think that he could go back to see Mia, or even back to the café and search for the girl. Her voice made him feel real. That's how Daniel pictured it over there, energy flowing free, while over here he was scratching at the same spot and waiting for a burst of energy, even if the bursts had been quite regular so far.

"Jac, where the hell are you?" he said to himself.

"I'm not talking to you. You pushed me away. I still have a ringing in my ear," he said. *"It's still ringing."*

"I did what? I thought you were being moody because I didn't ask Reuben if you could visit," Daniel said to himself quietly as he rushed down the flights of stairs to the foyer.

"Well no. That's not what happened at all. And I had a headache for hours, and when I did try and contact it was like walking into a wall then getting up and doing it again. Did I forget to mention the ringing?" he whined.

"You know I went *off the island,*" he covered and his mouth as he whispered, walking out of the building.

"You went to see her. What happened? They haven't killed you yet? Or are they going to?" Jac panicked.

"No, no, no. Well not that I know of. And yeah, I went to see her. It was amazing. I was so powerful, *think* being able to just do what you mind wants with little effort."

"As if. The only reason we have rules here is to keep us in check."

"Probably why nobody else can use it there. It's addictive."

"Have they even taught you about the Luminaries? Heck, didn't Erik or Roan not tell you about them?" Jac asked.

"Of course I know about the Luminaries, my teacher is obsessed with them. But *they* didn't say that you're not allowed off the island," Daniel said as he walked down the path towards the woods.

"Two thousand years ago when pure energy was found on the island there was this 400 year era of people enslaved and we had such little power, if any, the people on the island then took over and drove them away," Jac explained.

"How do you know that? And what does that have to do with the rules?" he asked.

"It was a shock to them, they hadn't aged in the 400 years they'd been here. Not to mention they'd cursed the land, saying that if anyone was to leave they would be killed, killed by the energy that they use, it's what governs us. Nobody can ever stumble upon us, and we can't venture out," Jac continued to explain.

"Who's been teaching you then?" Daniel chuckled to himself.

"Well I did go to the library with you, quite a bit."

Daniel's stopped silent as he stood outside the forest. He pushed stray branches from his face as he entered it. "Whoa. It's beautiful in here." He pushed his hands out as he reached for the pulse carried in each tree.

"Where are you?"

"One sec, Jac. I might have to push you away. I'm just doing something," his said monotonously, glaring straight ahead to a huge tree.

"No. I'll just—" it was too late Daniel pushed him from his mind.

He rubbed his eyes and glared at the ash coloured oak tree in front of him. He walked closer, his fingers tingled by his side and his palms were slick with sweat. He reached out with both hands and touched the cool skin of the tree.

A whoosh filled him with the same cool hardness of the wood inside the tree. He turned and watched the twisted roots dive in and out of the fertile soil. He smiled to himself, his heart took a dive and a couple of extra jumps in places they shouldn't.

He cooed to himself as he polished his hands across the wood, a piece of bark flaked between his fingers. He caught it before it fell, he pressed it hard in his palm. It crunched and crumbled, then settled on his skin, melting into him. "You feel that—energy?" he asked himself.

He closed his eyes. He could see better without looking as he gripped hold of another piece of bark. The heat of his breath tingled on his tongue. He rest his back against the oak and slid down to sit with the upturned roots.

"Next time you push someone, push them properly!" Jac said in a pseudo-angry voice.

Daniel jolted upright. He sucked at all the cool air around him and rubbed his groggy eyes. He coughed and fell to the floor, dropping the handfuls of bark he'd collected.

"What?" he asked. He rushed off out of the forest holding himself in his arms.

Daniel stared at his feet as he walked out. He bumped into Enek. "Sorry. Sir. I didn't see you there." He rushed.

"Hold up." Enek grabbed Daniel's arm. "Have you just come from in there?"

Daniel froze and turned to see Enek tapping his foot. "It's a project for R—R—Mr. Croft," he said.

"I'm surprised you got out so quick, or out alive," he chuckled, "some students have gone missing and don't turn up for days, or weeks, but we've got access to the field, well Reuben does, we can find missing students easier, and it's also handy for people *cutting* their classes, so don't cut class," Enek began to digress. "I've never been in there, so I don't know what it is scaring those kids half to death, seriously, like this close to death." He made a small gap between two fingers to show Daniel what he meant, but he wasn't listening.

"I'm gonna go," he replied and rushed off.

"Who was that?" Jac asked several times, each time stressing different words until he shouted.

"Something happened," Daniel muttered, "it was an amazing feeling, but it wasn't real. I want to go back in there—b—but I know better. The tree wanted me to just *attach* myself to it. It wanted me to just take—or *give* it all my energy."

"Yeah, you're not making any sense."

Daniel stopped and stood. He looked left and right. One way lead to his dorm, and the other to the main hall. He stumbled over his confused feet and fell into a hedge at the side. He pushed himself up and wavered before gripping the wall. He pushed a hand up against his chest and moved it to massage his neck and collarbone. Breakfast tickled his stomach and within seconds it made its way up his throat and out of his mouth.

"I can hear that. Really?! You're being sick...or are people poisoning you? Crap!" Jac boomed down Daniel's nervous system, causing his jaw to clench. *"I'm coming!"*

"No, no you can't," Daniel said as someone passed him and frowned. "For all I know, it could be because I went off the island," he said, cupping a hand around his mouth.

"That sounds about right; there are forces bigger than us. You can't see her again. Okay!" Jac said.

Daniel nodded to himself, but he couldn't just give up like that. "I'll try being *less* active," he said.

"Daniel? Are you okay?" Reuben asked, tapping at Daniel's leg with his walking stick.

"No." He turned, still crouched. He straightened up and wiped his mouth. "Think I ate something that didn't agree with me."

"Who were you speaking to?" he asked, tipping his chin.

"Oh, just myself, trying to figure out why I could be ill," he explained.

"So you *haven't* been in the forest yet then?" Reuben shrugged his collars and tightened his overcoat.

"Yeah, I—I—I came back out because I felt a little ill."

"Okay. Just get some rest and I'll see you in the morning. Don't forget. And if you're still ill we might be able to test some new methods to reduce it or remove it from your system," Reuben said, shooing Daniel.

Daniel nodded. "I'm sorry for being sick in your hedges." He crouched back over and teleported to his room, the whoosh of the energy he invoked sent his head spinning, He rushed to the sink in his room and threw up again.

CHAPTER TWENTY-THREE

DANIEL left his window open all night. He'd slept on top of his duvet and when he woke his skin was white. It shimmered a silvery blue. He didn't shiver, and his teeth didn't clatter. He looked down at his arms and tried to lift them.

"Eh." He struggled to move them, his bones had set like cement.

He raised a hand and flicked the sleep from his eyes. The sockets of his eyes were swollen and numb.

He climbed out of bed and grabbed a towel. Appearing in the shower room, he pushed open a cubicle door and let out a long drawn out yawn. His fingers shook as he turned on the shower. Steamy hot water jetted out.

He showered and when he'd finished almost fifteen minutes later he was refreshed. The steam settled his puffy his eyes and added a fleshier colour to his skin. He dressed and teleported back to his room where he finished getting ready.

The women who made the food in the cafeteria always saved a little extra for Daniel. And right on cue before they shut, she would produce a plate full of food for him.

"Thank you," he said.

"It's no problem, got to keep our own safe."

He sat down and scoffed the food. One eye on the clock and another on the fork spooning food in his mouth.

"Mr. Satoria," a man with white gloves and a black suit; a butler. He tapped Daniel on his shoulder. Daniel rammed the rest of the beans into his mouth. He turned. "Mr. Croft and his class are waiting for you in the foyer. Also, the cafeteria is now closed."

"Thank you," Daniel said after he finished chewing his food. The butler ushered him into the foyer.

Everyone turned to see Daniel, and it wasn't just Jasper in the class, Mark and Carlie had places as well, and a few others who he'd seen around but never spoke to before. They all stood behind Reuben. Carlie winked at Daniel and bit her lip like she always did. Jasper watched her do it, and Daniel rolled his eyes but watched as Jasper took a hold of Carlie's hand.

"We're all here now. I'm going to be taking you to a secret locale, some place very close to nature, some place where we can call a Luminary. Get one in the flesh," Reuben grinned. "Follow me."

There was chatter between friends, and an ear-splitting boom from Jac, *"how can he get one of them here? Daniel! What's he doing this for? I think for everyone's safety you should tell them all not to. Tell them to do something else."*

Reuben led the way; he opened a door beneath the stairs, a plain cupboard with two brooms, a mop and bucket, and a shelf with dirty glasses. He pushed the wall and a stone door revealed itself before swinging on a hinge, sending clouds of dust their way. "Not been used in a while. We all usually just 'port in and out," Reuben said, walking into the tunnel.

"I can't, nobody will listen, especially not to me," Daniel said quietly, following the crowd right at the end.

Daniel walked into the passage and the door slammed shut behind. For a moment they all stopped and stood in the darkness. Reuben laughed as orange light broke out along the walls.

They walked for about five minutes before all the lights died out again and another shone through from a door. Reuben pushed it opened.

"You need to mind your heads and watch your steps, some drops are larger than others, remember that you're going down in a spiral," Reuben called out along the line. He headed down first.

There was a natural glow from the rock, and the smell of damp was already sticking to the fabric of their clothes. Daniel let his hand ride the smooth rock column as he walked down and around it. He admired how clean it had been kept and how there were little green moss patches in places.

"Now that you're all here, you can 'port here for lesson, and only then," Reuben said, as everyone reached the opening at the bottom of the stairs.

"What if you can't teleport?" a boy asked from the front of the crowd.

"It's a shame, Ven, but you're talented in other ways. It's your earthly affinity which got you in this group, so don't let the fact that you're less than *mobile* get in the way," Reuben said.

Ven nodded, after all, it was still a compliment to be in the group.

"Are you listening to me?" Jac asked.

"Sorry, what?" Daniel blurted, louder than expected.

"Oh, nothing for you, Daniel," Reuben said.

"I think you should call all your energy in now. I think that you should do something to stop him from calling a Luminary, for all you know it could take all your energy away from you and then what? No, Mia. Ever again!" Jac pleaded.

Daniel glanced around the room, he didn't have a clue of what Jac was going on about, and then he locked eyes with Ven and felt sorry for him. Daniel butted his lips and kept quiet. He made note of how lived in the room felt; crates stacked on the floor with rags folded beside them, and candles on ledges.

"Gather round," Reuben called and whacked his staff on the stone floor.

They fell silent and came to a regimented circle. Daniel stood beside Mark, across from Carlie and Jasper. He turned to look at Mark's face. He was grinning like a child and looking over at Jasper.

Daniel clenched his jaw and hushed himself. *Chomp. Bite. Chomp.* Something had latched itself to Daniel. He felt teeth nip at the nape of his neck and sharp prongs pull on the sleeve of his energy. Jasper giggled and Daniel shook his head to pull away from the pain.

It was Mark, his hands were by his side as he strummed at the air. Daniel glanced down to see the faint glow on Mark's fingertips. Daniel gripped his hand and cracked his fingers.

"Ow!" Mark shouted, barging out of the circle to stand beside Jasper.

"Is everything okay?" Reuben asked. Daniel bit his bottom lip, expecting a comeback, but Mark shook his head. "Good."

"Yeah, do it again, rile Reuben and he might not do the lesson," Jac said in a panic-stricken breath. *"You can't let him go through with this!"*

Daniel coughed into his hands.

"Sir, aren't the Luminary sacred?" a girl asked. Daniel smiled at her, perhaps Jac had got to her as well.

"Very. And we all pray to them, or we should, and this is just like a prayer that we know they're going to get," Reuben replied, slipping a hand into his jacket pocket. "I have a special stone. This stone can call upon *any* Luminary, and they will appear, albeit not physically, but they will be here, and confined until we will them away."

"Ask him who he's willing through, ask him!" Jac's voice rang inside Daniel's ears.

Daniel coughed again, this time louder. "Who will come through?"

"The one with the power, the one at the head of the bloodline, but if you wanted to call for the ancestor you'd need another stone," Reuben said. He played with the stone inside the red velvet pouch.

"Oh. Why are we calling a Luminary?"

"Because of what Leigh said, Luminary are the seven most sacred people in existence, who would be of more value than someone to whom we send prayers to?" Reuben asked. He raised his eye at Daniel.

"Won't it anger them?"

"Do *you* think it will anger them, Daniel?" Everyone turned to Daniel as he flushed red and smirks formed on their faces.

Daniel shook his head.

"Good. We don't need weak links here."

"Yes, Daniel. Yes, it will anger them," Jac said quietly, like he'd given up. *"There's something dodgy about it. Just leave."*

"I don't think any of you are weak, if I did you wouldn't be here. This has never been done before, but this stone, this has been in creation for hundreds of years," Reuben said, holding the stone up, still inside the pouch. "You are the most gifted bunch at the Academy, and I believe that we have the power to summon a Luminary."

"I thought we were learning about energy stones and the healing qualities. Revolutionary things, being able to heal all those sick in the Lowerlands and letting the earth be your teacher. That sort of stuff," Leigh butted in.

"Oh, this is revolutionary, and the first of many classes, may I add. Besides, you'll go down in history as one of the people to summon a star, a planetary being, think of the demands, think of how we can control the wellbeing of all those sick, all of those people who have to die, just at the flick of a Luminary," Reuben chuckled. "Leigh, if you object to any of this, then you know where you can exit."

221

"No, I'll stay," Leigh said, with a grin on her face. Daniel finally placed her face, he'd seen her with Carlie, she was probably Mark's girlfriend or something, she certainly belonged to *that* crowd.

"You do realise that this is not what you want," Jac said, *"you want peace with these people. You need peace with them, if you go around acting all hostile then they'll never trust you again."*

"Never trust me again?" Daniel said under his breath.

"Don't do this, you can't do this."

He didn't know what Jac was talking about, but the Luminary were people who founded the power which he embodied, and from what he'd heard they were ruthless beings that enslaved an island and its natives.

Reuben picked the stone from the pouch; a dark polished yellow stone. "It was created with an acidic poison inside the core, and that makes escape impossible, well without first harming themselves. So to all of you who thought that their wrath would come crashing on you the minute they came, you're wrong." A hand rose to question him and he shooed it. Reuben broke through the circle and placed the stone in the centre of it. "Focus all of your energy into that stone, and I'll say a few words to summon," he paused in thought. "Mercury, a popular choice, I do believe."

The word, *Mercury*, it rang in Daniel's ears like the word had a layer of negative intent. His throat constricted and his skin pimpled, he closed his eyes, he couldn't put any energy into that rock. It was dangerous, and everyone in that room knew it.

"You need to *push* and *flex* your energy into it. Do not try moving it or calling out to it with energy, no heating it or taking it back into the earthy breadth beneath us. Just let the flow of energy pass," he continued.

Daniel opened his eyes. His fingers tingled by his side, and the tips spun beating veins of gold. They weaved through the air and aimed for the stone. He made fists of his hands, but the faint yellow glow of purity was now wrapped snug around the stone. The more the stone tugged, the more lax his fists became and the faster the stone reeled in his energy.

"Taking from this energy, I call out. I call out to Mercury. Mercury, show yourself, or may your blood turn black and the poisons of the stone *forever* dwell inside you," an enthralled Reuben let go of his walking aide and hailed his hands high above his head, "I call out to Mercury!"

The stone vibrated, clattering against the rock floor. A small tremor escaped and shook them. Daniel tripped over his feet and whacked his head against the wall behind him. Nobody noticed.

Daniel came to, rubbing the back of his neck as his eyes focused. He stared at the stone, it seemed to have split open as a gas poured out. The group gasped. A figure appeared hissing and scratching at the ground. *Mercury*, but half-conscious Daniel knew him as Karsar.

"What? Why am I here? And who the hell are you!?" Karsar snapped. The cuts on his fingertips from where he'd dug into the ground healed over.

Daniel scooted his back against the wall, keeping out of Karsar's view. He thought he'd brought himself some peace, but this wasn't peaceful at all.

"It's a neat trick," Reuben said.

"But you can't keep me here," Karsar said, smirking.

"I think *we* can." Reuben turned to face the rest of the class, they broke out in excitable laughter. "So who wants to see what else we can do? Who wants to command Mercury, tell him what you want, make him will it!" Nobody spoke up. Nobody wanted to be in the wrath of the Luminary. "How about you, Ven, we all know that you can't teleport, well he's the guy. Ask him, go on. *Tell him*. He can't say no."

Ven glanced from Reuben to Karsar; Karsar's eyes were black from that distance, just as Daniel had remembered them. Ven shook his head and butted his lips, he didn't hate the Luminary at all, the truth is, he prayed to them in his first year when he couldn't teleport and that's when his flare developed. He grasped a section of the elements far greater than anyone that's been before him at The Croft Academy.

"Ha. You called me to make his *wish* come true?" Karsar asked.

"No. I'm surprised you're even co-operating and not trying to communicate with the other Luminary. You've probably only just come into your power, haven't you?" Reuben asked.

"I've had it long enough to know my way out of a summoning stone," Karsar laughed.

"How often are you summoned?" Reuben lifted his eyebrows.

Karsar glanced from the floor and then to Reuben. "I've never been summoned, people fear the thought, let alone go through with the act."

"Oh, but you do realise that this stone is infused with a delicate balance of poisons, and you heard the little *threat* when you were summoned, right?" he asked.

Daniel sputtered from the back of the room, he continued to cough. They moved out of the way so Reuben could see as Daniel climbed to his feet and rubbed the back of his head. He felt a clump of hair stuck together. He brought his fingers to his face. It was definitely blood on them. He felt again, but there was no cut.

"Something you'd like to say, Daniel?" Reuben asked. Daniel glanced up, realising that everyone was looking at him, even Karsar.

That was the first thing he noticed, Karsar, glancing at him, looking straight at him like he had horns and was about to charge right through him. He sucked in a deep breath and his sight moved and met Reuben's. "No sir, I fell."

"Why don't you ask Mercury for something," Reuben said, "hmm."

"Umm." Daniel gulped. He wiped the blood on the back of his pants and looked up at Karsar, it was definitely him.

"No?" Reuben asked. "Anyone? Ven, guess we're coming back to you then."

Daniel could see a bright glowing fluid saturate the floor around the stone and Karsar's feet. Daniel noticed it as the colour of pure energy, but it might as well have been blood because it meant just as much. It was being wasted. Daniel glanced up at Karsar, his jaw tensed shut.

"He's a Luminary. You're looking in the eyes of a Luminary," Jac's faint voice, seemingly sharing the same body as Daniel for the moment as he partially left it.

All Daniel could think of was how people prayed to him, people prayed to Karsar, the guy who'd almost convinced Daniel that he was going crazy. He glanced down to the glowing pool of energy. It was growing, enveloping the feet of everyone in the room. Nobody could see it, and it didn't touch Daniel; it wrapped a ring around him.

"You have a bad feeling about this. I told you they'd be furious. Will him away. Do something!" Jac pushed.

"What like?" Daniel cupped a hand around his mouth and whispered. He glanced up at Karsar and shook his head.

Daniel gritted his teeth and sighed. All the wicks in all the candles burst as crevices of light died out. The room was locked in darkness. Daniel trudged his feet into the pool of pure energy. "I will you away, Karsar," he whispered as everyone fumbled in the dark.

"You did that! Mercury!" Reuben roared as the room returned to normal, and Karsar was gone.

Most of the group had vanished, teleported out, but Daniel, Jasper, Carlie and Ven stayed. Daniel stayed and played the part of equally shocked; he was, he didn't know if it was going to work.

"Where's he gone?" Reuben asked.

"Maybe the poison wasn't strong enough," Jasper said.

"Maybe you should just go home! That poison was the strongest toxin, and that clause, that *threat*, that was binding!" Reuben shouted. He closed his eyes and massaged the bridge of his nose. "All of you, *out*, now!"

CHAPTER TWENTY-FOUR

DANIEL teleported to the path outside the dorm building. The whole experience had left him dazed and planted to the spot. He rubbed at the throb on the back of his head and he felt the small globed bulge deflate.

He sighed and looked to the sky. It was chilly, yet the sunlight warmed him enough. He nodded and thanked it. Slowly, he reached the hallway. He heard a few brash and heavy footsteps up ahead, following by shouting and cursing. *Smash!*

Daniel froze, it had to be his room, and it had to be Karsar coming for him. He teleported in and threw a bolt of air in every direction. The last part of the mirror smashed and the duvet flew across the room.

"Jac?"

"Daniel," Jac said. "Jeez, I did tell you I was coming."

"When? You've just been telling me all this stuff about *them* and being all cryptic and everything and then you're here. Why didn't you tell me then?" Daniel sighed and sat on his bed. "What did you break?"

"A cup, it was an accident, and in my defence it was a lot more important than telling you I was in your room," Jac said. "Besides, you're the one that goes to the *fancy* school. You know how to fix stuff. Don't you?"

Daniel rolled his eyes and shook his head. "Just brush it to the side and I'll deal with it later."

Jac noticed the plimsolls on Daniel's feet and raised an eyebrow. "Really?" he grinned.

"Yeah, you have to wear them, or cut your feet open on the rocks," he replied. "Anyway, what are you doing here?"

"Because I said that I was gonna, and let's face it, you were chucking your guts up and blocking me out."

"I wasn't poisoned though," Daniel said with uncertainty. "Did you tell my parents you were coming?"

"Yeah," he said and hummed a laugh. He sat on Daniel's bed and then bounced up and down on it. "They sure do treat you like royalty here then."

"All of the rooms are like this," Daniel said.

There was a knock at the door and Daniel froze on the spot.

"Should I get that?" Jac asked, "or go hide?" he grinned.

"Yeah, go in the wardrobe, and take *that*!" Daniel shooed Jac and kicked his satchel to him as he climbed int the wall.

"It's roomy in here," Jac said as he slid the door shut. "Bigger than mine."

Daniel fumbled with the lock, although it only went one way. His worst fear had been Reuben with his all-knowing look. He closed his eyes and pulled the handle to open the door.

"I saw you today," Carlie said, bursting in through the door. She shoved a hand on Daniel's chest and pushed him on his bed, kicking the door shut behind her. "I saw all of that power you used, that was a—a lot of *power*."

"Why are you here?" he asked, swiping her hand from his chest.

She bit her lip playfully. "I came for you, silly!" she said, and rested her hand on his upper arm.

"Please, just go back to Jasper," he said, and brushed her hand away.

"He doesn't protest as much as you."

"How come you didn't tell me?" Jac whispered.

"There's nothing going on here," Daniel replied to them both.

She stood on the balls of her feet and kissed him on the lips. Daniel pushed her slightly; she fluttered her eyelashes and grinned. She stroked the right side of his face and turned toward the door, teleporting before she hit it.

Jac opened the wardrobe and walked out. He blinked and glared at Daniel with a bug-eyed look. "Are you sure there's nothing going on?" he asked.

"Listen, she's crazy, probably one of the reasons why Jasper hates me."

"And what happened to Mia?"

"Nothing, I like her and she likes me, but it's all too weird. I'm here and she's," he paused, "off the island," he whispered.

The phone in Daniel's pocket buzzed and tickled at his leg. He pulled it out; it was a message from Reuben. He read it to himself, and then read it out loud while Jac made a sly comment about Daniel having a phone.

"Reuben needs to see me now. I think I know what it's about," he said.

"Go on, tell me," Jac said.

"I set him free. I don't know what I did but I let the Luminary go," Daniel said, he opened his mouth to say something else, like how he knew it was Karsar and how he'd been invading his dreams, but that would make him sound crazy.

"Thank goodness! Well if you don't come back I'll presume you're in a ditch somewhere," he said.

Daniel glared at Jac and shook his head. He turned and was outside Reuben's door. He took a deep breath; the door was bigger than it had been. He wiped his sweaty palms on the back of his pants like he always did before combing a hand through his hair. He slipped the phone back in his pocket and exhaled.

"Come in," Reuben shouted before Daniel could knock.

Daniel opened the door, and before he could let go of the handle he slipped to the floor.

"I have an urgent matter at hand," Reuben continued.

"Oh, what about? I haven't done anything wrong have I?" Daniel asked, standing and brushing himself off.

Reuben chuckled. "No, of course not. I was supposed to grab you before everyone left this morning. It's about my nephew's girlfriend, Carlie. She seems to be looking at you. A lot."

"It's not what it seems," he said and waved a hand frantically to protest.

Reuben chuckled harder. "I know it's not, I'm actually protecting you in a different way by telling you this. Carlie leeches on the energy of others, she does not source from natural sources, although she would argue that we are *her* natural source," he grinned. "Jasper sleeps with replenishing stones under his pillow, they give him his edge, but you're stronger than Jasper, if she got to you then she'd take more and that would make it take a lot longer for you to be fully energized again."

"I think I'm following," Daniel said, after all Jasper's uncle said he was stronger. "Wait, how does she take energy?"

"Through touch, even if it's a brush against her, the littlest brush she might catch a hold of that and come on to you."

Daniel started to breathe heavily and his heart hiccuped in his chest. "Hm. She kissed me once. But I pushed her away."

Reuben pushed the glasses to the end of his nose and looked Daniel in the eye. "I should have known, I should have addressed you when I found out about your flare," he sighed. "We're not allowed to make statements to the school, telling people about students who are afflicted, like her, it's classed as discrimination. But it would have averted any crisis."

"I'm fine though. But what happens if she does get too close?"

"You'd die, I'm surprised you don't already know that, but I'm not the person you should be talking to about Carlie's condition. Marianne is in her room now, I think she'd be happy enough to talk to you about it, just tell her that I sent you and that it's about Carlie."

Daniel nodded. "Should I go there now?"

"Of course, unless you have any other matters to address."

It had made Carlie sound like she had some weird disease and he needed help getting rid. He debated on whether he wanted to go and see Marianne after leaving Reuben's room. He stood at the bottom of the third floor steps and glanced around at the different doors.

"Daniel, you have a look in your eyes," Marianne said, stood in the doorway of her room.

"I was just about to come and see you," he said, lifting his brow in thought.

"I knew something was up. Come in then," she said, gesturing with her hand.

Daniel pulled a seat from the lined formation they had been in for her next class. She took a seat opposite.

"So, what is it?"

"Reuben sent me down because Carlie kissed me," he said with a blank expression on his face. He was still slightly confused.

It began as a hum and then she chuckled. "I bet he told you that you had the plague, didn't he." She rolled her eyes. "My husband also sources from people, syphoning energy through touch because their receptors, the sixth one, is *disabled* so they can't get their energy in any other way. That's all it is."

"Don't you worry he'll take all of your energy?"

"No," she grinned. "Now, I'd like to ask you a question. How do you explain that you can do things other people can't, like the advanced stuff?"

Daniel had an answer for that question, it might not have been all that true, but it sure pointed to it. He was doing exactly what Carlie was doing, but only this time he was tapping into the source of a Luminary.

"It's all I ever did, while everyone's lives here have been cushy, I went to work with my dad. He works at the library in Faber and all I did was read books. I guess that's what everyone should do; the library's big enough for everyone."

She nodded along. "It's also a vault," she said and Daniel caught a whiff of peppermint from her. She pulled up her sleeve to look at her watch. "We're going to have to cut this short. I have a class in ten minutes. So, don't go near Carlie, but don't push her away either, you touching her has as much intent as when she touches you."

"Okay," he said. He stood and pushed the chair back in line.

Marianne fumbled inside a paperback. She pulled out a handful of wrapped sweets. "If you feel drained at all, take one of these. They pack a burst of energy when you're feeling low," she said. "And if you have any more questions we've always got tomorrow's lesson."

Daniel took the sweets and shoved them in his pocket. "Thanks," he said, and walked off.

Daniel found himself standing in the foyer. He could smell lunch being dished out. *"I'm hungry,"* Jac whined, almost as if he could smell what Daniel did. Daniel grabbed two plates, and filled them with sausages, eggs, toast, beans, and fried mushrooms. Nobody asked him, and before anyone could ask him he teleported back.

CHAPTER TWENTY-FIVE

THERE WERE no unsettling breezes or scorching heats, no windswept looks or clouds in the sky. Nobody walked the streets and no cars polluted the air. The world was silent. All the while Karsar cried inside himself for help.

In the corner of an alley, hiding beneath a cardboard box. Karsar curled up. He rubbed his hands together and blew into them. His pale skin, almost perfect with sickness with one single purple bruise beneath his right eye.

He'd spent the past few hours shaking as he tried to piece a picture of events that had happened. He couldn't. And one face was at the forefront of his mind. Daniel's face.

He told himself over and over, first in thought and then as an incoherent mumble. He didn't want anyone to find out, what would they think, what would they say about his power. *Laugh, they'll laugh. It's all—all his fault. D—Daniel's fault!* He covered his face with his hands and wiped away tears. He flinched as he brushed against the bruise. "Daniel," he mumbled.

"Satoria," a surprised voice said. Karsar's ears pricked as the voice trailed off passed the alley. He cocked his head to the entrance and saw a woman pass with pinks and blues in her hair, and like rain drumming down on a window it washed over him.

"Hey!" he shouted feebly. "Who are you?" he asked. He pushed himself up from the ground. "I know you!" he shouted after her, his knees buckling as he tried to run.

"Dammit!" she growled. She rushed off down another empty street.

"I know you! Wait!" Karsar ran after her, trying to fix the clothes he was wearing to make himself look more presentable in front of a girl.

She stood still and turned. "Listen! You need to stop doing *whatever* it is that you're doing!"

"Aryana?" he said softly as he stopped in front of her. They went back a while, in fact she'd found Karsar sitting in a gutter afraid of himself, just before Richard took him under his wing. "Why are you here?"

"The same reason you are," she replied.

"I live in the city now."

"No, for Daniel!" she said and whacked him in his chest. "Don't play stupid."

Karsar took a step back and scrunched his face. He put a hand over his chest and tried not to show that she'd hurt him. "You, you're here for him?" he asked, almost grinning.

"He needs to make a decision; he'll need to know both sides. You know that."

"Well you can't tell him. You *know that.*" Karsar rolled his eyes. "It has to be someone in his bloodline, his guardian."

"So let them and stop interfering!" she pushed through her thinning lips. She took a deep breath and looked Karsar up and down. "Is it bleeding?" she raised an eyebrow.

He took a deep breath and pulled the bottom of his shirt up, there was a clean white piece of cloth taped to the side of his ribcage. "It heals every now and then." He pulled at it and a bit of blood dribbled down his finger and abdomen. He didn't look at it. The warmth of the blood had his throat constricted; he gulped hard at a knot inside and pressed the cloth against his skin. "I've slowed the rate that it bleeds, but it won't heal now."

"You're lucky you haven't bled out, and then maybe the title would go to someone more fitting of *luminary.*"

Karsar snarled. "I'm not going to. How do you even know that could happen?"

"You know I read, and I'm in tune to the generations of knowledge from my family. Like you should be. Plus, we all felt it, we all know Daniel's gone through the second stage."

"I don't have any living relatives, and that *palace* in Greece, wherever it is won't reveal itself. All of this is your fault you know."

"You were the one fearing for your safety because things kept on happening around you. I was only 13 at the time and I travelled across the world because of what I felt."

Karsar shook his head. "You shouldn't even be here."

"I'm staying here because this is the only other place that Daniel knows."

"I'm sure I can send you a postcard to Australia when he comes back."

"I'll go back if you tell me why Daniel was here."

"You're wasting your time, Aryana. I don't think you should be here, there's already a lot of tension and you're just going to make it worse."

"Me? You're the ones keeping secrets, and you would have never told us about the seventh. But you tried to keep it a secret anyway. Orlana knows, so let's play fair, even though he'll join us. I know that."

"You know that? Really."

"So you think he's going to want to destroy the island where he grew up. You're stupid in thinking that."

"Just go."

"Don't die on us now," she said, smacking his chest. He coughed and pushed at the pain. "I'll go, when I'm sure that Daniel knows the whole story."

"When Elisa knows you're in the city it's only a matter of time before Richard invokes the ruling."

"Shut up. Daniel will find out that there is a *good* to all of this." She turned and teleported.

"There is no good, only lesser evil." Karsar chuckled to himself. He teleported to his apartment.

Richard stood by a window, watching the street below. "Did she take it?" he asked.

Karsar hauled himself on his bed. "Yes," he snapped. "Get these *demons* out of my head!" He clutched at the wound on his side as the blood leaked from the bandages.

"Elisa said, wait it out. We're your peers, not your carers."

Jac woke the next morning, groaning at the sound of Daniel's alarm. He flailed his arms and stretched his legs, twisting in the sheets Daniel had stolen from linen closest at the end of the hall.

Daniel hadn't slept all night. He'd cleaned his room, and fixed both the window and the mirror. He ended up in the washroom, soaking in a long hot shower. He tried to find the building where Mia was staying but he'd failed at teleporting out.

He couldn't make calls to her. Or search for her on the Internet. He didn't know if she was okay, or if Karsar had gotten to her.

"Daniel!" Jac groaned.

Daniel appeared. He was wrapped in a towel with his clothes bunched up in his arms. He turned the alarm off. "What?" he asked, shivering in the cold air.

"I just wanted you to turn the alarm off."

Daniel chuckled as his jaw chattered in the cold. "I'm gonna get changed and then get breakfast." He turned the alarm off before pushing his head through a t-shirt and sniffed at the lavender scent in his clothes.

"I'll have to get up then, won't I?" Jac huffed.

"No, but you will if you want some breakfast."

Jac sighed. He lifted his head from the pile of sheets he'd used as a pillow. "Should I come down with you?"

"I'm sorry to say this, but you're going to be confined to these four walls until you leave," Daniel said.

Jac glanced around the room and sighed harder. He had so much that he wanted to tell Daniel but there was never the right moment, or feeling from inside that told him it was right.

Daniel was usually let in early so that he could have the first pick of the food, but this morning everyone seemed to be going in early. He glanced up at the clock on the wall inside the cafeteria. At this rate he wouldn't be able to take Jac anything back *and* see Marianne before lesson started, although he only had one question left to ask, he wanted to know if there was any way he could repel himself from Carlie.

Daniel grabbed a tray from the pile and queued with everyone else. People continued to make sly comments about him and the staff behind the counter. He shared sympathetic glances with the workers; they were a long way from home and probably have been since taking the job, the highest paying job they'd ever get. Daniel pushed away the thoughts of other people as his stomach rumbled. He piled food on a plate; sausages, buns, strips of bacon, and poached eggs. He took two sets of cutlery from the stand at the end of the aisle and turned. He barged into Tanner.

"Watch it!" Tanner shouted. His tray wobbled in his hands.

Daniel took a deep breath and backed away. He didn't have the time to start anything.

"Scum," Tanner muttered as his lips curled.

Daniel shook his head and tried to forget. He grinned, he couldn't forget and he pushed into Tanner, flicking his tray up with a little energy. Tanner yelped as hot milk from the cereal wet him, leaving tiny welts form up his torso.

Daniel smiled as he watched Tanner drop his tray and the rest of the milk splash up his pants.

"Oi!" Jasper shouted.

Daniel turned and teleported before it could escalate.

"Did you hear them?" he asked, placing the tray on his bed.

"Who?" Jac asked, folding the sheets.

"The people in the cafeteria, I got my own back, although I doubt it will stop them speaking about me."

"I can guarantee that they'll always speak about you, you left an impression," Jac said. He looked at the tray and tucked into the food.

"Sometimes I think I should have stayed at home and just gone to the library with my dad," Daniel sighed, putting a sausage and a few bacon strips on a bun. "I'll eat this and then I best get to class. And you best be listening in."

"It's not that easy y'know. I have to concentrate," Jac said, chewing on a sausage.

"You don't have anything better to do," Daniel said, before taking a huge bite out of his sandwich. He nodded at Jac and disappeared.

There were a few people standing around outside the classroom. Daniel walked through everyone as they huddled close to the door, he tried not to push. He sat in the front row and finished eating the rest of his sandwich. The snide comments ambled in on bitter tongues and sat around him. It was comforting to know that Jac was listening and Jac had a temper when he wanted.

Marianne walked in, she smiled and nodded at Daniel. "Today we're going to be talking about legends," she said, taking a seat and facing the class.

There was excited chatter from the first two rows, nothing about Daniel, it was about the lesson, how they'd looked forward to this lesson since they started. The rumour was that this lesson had been the one when teachers entrusted information that the rest of the island didn't know.

Marianne talked for some time, telling the class what they'd already learnt until something caught Daniel's ear and he paid more attention.

"People used to deal in Luminary blood, sometimes it was normal blood and other times it was animal blood. It killed a lot of people; they thought that a little bit of it would allow them to soar just like the Luminary. There was a bit of real Luminary blood in circulation though. That killed people as well," she explained to her captivated audience.

Is that why Reuben was trying to get Karsar? I bet Karsar thinks it was my idea. I think I should tell him that it wasn't. I should probably summon him in a dream.

"With the Luminary blood people would try to take down the pillars of power by summoning them through prayer or a group invocation," she sighed, "they'd try to get them to will all their power away. However, only the most foolish people would try and get the attention of a Luminary, because it would never end well."

Daniel turned, hoping to see somebody that had been with him in Reuben's class yesterday. He was the only first year that had been there, so he wore the sickly pale alone.

"Who would our prayers go to?" a girl from the second row asked.

"We pray to the planet, not the planetary person. Each Luminary has a planet to which they are tied to, or as we've hashed over before, the Sun, so when we pray it's like our calls are being diverted first," Marianne replied, combing through the end of her plait. "Nobody knows the name of a Luminary, if you did it would be easier to call to them. They're probably living in some fancy castle somewhere, somewhere *off* the island."

Daniel frowned as Karsar's face flashed before his eyes. He could see his face clearly in his mind, the horror when he thought he was going to be trapped forever.

"So they don't listen to our prayers?" she asked.

"Of course they listen. It's our need for energy that gives them the power that they have, so of course they listen to our prayers."

"Oh, but what if we—" the girl began.

Marianne held her hand up and the girl fell quiet. "I have something interesting to tell you about Luminary blood. It's still sold today in the markets, and there are poor sods who will barter for a vial of it, although it's almost certainly poisoned so that you're susceptible to being controlled."

"People do that?" Daniel asked.

"Yes, every day, in fact. It happens in the City mainly, where money is money and everyone wants it," she replied. "Besides, you can't take the blood of a Luminary, they have guardians, born with them and they'll die for them. They are ruthless people, but you'll never come across one in your life. You might in a dream after you've prayed for something big, like love, a saviour, or prosperity."

It wasn't long before the lesson was over, a few students had stayed back to ask Marianne more questions. Daniel had stayed as well for a momentl, but teleported back to his room when he realised that he couldn't talk privately with a queue behind him.

Jac was laid in Daniel's bed, his eyes closed and his arms folded over his chest.

"She's right you know," Jac said.

"Who?" Daniel asked.

"Your teacher."

"Oh," Daniel nodded, "why do have my phone?" he asked, looking at the phone in Jac's hand.

"Mia called, she seems nice."

"You answered my phone?"

"Yeah, it kept ringing so I pressed one of the buttons and hoped for the best, then her voice came through," he said, passing Daniel his phone.

"I tried to call her last night," Daniel said, pressing buttons to call her. He held the phone to his ear, listening to the dial tone.

It rang once before Mia answered. "Daniel?" she said.

"Hi," Daniel said. "I tried calling you last night, but my calls didn't go through."

"You probably have crap signal," she said, "I had fun talking with your friend—" she trailed on.

Daniel creased his brow and scratched the top of his head. "How come I didn't hear anything?" he asked, looking at Jac.

They both answered him. Jac shrugged. "I did try to tell you that the phone was ringing," he said.

"—I don't know," Mia giggled. "Is your friend like you? He said you spoke about me, *telepathically*. Can he do the same things you can?"

"Yeah, we all can. Everyone on this island is full of energy and power and, I don't even know why you can't do it," he said.

"What did she say?" Jac whispered and Daniel raised his hand to shush him.

"I wish we could too! Then I could fly," she giggled. "Oh my—your friend said you summoned some god, guy, person."

"It wasn't as big as he made it out to be. In fact, it was nothing."

"The way your friend—"

"Jac," Daniel interrupted.

"Yeah, the way Jac put it, it sounded like you fought off a shark with your bare hands," she laughed.

"I'm hungry," Jac whined, flopping on the bed.

"I have to go, Jac can't leave the room and I need to go and get lunch for us. I'll phone you back later though."

"Sure, but if I don't answer then my father's probably taken it from me," she said and hung up.

"Bye," Daniel said as fast as he could and then pushed the phone into his pocket.

"So you're the one who got into this school, not me," Jac grinned.

"Whatever."

"I'm just trespassing."

"And eating all the food, and making a mess and—"

"Okay, okay. I'll give the room a bit of a clean and I'll try and eat less."

"I'm joking, you can eat as much as you like, I'd rather you were fed than some of the people here."

"Well, I am the only one who truly knows the meaning of *slumming* it," Jac grinned. "Are you going to get me something, or do I have to starve?" he asked, holding his stomach as he curled up in the fetal position.

CHAPTER TWENTY-SIX

DANIEL made his way back to his room with two brown paper bags. The servers must have caught on because they gave him double without him needing to ask, that or they thought Daniel needed to bulk up some more.

Three loud bangs rasped against his door. Daniel knew it was his door, there was something in that echo he'd heard before. Jasper's voice was the next thing to tremble. He demanded that he opened it. It was definitely his.

Daniel teleported back to his room. It was clean and empty.

"There are some people wanting to get into your room," Jac whispered.

"Where are you?" he asked.

"I'm hiding in the closet."

"Come out then, I'm back now. No wait," Daniel opened the closet and threw the paper bags inside. "I'll see what they want."

Jac was stood, startled to see Daniel's face when the closet door opened. He closed it as Daniel rushed to the door.

Daniel unlocked it and Jasper tugged on the handle and pushed it open. "What do you want?" Daniel said.

"Are you sleeping with Carlie?" Jasper asked. His forehead turned red and his lips thinned as he asked him again.

"No," Daniel laughed.

Jasper took a deep breath and then punched Daniel square in the mouth. He stumbled backwards and held his jaw. He pushed it side to side and rolled it until it clicked. He could taste the iron from the blood and see the light red gloss over his fingertips. He stumbled forward and the door slammed shut as he walked out into the hallway.

"I think it works," Mark said. He looked down at Daniel's feet.

"What?" Daniel asked. He looked to see three stones glowing around him. "What is it?"

"Why, does it hurt?" Jasper grinned. He turned and high-fived Mark.

Daniel reached out to touch the spectral film that had cased him. He pushed his fingers through and tore a hole, his hands blistering and turning red.

"Don't. Because that *will* hurt," Jasper said.

Daniel clenched his jaw harder as the pain touched his nerves. He continued to rip at the barrier, but it kept on filling back up, even over his fingers.

"What is it?" Daniel asked. He rubbed his hands together and watched them heal.

"You people shouldn't have power. So you gotta give it up. Give it all up," Jasper said.

"Why? Why don't I deserve power but you do?"

"I deserve power because I have wealth, but for you it is a way to get by, therefore if your power goes, then you're gone," he replied with a snort of enthusiasm.

Mark sliced both hands through the air, and moments later Daniel fell to his knees. He turned to see blood. It soaked the back of his jeans and pooled on the floor.

"You'll heal," Jasper said, watching the horror spread across Daniel's face.

"But why are you doing it!" he shouted.

Mark swiped his hands again and acted like he'd hit something, but tore right through it. Slowly, a light red line broke open on the back of Daniel's hand. It covered him in more blood. He was used to the pain it had been no more than a tickle to his skin.

"You're at your weakest when you're cut, or bleeding. So I wouldn't try and use any of that *flare* of yours in there," Jasper laughed.

Daniel's body burned at the cuts he'd endured. They'd stop healing over swelled. He held his fingers up to his face as he watched them turn blue and blow up like ripe aubergines.

"Jac!" Daniel stifled as he coughed into his hands. "Can you hear me?"

"Yeah, what's up, I'm eating," he replied, chomping on potato waffles.

Daniel's teeth chattered in his mouth. "I don't care who sees, come and—come and—help."

The door of the dorm burst open and all heads turned to Jac. He stood with his hands in fists by his side. He scowled at Jasper and Mark as they stood laughing. They looked up, stumped.

"You have a friend?" Jasper asked.

Jac stared at them. He prided himself on being the quick one who'd survived surprise attacks and lived in the forest for all those years. He glanced at Daniel, hunched over with his hands tucked against his stomach. He didn't have anything to say.

"Jac?" Daniel grumbled.

"No!" Jac shouted. "Who are you? What are you doing?" He kicked one of the stones but it stayed intact.

"Just messin' with our *friend*," Jasper grinned. He took a step back.

Mark lifted his hand into the air. He twisted it like he was pulling a lime from a tree. Daniel fell harder on the ground.

He groaned as the cuts on his body opened a little more. His skin now a light shade of blue.

"It won't properly hurt him," Jasper said.

Jac kicked the stone again and it inched away slightly. Daniel continued to force himself to the ground, coughing and cowering into his arms.

"What have you done?" Jac shouted through gritted teeth.

"Nothing you do can stop us taking *all* that power."

Jac shook his head; he knew differently, he knew that they couldn't take any power, and even if they tried to sample it they'd keel over and wake in a hospital room without any recollection of who Daniel even was. He smiled at the thought.

"You will regret trying!" Jac said. He glanced from them to Daniel. He noticed tiny crystals from inside the stones glow and explode with colour. It was a gut instinct as he stomped on the stone and shattered the hold they had over Daniel.

Jac dodged Jasper's fist as he aimed for his jaw. He fell forward slightly. "Take a beating. Bet you're scum like him!" he shouted.

Jac took the chance and pulled Daniel from the ground. He ushered him back into his room and left the trail of blood smeared across the floor outside.

He turned and caught a punch to his torso from Mark. He wheezed and ground his teeth as he tried to remember everything he'd learnt. He coughed. "Just wait!" he shouted after them down the hall.

"You couldn't hurt us," Jasper said with snarl.

"We hurt you though," Mark laughed.

Jac clenched at his abdomen as the pain found a comfortable place to sit. "Well done," he said and rolled his eyes.

"Scum, just like Daniel!" they shouted.

Jac grimaced; he looked at the crushed stone on the floor and shook his head. "You're the scummy people around here." He walked back to Daniel's room and locked the door.

Daniel laid on his bed with his arms clutched against his chest. His body had taken on a more fleshy tone, but there was still a tint of blue in the ends of his fingertips.

"What did they do?" Jac asked

"I didn't think they'd go that far," he said. "They wanted to *kill* me." He coughed at the knot in his throat.

"They won't be bothering you, not when they know who you really are. I need to tell you something, Daniel."

Daniel laughed weakly. "What did you do to them?"

"I stood strong, I rooted myself. That's *not* what I need to tell you. This is something you need to be fully functioning for. You need to listen to me when I tell you this. Are you listening?"

Daniel looked up at Jac and nodded.

"I've been trying to think of how or when I should tell you. I'm not sure how, but it was either me or your dad, and he said I had to tell you," Jac said. He sat down beside Daniel.

"What is it? Is it—Is it—" Daniel stopped as several sharp knocks rapped against the door.

"I'll hide," Jac said.

It was too late, Reuben pushed the door open, jolting from its hinges. He walked over with Jasper and Mark behind him. They were both holding their bodies like they'd been seriously injured.

Jac stood still as they joined the room. His eyes popped open and glared at the three of them. He glanced down at Daniel and all he could think about was how he needed to tell him that he shouldn't be afraid, that he shouldn't be their inferior.

"You!" Reuben shouted. He pointed at Jac.

"I've done nothing wrong," Jac protested.

"Trespassing and hurting *my* students. Well that doesn't seem like nothing," Reuben said.

"They were hurting him first. They cut him pretty bad, they had him on his hands and knees," Jac said, throwing his hands in the air and pointing at Jasper and Mark.

"Is this true, Daniel?" Reuben asked, combing a hand through his slicked-back black hair.

"Yes," Daniel said. He sat up and thousands of little electric bullets jammed inside his chest. His eyes started to tear up from the pain.

"Do you have proof?"

"Yes," he said. He moved off his bed and tried to stand. He turned to show Reuben the back of his jeans. There was no sign of blood; he then noticed that there wasn't a trail leading into the room and nothing outside it either.

"You're lying," Reuben said.

"But there was—they had me in this force field square and they said that I didn't deserve what I had, and that I was, *scum*," Daniel said in a forceful tone.

"Is this true?" he asked his nephew. Jasper shook his head. "Why would my nephew lie to me? And why is he on *my* land?" he pointed at Jac.

Jac stuttered as he tried to think up an excuse. Reuben's nostrils flared as he raised his staff from the ground. He took a swipe at Jac and before it made contact, Jac had vanished.

"And I revoke your access to go off the island and off the campus!" he shouted at Daniel. He turned, and a second later the three of them vanished. The door picked itself back up and secured itself in place, "and you're being locked in!" his voice came again and roared inside the room.

Daniel's heart raced around his body. His fingers shook as he shoved his hand into his pocket and pulled out his phone.

He called Mia. "Meet me!" he said.

"I'm having dinner, I'm nearly done though," she whispered.

"*Mia*, off your phone at the table," her father shouted in the background.

CHAPTER TWENTY-SEVEN

DANIEL stood on the ledge of the tall building where Mia lived. He let his feet itch over it, closer and closer, his toes hung, clutching to the stone. He closed his eyes and let the air whip around his face. He threw his head back and glanced up at the half crescent moon. *So bold. So powerful. I bet you don't have troubles,* he thought.

The squeak of the hinges from the door on the roof startled Daniel. He turned and jumped to the roof. "I could have fallen," he said with a smile.

Mia peered out of the door and saw Daniel. She grinned. "You didn't," she said. "So what happened?"

Daniel glanced to the ground and back up at her, she was waiting for an answer. "I feel stupid saying this. I was beaten up," he said, "and then Jac was taken, I don't know where he's gone, I can't talk to him or anything. And Reuben revoked my permission to come here."

"You—you have to go then," she said.

"No, you're the only one I can speak to about this."

"Yeah, and I want to, but I don't want you to pay for it. I don't want you to die." She walked closer, taking his hand. "Just phone me."

"They can try to kill me. They can try," he said.

"Go back," she said and placed a hand on his chest.

He gripped her hand and pulled her to the ledge. "I want to show you something," he said. "They said I shouldn't do it, but you know what, I'm gonna." He peeled her hand from his chest and turned. He took a step and stood tall. He looked over.

She gripped the sleeve of his jacket. "You're not going to jump off!"

Daniel brushed her hand away. He unzipped the jacket and took it off, throwing it beside the vent on the floor. His chest was goose pimpled as the cold took a hold. He shivered and rolled his shoulders, there were several cracks and clicks, and as Mia watched, two huge arched wings formed on Daniel's back. The feathers were darker in colour; it had been a while since he'd projected that much energy out of his body.

"You're an angel," she whispered. "Am I dead? Are you taking me to heaven? *Did I jump?*"

"No, what are you talking about," he laughed, "I'm not an angel or from heaven, but I can grow these and people have said that it meant I was special."

"Oh, I—I—I knew that, yeah, you are pretty special."

"The first time we met you were ready to jump. Would you have gone through with it?" Daniel asked.

Mia's smile faded and she looked away, anywhere but into his eyes. "I don't know."

"Well, do you want to know what it would be like to fall?"

"I'm scared of heights."

"Then it's lucky for you that I can use these," he grinned as the wings on his back spanned out.

Mia took a deep breath. "Will they carry us both?" she asked with a nervous smile.

"You're probably lighter than Jac and I've saved Jac quite a few times with these. So yeah, probably," he said. He held his hand out for her.

She took it and he pulled her up to the ledge. "What do you want me to do?"

"Climb on my back," he said. "But don't strangle me or lean on a wing. I don't think there's anything worse than spinning out of control; I should know. It's *happened.*"

Mia rolled her eyes at him as her grip on his hand became tighter.

"Hop on," he said, turning on the spot so she could jump on his back. She was almost pushed by a wing but she didn't let go of Daniel's hand for even a second.

"Are you sure it's safe?" she asked as Daniel knelt slightly. He wrapped her arms around his neck and when Daniel stood she swung her legs around his waist.

"Trying to stop the circulation?" he croaked. He coughed and Mia loosened her grip around his neck. "Are your eyes closed?"

"No," she lied through her gnashing teeth.

"Good, because I'm closing mine," he said and they toppled from the top of the building.

They were falling, slicing through the air, their streamline bodies created a vacuum of intense g-force. The pressure kept Daniel's feathers sleek and Mia's hair stuck to her scalp. She burrowed her head in his neck, and kept her eyes closed and her mouth shut. She stopped breathing.

The butterflies in Mia's stomach were too much. Her chest thumped against her vocal chords as she tried to speak. "O— open your eyes," she spat, lifting her head slightly.

They'd fallen halfway down the building before Daniel swooped back up. The force tugged at Mia as they gained height. She wrapped her legs around his waist tightly. Daniel dropped again and this time her arms around his neck jolted like the mouth of a snake.

"Mia, it's fine," he said, easing his neck out of her strangulation.

"Just—just slow down," she said.

"Don't worry, like I said, they've only failed me once."

"What if people see?"

Daniel slowed to a hover, half-way between the road and the roof of the building. "They might, but nobody will say anything for fear of being thought of as crazy," he smiled. "Should we go see them?" he asked, and before she could answer he'd already swooped and headed for the road below.

Her arms pulled tighter around his neck again, reining him in before a witch hunt began, that or her fainting. "Please, can we go back?" she shouted.

There was a pop. A fizzle. Colour faded out of Daniel's eyes and before he realised what had happened, someone had spotted them, almost like someone had taken a photo. He dropped just above the people and darted over their heads. He was following a trail of popping lights.

"Up! Up! Take me back!" she shouted.

"No. I can't. It's her," he said. He caught a glimpse of the girl, she was moving just as fast as he was. A faint flare to the rest of the people.

The girl stopped and turned to look at him. It was the girl from the coffee shop, the one he'd shared thoughts with. She was like him. She had to be like him, there was no other way Daniel could process how she moved through the crowd or spoke to him.

He halted in the sky as she entered his mind. *"Don't come any closer! You'll expose us all; at least I can clean this up! Just go!"* she boomed throughout him.

He pushed higher into the sky, repeating the word *'expose'* to himself in a mumble. He wasn't thinking properly, he was angry at Reuben. She wasn't angry like him; she didn't mind him being off the island. He realised what he might've looked like, a seraph, a winged boy, swooping down over the town.

He reached the roof of the building and landed on his hands and knees. Mia jumped off and playfully hit him. "That wasn't funny," she said. Daniel turned his head slightly to see the huge grin on her face, only thinking himself, *no, it really wasn't.*

He stayed on his hands and knees for a moment and then a huge gust of wind knocked him, taking the first feathers from his wings. He molted as the wind picked up and hit him in all directions, each gust stole a handful of feathers. It picked his wings clean until all that was left were the bone. They receded back into his body and left gaping pools of blood in their place.

Mia had asked several times if he was okay, each time she asked her voice was more strained. "Why are you bleeding?"

"I'm fine. Really, I am. The bleeding happens every time; it will heal over and look like it had never happened." He looked into the sky and watched his feathers being taken away.

Mia caught a feather. She stroked the side of her face with it. "How come they're—" she turned around to see Daniel standing beside her.

"Usually they come back inside," he said. "I guess my power isn't as self-contained out here." He looked into her eyes, and touched her hand. He turned his head to the long feather. "Keep it."

"I'm gonna," she began. She turned to look at him, and as she turned, he kissed her. She pulled away. "Um." She kissed him back. "I think you should get dressed now."

"It is getting cold," he laughed, tucking his hands under his arms.

Mia picked up the bundle of clothes and chucked them at him. "I can't believe it. And you even did it half-naked."

"Well, I was warm when I did it. Probably because I wasn't exactly human, I was more bird than I was boy. My blood changes and everything, my senses become sharper and my skin, well I'm not sure about that, but I know it means I can stand very, *very* cold temperatures," he explained, slipping the t-shirt over his head.

"Are you going to tell me what you are then? Bird boy," she said and brushed the hair out of her face.

"I'm human," he grinned, "in fact, I'll probably be dead tomorrow if the law has anything to say about it," he grinned, and that soon faded as he realised it was true.

"I doubt it. He wouldn't have given you this privilege just to kill you. He's knows that you're special, just like I know you're special. But you'll still have to call me tomorrow, to make sure that you're alive."

They kissed again before she left through the rooftop door. Daniel sat on the ledge of the building for several minutes. He thought about the girl he saw in the coffee shop, the same girl he'd just seen. He didn't like her, not how he liked Mia. This girl made him question himself, she was like Karsar. *Was she another Luminary?* He gasped at the thought. *She was, she has to be.*

When Daniel got back to his room he was alone. It was the evening now, almost time for dinner, but he wasn't going to step another foot outside that door. He'd contemplated going home, going to see his mother, but she'd only be more worried than she needed to be.

He curled up in a ball on his bed, cocooning himself in his duvet as he let himself drift off. He fell into a blissful slumber.

The white surrounded him. *"Come with me,"* a heavenly female voice yanked him. *"Come—come—come with me,"* it pulled again, this time waking him.

"Hello," he said. He pushed his hands out in front of his face. Something clung to his fingers, white sticky fluff. It was taking over his body.

"Stay still," the voice drowned his ears.

How? He thought.

A warm rasping breath caressed the nape of his neck and the back of his ear. "You're born wrong. You're born strong. The scum is that beneath you. Not right through you. Errors of size, have been dealt. Skin and flesh, will always melt. Try to realise, what's been done. Think on your feet, little one." A woman, made of mist logged features spiraled around him.

Before Daniel realised it, he was breathing the smoke in, and out, in, and out. Getting light-headed, he pinned his eyes open to get a better look at the woman's face.

"I don't understand," he murmured, his head rolled.

"You're stuck. Go un-stick yourself," she said, and vanished, taking the fluff that had enveloped him.

CHAPTER TWENTY-EIGHT

DANIEL stood before Reuben's office door. He stood silently, waiting for the nerves in his body to calm. He held a hand up to knock, but it flew open in anticipation. Reuben's face was covered in pulsing veins.

Reuben slammed both of his fists down on his desk. "What are you waiting there for?" he asked. Daniel jumped and hurried into the room as the doors shut behind him. "You broke the rules!" Reuben thumped his fists again. "What do you have to say in your defence?"

"Um. I—I—I was angry."

"Oh, so that's okay then, I went out on a limb for you, Daniel. And I might have been fine if you didn't pull that *little* stunt. It could've exposed us all."

It had occurred to him, he knew what he was doing, and he kind of wanted to be caught on camera. He glanced behind Reuben to the grey cloudless skyline. He thought, *they're probably paying a price much worse than mine. Is there anything worse than death?*

"Did someone see me?"

"Did someone see you? *Someone?*" he laughed.

So it's true, someone else is going to pay a price worse than death. Daniel butted his lips together and blinked away the tears from welling in his eyes. "H—How many people?"

"It doesn't really matter, does it? Do you feel bad for what you've done? You put more than just your own life in danger, and you still don't really understand the repercussions of that. People can lose their lives over this, Daniel."

"But you don't have to say anything. I promise I'll stay on the island."

"If it was up to me. But it isn't, the footage went straight to the City."

"What if the Luminary doesn't want you to kill these people?"

"We do this to please them, so of course they want us to. However, I'm willing to get those in charge to just erase the footage."

"Are you g—g—going to kill me?" Daniel asked, the back of his legs tingled. He remembered telling Mia that he was happy to accept any punishment. He wished he hadn't lied to her now.

Reuben snorted and threw his arms back as he lounged in his leather office chair. "No," he said, "but punish, yes. I need a vial of your blood, for insurance purposes, in case this comes back to bite me."

The glands in Daniel's throat throbbed as he choked on Reuben's reply. He looked up, his eyes pink from the need to cry. He nodded. He didn't have a care for what Reuben needed his blood for, as long as he wasn't going to die.

"You're not going to class today, but the rest of your week will stay as planned, including Tuesday," he continued.

Daniel nodded in agreement; there was no room for him to protest. Reuben gestured for him to approach.

"I'll need that blood from you now," he said. "Aren't you going to ask why?"

Daniel paused, wondering whether or not it was a trick question. "Why?" he asked.

"Removing you from the *map* was temporary, this can make it permanent."

Did that mean I could leave whenever I like? He mused.

"Right, let's get this underway. And then afterwards, you will go and get your breakfast and you will take it back to your room and eat it, and only come out when it's time for lunch," he explained.

Reuben pulled Daniel's arm close, he pushed his sleeve up. He looked Daniel in the eye, and with one smooth flick of his wrist there was a cut across Daniel's palm. Reuben held Daniel's hand over a small pyramid-shaped glass where the blood trickled down his fingertips and drip by drip, the blood filled the vial.

Reuben shooed Daniel away when the glass was full. "Go get your breakfast," he said, screwing a cork into the top of it.

Daniel hurried off. He cradled his bleeding hand in his arm.

"That *should* heal," Reuben shouted after him.

Daniel didn't stop for breakfast, and even though the blood loss had made him weak, he managed to summon vibrations to teleport him back to his room.

"Screw him! I did nothing wrong!" Daniel shouted. He wiped the tears from his face and smeared the blood from his hands in its place.

He finally calmed down and sat on his bed. He'd tried several times to get a hold of Jac, but every time he felt close, an abrupt wave of white noise crashed down inside his ears. He tried again, and again, and soon after he came down with a heavy nosebleed. He called it quits.

He did nothing, he could do nothing. The lady in white, and the man in black were the only people he could meet, and they were in his dreams, so he decided to sleep.

Daniel woke, seconds before his alarm could chirp. He gasped and rolled straight out of his duvet to the floor. He took a deep breath and sighed, glancing at the time; not even enough to get a quick shower. What worried him even more was the fact that he'd slept for 18 hours and his stomach scratched at his insides.

"Jac!" he called out. He closed his eyes and tried to push the name.

Daniel sighed and walked over to the sink. He picked up the dry flannel from across the faucet and wet it with cold water. He blotted his face and body with the cold flannel. There was a wave of instant pleasure as he wiped at his sweaty skin.

He dressed and rushed out of his room. He grabbed a quick snack from the cafeteria before it closed and headed straight for the stables. Although he was told to skip all lessons, he didn't want to miss out on something he'd already missed too much of.

Daniel walked into the stables and Enek looked over. He smiled as Daniel sat on a work bench behind the rest of the class.

"Today, we're going to be fighting in our animal forms. We must all learn how to do it, and we must all learn how to do it well," Enek said. He formed a circle from the class around him, and encouraged Daniel to join. "Even if you're an elk." He turned around to a small chubby girl and grinned. "I've been advised on pairings, and your opponents will be the one who you can learn something from."

Jasper glared at Daniel and snarled. It was a sudden feeling, the feeling that he knew what was going to happen, Daniel would be paired with Jasper, and the school knew how that went down last time, besides, Daniel didn't even shift form that time. He tried to return the same snarl, but his stomach knotted; it felt like it was chewing on itself, and the expression Daniel gave was not a powerful one.

Enek reeled off a list of names. He got to Daniel's name. He hummed and bit on his lip. "Daniel, you're with Charles," he said.

"Huh?" Charles said.

Daniel recognised him, he was from his Tuesday class, but he seemed nice there, now, here, the look on his face was that of someone who'd been told his whole family had been massacred. Daniel didn't know much about Charles, his animal form was the snake and he was friendly with the teachers.

"Enek," Charles said. "Our animal types are off," he protested and swiped a hand through his gelled back hair.

"Oh. How do you figure?" Enek asked. "Are you the teacher?"

Charles flared his nostrils and stared at Daniel from across the stable. Daniel was relieved; the look Charles gave him was nothing in comparison to the cold stomach wrenching ones that

Jasper seemed to throw around. This gave Daniel a chance to release some anger, and he was suddenly a bit disappointed that he hadn't been paired with Jasper.

Each pair took a different section of the barn. Charles' lips curled as he met up with Daniel. "You do know my venom is dangerous, right?" Charles said.

"So guys, I want you to keep this clean, no other use of energy and no weapons. If you do *kill*," Enek grinned, "then you too will be killed. Even if accidental, you know your own threshold and must submit if you've gone too far, similarly if you think you're going to kill, pull back. Now, on with the show."

The thought of death took Daniel back to yesterday morning where he feared that his own life had come to an end. And then his thoughts whirled to Jac, he'd only ever killed with Jac, and most of the killing was done by Jac. Daniel would fly, swoop down and injure with his talons, but the smell of blood made his stomach acid bubble. Even now, just thinking about it, he clutched at his abdomen.

"It can sometimes inhibit your other abilities, and even keep you in your animal form," Charles continued, "are you sure you want to do this?"

Daniel grinned. "I'm ready."

Within seconds of Charles rolling his eyes he landed in a heap at the ground as a snake. Daniel jumped back as the snake cocked its head and readied itself to strike. The snake was huge, and its glossy skin was coloured in whites and blues, not easily camouflaged.

"A little warning," Daniel laughed, "but what pretty colours you have." He took a step back and morphed into a huge eagle with a silver beak and golden talons.

Daniel snapped his beak as Charles squirted his venom. They both took on defensive stances across from each other, and before they could figure it out they'd taken to the centre of the stable while others fought around them.

In a corner Jasper as a lion clawed at the elk. She tried to kick him in the face with her hoof, but that didn't work and Jasper kept on clawing. He hit her, but his claws were retracted, so he'd only petted her with a soft paw. She skipped across the straw and smiled to herself. Jasper's claws were out this time and he swiped again. He scraped her leg. She whined and shifted back, giving in to the pain. She picked herself up from the floor and slapped the lion across his face before rushing away with a limp.

Daniel took to the air. He flapped, and shot gusts down at the snake. He sliced through them and squirted blasts of venom up at Daniel, but they didn't reach.

"Daniel! I said fighting, that's a defence tactic up there," Enek called from the balcony in the barn.

Daniel cocked his head to Enek and nodded. He knew it was right, he knew that he had to get into some real fighting. He looked back down at Charles slithering across the ground.

Jasper pounced and grappled Daniel out of the air.

"Get off!" Daniel shouted in a squawk.

Jasper pawed him and pinned him down by his wings. Daniel pecked at Jasper's neck and pulled out a clump of his fur. Jasper yelped and rolled off Daniel.

They glanced up at Enek; he shrugged and grinned, and held his hands up like there was nothing that he could do about it.

Daniel now had two people after him, a lion with a bite and no venom, and a snake with no bite but enough venom to kill. It was in the split second when both Jasper and Charles exchanged glances and Daniel realised they would both rather go on the chopping block than have '*scum*' continue to study at their Academy.

Daniel turned, he was ready to catch some air when something hit him. Jasper's claws were inside his wing. Daniel tried to flap. He whacked Jasper around his head, but the lion hit back, this time the claws sunk into Daniel's skin and his blood wet the feathers. Daniel screeched in a low-pitched whine. It drove them all crazy as they writhed out of their animal forms and a small congregation stirred by the barn doors.

"Which one's Daniel?" a newcomer to the audience asked.

"The one crying," a girl replied.

By now, everyone else had stopped fighting to watch what was happening. They kept glancing from Enek to the fight, and from his half-smile, it seemed he approved.

Daniel screeched once again, it made everyone flinch, except for Jasper and Charles. Jasper tried to roar back, tried to roar louder, but it was nothing in comparison. The snake hissed and lifted its head. It bobbed and weaved, threatening to fire its toxins.

"Just shut him up," someone shouted.

The snake threw its all at Daniel and wrapped itself around his neck. Daniel went silent as he tried to peck at the snake. It had constricted his throat and only whimpers could be heard as Daniel opened his beak to screech.

"Finish him!" someone started, and then they all began. "Finish him! Finish him!"

I'm finished, I'm finished! Daniel shouted at himself. His breathes hitched as he couldn't swallow. He flapped his wings aimlessly. He dropped to his knees and whacked himself. He tried to get a feel for the snake around his neck.

"Enough!" Enek said, waving a hand from the balcony.

The chanting stopped and everyone glared at him.

"Go on, shoo," he said, flicking his wrists and sending the barn doors shut. "And you three, *shift!*"

The snake became loose and dropped from Daniel's neck. Jasper and Charles were back to normal within the instant, while Daniel stayed on his hands and knees, choking as his exterior dripped around him. There was a shared gasp between all the students, and then as they watched Daniel squirm up from the ground, they stifled hands over their sniggers.

"Out! All of you," Enek said.

They hurried out and left Daniel alone. He was surrounded by clumps of feather on the floor of the barn and the remnants of his excess bones.

I should have skipped the lesson, he told himself.

CHAPTER TWENTY-NINE

DANIEL stayed in the barn, he wandered around in his head and in thought. He wondered about what had just happened. He'd almost been killed, his arms were bruised purple, yet he didn't get a scratch on Charles or Jasper, and then he thought about how full of himself he was.

"I'm going home," he said aloud, "there's nothing keeping me here now, is there?" he rubbed the bruises on his arms. "And I need to find Jac, and I can probably go home and he can teach me what he knows. I can go to the libraries."

"Sounds good," Enek said from the balcony of the barn.

"Oh," Daniel sighed. He picked himself up from the floor. "I thought I was alone."

"You know, people would kill family members to be at this school," he said, and walked down the ladder. "And Reuben chose you. So you must be special."

"I'm not special," he said. "People keep on saying that like it means something."

"Well, we've all heard the story of how you nearly died, several times over at this point. That's kind of special."

"So, Reuben tells you everything?"

"No, not everything, he doesn't tell us why he favours you over his nephew, and Jasper knows it as well, that's why he's acting out."

"I still think I'm gonna go, there's nothing keeping me here. The classes that I go to are full of people who talk about me, and the teachers are constantly *glaring* and I already know what they're talking about."

"See. That's special."

Daniel shook his head. Enek gave him a hand as he found his footing. "I was so excited to come here," he said, "I've started to fill my journals with things I eat, or things I see, like *oh, another bird flew past my window.*"

"I think if it was anyone else, they would've left already," Enek said, he hauled the barn door open. "Are you really planning on leaving?"

Daniel walked out of the barn. He turned and bit his lip. "Who knows what's gonna happen, I might end up being thrown out of my bedroom window."

"Don't put ideas in their heads now"

In the daylight Daniel could see the bruises on his arms. They looked darker and welts had popped up around them. He held his hand over his eyes as they adjusted to the light and he looked into the sky. *I can go anywhere*, he told himself.

"Oh, there he is, I thought he was going to die," a passer-by whispered to a friend.

Great, I think they were betting on that as well, Daniel whinged.

He made his way to his room. He walked as slow as he could. He wanted to enjoy the day but not the company the outside brought. He swiped his card to unlock the door and smiled as he realised he hadn't done that in a while. His room was dark from the drawn curtains. He flicked the lights on and found Carlie, sprawled out on his bed.

"Get out! What are you even doing here?" he asked.

She winked. "For *you*, silly."

"Really. I'm fed up this. What are you even doing?" he asked. "Just leave!"

She huffed. "You're no fun." She climbed to her feet. "Y'know Jasper hates you right. So, how about you get back at him?"

"I don't know what you do, but I know that you *take* from people, yeah, you *take* their energy," Daniel said, "so what is it about me?"

"Exactly, you're powerful, stronger than Jasper, heck, even Mark's stronger than Jasper," she said, "I should know. I was close to draining Mark."

He closed his eyes and nestled his fingers across the bridge of his nose. "You're crazy. But you weren't born crazy," Daniel said. "You've created it, all on your own." He ushered her out of his room.

"Huh? I do *this* for the thrill, and just because I know a good time, doesn't mean that I don't know how to settle down. Why are you being so *precious* for," she grinned and pushed a hand up to Daniel's chest to feel his heart pounding.

"Yeah, I don't care, just leave!" he slapped her hands from his chest.

"Are you hoping to," she winked, "with that girl?"

"Who?" he asked. "Mia?"

"Mia?" she asked with a smile. "Soon, all your other ties will be gone, and then you'll want me. In fact, you'll want me more than I *need* you."

Daniel frisked himself for his phone, but he didn't have it. "Where's it at?"

Carlie huffed and left. She ran down the hallway giggling to herself.

He slammed the door shut before he began throwing things around. His duvet was on the floor, followed by his pillows, and the bed sheet. He searched around the frame of the bed to see if it had fallen down into it. He checked under his bed, and saw Jac's sheets from before he'd been so violently confronted and shunned somewhere he couldn't reach.

A buzz came from the drawer of his bedside table. He yanked the drawer and there was his phone, glowing as the 'low battery' sign flashed. He sighed and picked it out, but there were no missed calls, no text messages or anything. He typed Mia's name in and phoned her.

"Hey," she answered.

He sighed. "You're fine?"

"Yeah, why?"

"I think people know about you," he said.

"Well yesterday you told me that people spotted us, it would be hard for them not to have caught me on your back. I mean, I was strangling you almost," she chuckled.

Daniel pulled the grille of the phone away from his face. He was thinking of ways to word it, he told himself that he couldn't come off as paranoid. He couldn't. He pushed the phone back to his ear.

"I need you to stay at home, just be ill for a few days. I'll try and see if you're in any harm. Don't worry though, you're probably not, but just to be safe," he said. "A precaution."

"Okay. Are you sure I should stay off?"

"Yeah, pretend you're ill for a few days or something."

"Fine, but you're gonna to have to come back and see me," she said.

"Okay."

"I need to go, dad's just shouted me for dinner."

"I'll phone you later." He ended the call.

There was a knock on his door, and it was times like those he wished he had a peephole in place. The knock came again, stern and solid.

"Who is it?" he asked. He stood with his hand on the door handle.

"Lunch," a girl said.

He let his heart rest back behind his lungs as he pulled on the door handle. The door whacked him in the face as Mark and Jasper barged in. Daniel heard a girl whimper her apologies.

"This is getting old!" he spat in frustration. His jaw tensed and the bruising up his arms itched.

"Again?" Jasper laughed.

"What now?" Daniel asked

"Coming onto Carlie like that, she doesn't like *you*," he said.

Daniel grinned as he looked at Mark and noticed the humility behind his eyes, because he knew just what she was like.

Jasper swung for Daniel's face. Daniel dropped to his knees to avoid the swing, and Jasper stumbled forward from the force.

He went to hit Daniel again and missed. Mark grinned, but when Jasper glared at him he joined in on the attack.

"I'm going to Reuben," Daniel said as they both closed in on him.

"Go for it, he's my uncle, he'll probably praise me for scaring the runt," Jasper laughed as his hands eased by his waist. "Besides, this is retaliation for your friend who wasn't supposed to be here. You know how long it takes to heal?"

Daniel found his question funny. He knew how long it took to heal, everyone knew their own healing time, but not many people knew each other's. Jasper swung a fist and caught Daniel at the temple—he flopped; his body poured like jelly as he hit the ground. Mark kicked him and they both ran away.

"You're both weak," Daniel shouted out after them. He pushed his door shut and hauled himself to his feet. "You're both weak."

Daniel fumbled around and called Reuben, he told him about what had happened and Reuben reassured him that they would be dealt with severely, and they wouldn't be allowed to go near him again.

He pulled his bedding up from the floor and wrapped himself in it. He dropped his head to his pillow and closed his eyes.

A crackle came an hour later, it gnawed at Daniel until his eyes shot open and his spine became tight. He pushed his chest out and groaned as white noise ate into him. It sent his eyes fluttering into the back of his head and his muscles contracting.

Seconds later, the noise stopped and Daniel's body dropped. He took a breath and clamped his hands over his head.

"Can you hear me? Jeez, just—" Jac's voice came through as Daniel's eyes watered and ears popped.

"Yes! Yes! I can hear you!" he said, relieved at the cool prickle soothing over his body.

"Finally. You don't know how long I've been trying to get through." Yet Daniel could have guessed. However, Jac wasn't in a state of constant worry about whether there was a body lying in a ditch besides the mountains, not like Daniel had been worrying that much.

"What happened?" Daniel sat up in his bed with a hand pressed against his head.

"Where to start? I fell through several layers of trees and broke my arm, but I didn't know I was still in the Upperlands until a man tried to kill me, he thought I was some bird or something. Anyway, he saved me and then told me my way back to the Academy. Apparently he shares my same hate for Reuben or he would have killed me."

"Are you okay? Where are you now?"

"I'm near the gates, but I should be inside by the morning. So what happened when I left?"

"I went to see Mia." Daniel took a deep breath. "And then I nearly exposed the island to the *rest* of the world, when I got back Reuben was real angry, he even took some of my blood."

"Blood? He took some of your blood?"

"Yeah, he said that it was in case I did anything stupid. Why?"

"Dammit, Daniel! You're at the school of all that is knowledge and you don't know the importance of blood yet?"

Daniel ground his teeth, he could feel the lecture coming on from Jac as his heart and head throbbed in consecutive beats. "Well, we touched upon it."

"Don't you remember all those stories about people? The people whose blood had been hexed? Do you remember the end, or the middle? Or the part where their power slowly killed them, and yes, in the end they died."

"That was just a horror story though."

"No, it wasn't. I need to talk to you, now!"

"You are." Daniel frowned.

"I knew you shouldn't have gone to that school. I could have taught you, at home, in fact, you could have lived with me. I even asked your mum, but she didn't approve. She told me that if the Academy didn't want you then she wouldn't have had much've a choice."

"But Jac, I've learnt so much, and I know you know lots of stuff an' all, but—"

"At least I wouldn't have tried to hurt you!"

Daniel closed his eyes as a low hum vibrated in his head.

"I really need to tell you something, face-to-face."

"I'm getting a bit of a headache, so I'll speak to you in the morning, y'know, if you get passed the security."

Daniel's head went light as he severed the connection. He laid back and blinked, each time his eyes stayed closed for longer.

A wisp of smoke touched his face. He opened his eyes and his vision was fogged. He jumped up at the thought of being gassed out. He waved hand in front of his face and he couldn't see it.

"Help!" he said, from the croak in his voice.

A giggle caught his ear and he turned. The smoke fizzled out as he caught a glimpse of a girl running behind a light orange clay wall. He spun around and took the new scenery in. It reminded him of something Karsar would've done, if he'd been into the lighter and brighter colours.

He started to lose himself in the new scene as he rushed off behind the wall to find the girl. He followed her trail of faint giggles and hums. He kept catching up to her, she would slow down, enough for him to get a glimpse before speeding off again.

She stood right in front of him. Her face, he knew her face, the one who had almost cost him his life.

"Hey, hold up!" he said, chasing her again.

The sunbeam concentrated on him. Daniel glanced up to it as it left dark spots in his sight. He rushed after the girl who trailed a finger across the orange wall.

He copied her. The tips of his fingers tingled, and as he stopped to take a look at them, he noticed thick red welts on them.

She continued to giggle and run her hands along the wall, smoothing over lumpy orange clay like a professional.

"Please, just stop!" He gasped for air and clutched his chest, bending over. He tried to reach out for her.

She tripped up in front of him. He rushed over and she looked up at him. He stood over her to get a full view of her face. She gripped him by his t-shirt and shoved her hand over his mouth. She replaced it with a single finger and then shushed him.

Her childlike body and face morphed. "I'm sorry. I'm not allowed to be here, but everyone seems to be playing dirty. Nobody but those key to your power can tell you, so get away. Get out of it!" she shouted from behind her gritted teeth.

"Who are you?"

"Ary—Aryana. But I can't say anymore. When you know, you know, and I'll come find you."

"You live outside the island, and you haven't been killed."

"I'm sorry, Daniel, I'm sorry, I can't answer your questions, but when you're free of your ties, then I will answer your them.

Don't worry, I *will* find you, but I'm not promising that we can meet back here. If they find me, or even know that we've talked, there will be a *filthy* war ahead," she said.

"But you said I was *him*. Who?"

"I've said too much, I can't intervene." She looked into Daniel's eyes. "It wasn't a coincidence we met in the coffee shop. I needed to know."

"You're confusing me, please, just, *I need to know.*"

She grinned and turned. Daniel reached out to grab her hand and it became dust in his fingers. She was gone, and the reality around him saturated his body in the dust and sand.

CHAPTER THIRTY

CLICK. "Daniel." *Click.* "Daniel." *Click.* Jac continued to snap his finger above Daniel until he groaned and waved a hand in the direction of his alarm clock. The snapping became louder, and Daniel heard his name being called with better clarity.

"Daniel. Get up!" Jac said. He sat by Daniel's side.

Daniel shot up and slapped a hand against his forehead. "I'm in bed," he said with a smile. "Why didn't you just wake me?"

"I didn't want to shake you in case you attacked me or something."

"Oh," he said and scooted up against the wall. "How long have you been here?"

"Not long, a couple of minutes. I climbed through the window," he said. "I unlatched it this time."

Daniel yawned. "Did you climb?"

"Yeah, but it was easy. Anyway. I needed to tell you something. I saw your dad and he—"

"What? My dad?"

"Yeah, he was worried about you being hurt in the school fight. You're big news in the Lowerlands. Well, it was you, right?"

Daniel scoffed. "So, where's my dad at now?"

"He's at home, he had to work, although he wanted to come up and visit. I told him I was coming, and you know, I think he was reassured."

"Ah, that's all I would have needed was him getting into an argument with Reuben. He worries about me too much."

"Yeah. Well he needs to."

Daniel climbed out of bed and dressed while Jac sat on the edge of his bed lost in thought.

"I think I'm healing a lot faster now," Daniel said. "How does my face look?" He combed a hand through his hair and ruffled it up. "How long does it normally take you to heal?"

"Like usual. And I'm fairly quick. Although I do get those days when it's really slow," Jac said. He rubbed at his arm. "I could have broken it, like, forever, and ever. But I'm lucky it started healing as soon as ligaments came loose. Why?"

"Just wondering, I always thought that over time you just healed faster and faster."

"You should know, this school is fancy as hell. But *no*, it's in your blood, in fact, there are a lot of things that determine who we are, and it's to do with our *blood*."

"Oh, god. You've been talking to my dad, haven't you?"

"Yes, no. Why?"

Daniel raised an eyebrow at Jac. "Because I know he's told you the story."

"So you know then?"

"I don't believe it. He's been telling me that story since I was little."

Jac nodded. "You did end up here though."

"Yeah, but he said I'd do great things with *power*, and I haven't done anything great yet, except take a beating and not retaliate. Or maybe one of the great things I do is beat Jasper."

"Well then do it and see if that is one of the great things your dad was talking about. But I still think he means greater things." Jac smiled.

Daniel shrugged. "My dad reads a lot, so, you shouldn't really believe anything that he says. And anyway, I can't pick a fight with him because if I hurt him he's got Mark, Reuben, and a bunch of other people."

"So you're thinking of the repercussions now." Jac grinned. "Well, you only have to ask. I'll happily kick the crap out of him for you."

Daniel shook his head. "No, you can't. Reuben would probably *kill* you, and Jasper hasn't even attacked you for *nothing* yet."

"Well, that's because I don't go to school here," Jac said. "You know you don't have to stay, we can find our own adventure, like we said we would."

"I can't let you do that. And no, I can't leave, I'm learning a lot," he said, finding the clean clothes out of his pile.

"How to take a beating," Jac laughed. "I'm kidding, of course."

"Ha," he said. "I'm staying here."

"What? Here? Where everyone hates you?"

Daniel bowed his head and hummed. "I do miss home."

Jac sighed. "See, you have it rough."

"Plus, I never had nightmares at home. And now I'm having full lucid ones."

"I want you to come back with me," Jac said.

"Seriously. I can't. So much has happened here that I can't just leave. Yes, a lot has been bad, but I wouldn't have met Mia if I didn't come here. And I wouldn't have started to have the nightmares, but they're starting to make sense."

"Everyone has nightmares. They don't mean a thing," Jac said.

"No. They do, Jac. Last night a girl, I forgot her name, she started to ramble on about knowing something and not being able to tell me. It felt so real. And I've seen her before. Off the island. I want to know what it's all about."

"What are you talking about? What happened in your dream?"

Daniel explained his dreams, and they talked again about blood. Jac usually humoured his abilities, he'd always been strong in his will, but something about knowing Reuben had a vial of Daniel's blood made him nauseous.

"Daniel, I think those stories were true. Daniel, you're probably not going to believe one word, but—" before Jac could finish, Daniel disappeared.

Daniel found himself wobbling on his feet and taking in his surroundings. He stood in Reuben's office, and in front of all the teachers. They were all waiting behind Reuben's desk. He was seated, his fingers interlocked and laid on his desk while the teachers behind him clasped their hands against their chests.

Daniel scanned their faces; each teacher had the same look, the same teary red eyes, and inane grins against their clenched teeth. "Hi," Daniel said.

"We knew it!" Reuben bellowed and all the teachers gasped in shock. "Why didn't you tell us?"

Daniel took a step back. "I'm sorry," he managed to say, after he opened and closed his mouth several times. He glared up at them and a stream of light poked him in his eye. He took another step back and wobbled on the balls of his feet.

"No!" Jac shouted. Daniel winced and clenched his jaw.

"Is everything okay?" Reuben said, "Take a seat, Daniel."

"You know?" Daniel asked. His heart lodged itself in his throat, and his face started to burn red.

"I need to tell you something!" Jac shouted again, *"you must hear it from me! Damn it, Daniel, I thought you said you knew!"*

"I know part of the Luminary codes states you shouldn't give yourself away to normal folk like us," Reuben said.

A drill of white noise touched Daniel's core, and reverberated through his bones. "What? Sorry."

"You're a Luminary?" Reuben said. "Right?"

The white noise had a voice, Jac's voice, and from it bled every curse word under the sun. It pierced Daniel, his nose bled. He put a hand to his face and wiped away the blood. He stared out at the people behind Reuben's desk. They were clapping but no sound came.

"We shouldn't have confronted him." Enek said.

"Nonsense, he's come to see *his* people, and we found out his secret," Reuben chuckled.

JOSEPH EASTWOOD

Their voices went over Daniel's head, but inside he could hear the synapses spark and pop, just as his pupils grew and shrunk, and his mouth dried and gush with saliva. He pressed his hand against his mouth and wiped at the drool. "I need—I need to go."

"Of course, anything," Reuben replied. "Be back soon."

He wanted to protest, and as he stood from the settee to waver at the comment he disappeared and fell face flat on his bed.

"How could they!" Jac said, grinding his teeth and flailing his hands in the air.

Daniel sat up, he could barely open his eyes and when he opened his mouth a trickle of saliva dribbled down his chin. "Jac," he said, trying to stand but toppling.

"It incapacitates you. That is what it does. It's in your genes, it's in each of your little—" he made hands look like pincers, "just snapping away and its hit a nerve. You should recover, but I was supposed to tell you." Jac sighed as he sat on the edge of Daniel's bed, besides him. "I can still tell you."

"I don't know. Th—th—think they poisoned me. They lied." Daniel said. He sucked in deep and clenched his jaw after speaking.

"You are a Luminary. Saturn. Satoria," Jac said. "You need sleep, Dan. Don't forget." He looked at Daniel. Red soaked

298

through his white t-shirt from his chest. Jac shook his head and bit his lip. "You won't forget, Daniel. You are a luminary."

"Take me home," Daniel said. He tried to keep from sobbing but tears fell from his eyes. Jac continued to watch as the t-shirt soaked up the blood.

"Go to sleep." Jac placed his hands over Daniel's eyes. He could feel their bond, he tugged and pushed Daniel into a deep sleep.

Jac peeled the damp cloth from Daniel's chest as he let out a loud moan. The cloth had reopened wounds and little streams of blood trickled down the sides.

"I'm sorry," Jac said. He glanced over at the weird 'h' across his chest, it was similar to the one that he'd found on his wrist weeks ago.

"Where am I?" Daniel asked. He tried to lift his head and winced at the pain.

"We're still at school. When you can get up we'll go home."

"No!" Daniel frowned. "I need to see Reuben first. Ow. What is that?"

"It's a scar on your chest. I'm sorry you found out like this."

He tried to open his eyes wider but it was still dark and the lamplight was dim. He pushed back on his neck to see it, but all he could feel was the pain of the skin stretching as he moved.

"I guess it all really happened then, didn't it? It's all true, isn't it?" Daniel said.

"Yeah, it's true, you're a Luminary, and you weren't even meant to be born on this island."

"I'm not—" Daniel said. He tried to protest as hot prickles rose up the sides of his neck and poked him in his cheeks.

"Don't fight it, it will hurt you more. I know things about your family that I didn't know weeks ago, I'm not from a bloodline like you are. I'm from something else. I was *chosen* to be your guardian."

Daniel smiled. "I didn't choose you," he tried to laugh. He pushed himself to sit against the cold brick. He hissed.

Jac stood and looked over Daniel. "Can you see it now?"

"Where?" he asked. He looked down at his chest for several moments and stared at the open cuts. Blood continued to pump out and roll down his chest.

"Did they cut me?"

"No, it's your heritage, it's your *emblem*."

"So, so, who did this?" Daniel threw a hand to his chest and clenched his skin between his fingers as blood poured harder. He bit his tongue in the pain and pulled his hand from his chest.

Jac closed his eyes and shook his head. "It means that you're one of *them*."

"No! You don't know that."

Jac set a finger on Daniel's forehead. "I know it because the guardian's before me knew. I am your guide, but this isn't how it was supposed to start, nobody was supposed to start on this island."

Daniel choked on a breath as Jac removed his finger. He shook his head slowly and turned to face Jac. "Okay, I know it's true. It's too right to be wrong."

Jac smiled. "Great. Now we just need to get you all healed up. We have to leave, if word gets out, they'll do and try anything to keep you here."

"So what happened?" Daniel looked at his fingers covered in blood. He glanced down to see the mark, half-scabbed over and looking like someone had burnt him.

"It happens when you find out. It's to scar you so that you never forget, and it's that painful that you can't," Jac said and rubbed at the scar on his wrist. "That's what I was told anyway, I think it's as a sort of identification."

"Saturn," Daniel said as he traced a finger around the sensitive ridges of the cut.

"You're one of seven, Dan."

"Why didn't you say something earlier?"

"I wanted to. I came here to tell you, but you had a lot of stuff going on and I wanted you to have a last few days of being a normal person before I dropped *this* on you. Well, before they did."

"When can we go? I don't want to stay, it all feels too wrong, when they all spoke to me like I'd won something, and then I felt like I was about to die. We need to go."

"We can't, your dad knows about you giving your blood to Reuben and he told me that I had to get it back off him. Blood is sacred, you know that, right?"

Daniel nodded. "Now I feel stupid for coming. I should've stayed at home, and you should've taught me like you wanted and then when you found out about all of this there wouldn't be much drama and we could have left the island peacefully."

"But you met Mia here."

"And her life is bad enough without me in it. Why couldn't my dad have told you before I left?"

"He didn't want to tell me at all, he never wanted you to find out, and your mum never knew either, she still doesn't."

There was a knock at the door. "Dinner," a woman said. Daniel and Jac exchanged wary glances for a moment, and then Daniel nodded for Jac to get the food. Jac opened the door slightly so that only he was in view. The woman passed him a tray full of food through and before hurrying off she giggled and gave a curtsy.

"Well, someone likes you," Jac said, balancing the tray with one hand before shutting the door and locking it with the other.

He sat the tray down on Daniel's bed, there were several bun rolls with a small pot of butter, and on a larger plate there were strips of thick crispy bacon, fat greasy sausages and two juicy chicken legs glazed with honey.

"I made friends with the kitchen staff," Daniel said, wiping his bloodied hands on his bed sheets.

"Eww, use this!" Jac pushed a bowl of warm water in front of him. "Clean your hands properly."

Daniel raised an eyebrow. "It's only a bit of blood." He rinsed his hands with the warm water, and wiped them on his bed sheets.

"Just because you're a Luminary it doesn't mean that you can't be ill."

Daniel started to shovel the food into his mouth, "*ooing*" and "*aahing*".

CHAPTER-THIRTY-ONE

JAC PUT Daniel straight to sleep after he'd finished eating. It was easier that way, it saved Daniel from moving around and disturbing the fragile scabbing process on his chest.

Jac stayed up through the night. He listened intently to the voices of the people who'd gone before him, people like him, fellow guardians. They let on that they could see the past, the present, and even future events, but they could only let on about the former two.

"How long will it take to heal?" he questioned. The voices replied, without words, they embedded images and video reels behind Jac's sight.

They'd told him to put Daniel to rest, he needed as much time as possible to heal, and he slept all weekend, stirring and waking slightly for water.

"Jac," Daniel said in a cough. "You better stop doing that."

Jac spooned the last of the chocolate yoghurt in his mouth. He hummed and licked the spoon. "Glad you're awake. You look like you've healed okay to me. I needed to make sure you were well rested."

Daniel coughed harder. "I feel better," he said and pushed himself up in his bed.

"Nobody has been in. They couldn't even if they tried," he said. "I feel like there's so much—so much *power*, and I can feel it in everything and everyone."

"That's what it's like off the island," he laughed. He pulled a hand up from his duvet to feel his chest. He caught his smell. "Oh, jeesh! I need a shower."

"I wasn't going to say." Jac grinned. "How does your scar look?"

Daniel peeled the duvet from his chest and glanced down at the symbol in his skin. He looked at Jac and glanced back to the scar. "It's scabbed quite well."

"It should've healed over by now, you should peel it in the shower or something. But before that, you need to eat; you've been asleep since Saturday."

Daniel turned and squinted at Jac. His eyes were glassy and his face flushed red. He puffed out his cheeks and threw his head over the side of his bed. There was a splash and then Daniel choked a couple more times as he threw up on the floor. Jac turned his face away and took a deep breath. He held it.

"You best shower first," Jac said.

"I need to eat though."

Jac walked over to the closet and picked up a towel. He passed it to Daniel, trying not to look at the sick on the floor. "Just go have a shower, food should be here by the time you've finished."

Daniel nodded. "What day is it?"

"Monday."

While Daniel showered. Jac tried to tidy the room. He tapped into excess energy he'd been storing for the right moment, and that moment came when Daniel's sick made the room smell.

Daniel burst into his bedroom. He was followed in by two women carrying huge platters covered by silver lids. They placed the platters on the freshly made bed and hurried off, giggling to each other and going red in the face.

They pulled the lids off to find that this wasn't their usual dinnertime meal, this wasn't at all like the foods they'd previously eaten. There was duck, glazed in honey and orange with a crisp, well-cooked layer of skin. And as Jac pulled the other metal lid, he revealed several smaller dishes, steamed vegetables; broccoli, carrots, potatoes, green beans.

Daniel picked up a plate and spooned the vegetables on it. Jac cut into the duck. His mouth watered as he watched the grease trickle down its side. Daniel held his plate out as Jac cut several thick slices off for him.

Beside the duck there was a dark brown sauce. Daniel dipped his finger in and stuck it in his mouth, he "*ooed*" and "*aahed*" as this new sauce touched his lips, at first there was vinegar, and then spice, and it struck him with a fruity kick.

"People are so nice now," Daniel said, dipping his finger back in the sauce.

"Don't be fooled, they'll try and have your child, and then run away and blackmail you for money, telling you how they'll kill the child if you don't pay them. They'd fail of course because your child will have Luminary blood," Jac blurted.

"What?"

"I don't have a clue. *Well*, I do. It's this store of knowledge about your family and heritage, and stuff. You also have a castle, y'know."

"We can't leave the island though. You heard them, didn't you? They'd kill anyone who left."

"And what part of, you cannot die, don't you understand. And I won't die until I'm of no use." Jac grinned.

Daniel hummed and took a bite of the duck. He was silent for a moment as he chewed and swallowed, and looked back at Jac. "I think you'll always have a use."

"Hah. That's reassuring," he said, "I can hunt big game without worrying about being killed now."

"Really? The biggest game that isn't a shifter is an elk."

"Yeah, well we're not staying here I've already packed your stuff, and we're leaving, as soon as you've eaten."

"What? And where the hell are we even going?"

"The castle? Apparently you have lots of money there. So why not."

Daniel eyed Jac. Everything was too surreal and he'd played it out like a sick dream, now set in stone. Sometimes there wasn't meant to be an answer to everything, sometime things had to play out on their own. He gulped at the build-up of stress in his throat.

"I can't leave without getting the blood from Reuben. Plus, the food here's delicious. I'll get it off him tomorrow when I have class."

Jac nodded; he didn't want to be there when Daniel broke that news, and he knew that if he was there he'd end up fighting.

"I still can't shift though," Jac thought aloud.

"Most people can't. You know that."

"Yeah, but. *Luminary*. *Guardian*. I should be able to at least shift a little."

Daniel chuckled. "Well when I learn how to use my *Luminary* power, I'll give you an animal."

"That's more like it!"

There was something else going on behind the whites of Jac's eyes, something that he smiled and figured would pass, but this wasn't going to pass. The inside of his mind had become a mess since his guardianship started. It was like an abandoned library; the floors were scattered with stray papers, and every other moment a gust of wind would throw something at him.

A tea-stained piece of paper slapped him. He read it verbatim: *a Luminary may not possess their ancestral power until the age of 18, when the development of their physical body should be complete. Luminaries should reach this age before being given any roles and responsibilities, or continuing the succession of a forefather's title.* The paper was torn at the bottom, and another hit him: *a guardian may also experience lapses in ability due to the information needed to survive being stored in them.*

Daniel glared at Jac out of the corner of his eye. "What's up?"

"I feel a little sick, and I guess cleaning yours up didn't help."

"Just eat something. This is *amazing!*" Daniel said, and licked the tips of his fingers.

Jac smiled and rubbed at the mark where he'd been scarred on his wrist. It slowly prickled his skin and itched. Jac tried not to touch it, but the scar was glowing and turning red. He blinked and glanced back at it. There was no bubbling, or rippling, but

the sensation had eaten into his skin and he could feel it long
after it had disappeared.

CHAPTER THIRTY-TWO

TUESDAY afternoon came quick enough, and Daniel made his way to Reuben's office. He'd prepared a speech, ready to tell Reuben that he was leaving and that he knew who he was now. He was also going to tell him that he wanted his blood back, and he'd fight for it.

"Mr. Satoria," a woman said. She bowed her head at Daniel as she rushed out of Reuben's office. "Your class is waiting in the teaching room beneath the school."

"But I need to speak with Reuben privately," he said. He called out after her as she rushed off.

She didn't turn to reply or even acknowledge that she'd heard him, she continued on in her strides. Daniel rubbed his clammy hands against his pants. It meant he'd have to walk back down those 3 flights of stairs, and then down another flight to the room, all the while, debating with himself about how he was going to tell Reuben; the man who had a vial of his blood.

"Stop thinking, start doing!" Jac said, a snigger escaped his throat.

"Yeah, I'm a Luminary. I shouldn't be scared. Right?"

"Like I said. Stop thinking!"

Daniel walked back down the three flights of stairs and made his way down to the room beneath the school. It gave him the creeps, especially since the last time he was down here they'd summoned Karsar, *and what could be worse than annoying a Luminary. Well, I guess finding out you were one, that was sure to top it.*

"Ahh, Daniel!" Reuben shouted.

Everyone turned to him. His classmates stood around in a circle, and all the teachers had congregated in a corner. They whispered and shared gasps.

Daniel bit the inside of his lip and smiled. "Hi," he said.

"Oh, come in. No need to be shy anymore. You're welcome here. And we want to embrace you. We *all* want to embrace you," Reuben said. He took a step out into the centre of the circle of students.

Daniel gulped.

"Just tell him how it is, and then get back here and we can go."

There was something unsettling about how dark the room became when the door was shut behind him. He walked further into the ring and stood opposite Reuben. He glared into his eyes before noticing that the ring of people surrounded him.

"We're all so happy to be in the presence of a Luminary. It's invigorating. You're just what Templar needs to restore the faith in prayer."

"I'm sorry. I'm still getting used to this, I don't really understand how it all works," Daniel said, glancing around the room with his eye on a way out.

"Naturally you want to leave and join *your* people, right?"

Daniel nodded.

"Yeah, now agree with him, take the blood and poof your Luminary ass back here!"

"We don't mean to sound anxious or needy, but can we have your blessing?" Reuben asked.

"My blessing?" Daniel said in a mumble.

"Yes, the highest form of energy that can be bestowed upon a person, and with it, we can travel and spread news that the Luminary folk are back, and they want us to send prayers to them." Reuben said, his words were calculated on his tongue. "You do know the others, right?"

"Yes," Daniel said, "yes, I know them."

"Good."

The circle grew as the teachers joined, some more willing than others; Enek's hands were bound together, and a dirty rag had been shoved in his mouth. He tried to shout through it, but it only voiced faint mumbles. He was kicked into the centre.

"What's going on there?"

Reuben pulled the rag from Enek's mouth. "An offering," he said.

"Please," Enek begged. "Don't do it, Daniel. Don't."

"I'm—I'm—what is this?" Daniel asked, shaking his head.

Reuben shot Daniel a sideways glance and a smile broke out in the corner of his mouth. "You want someone else?"

"No."

"Daniel," Reuben said, resting a hand on his shoulder. "You're going to give us it. Your essence, your being, and we can do this the hard way, or the increasingly *hard* way." Reuben's hold on Daniel's shoulder tightened as he dug his fingers in.

There was a shared gasp among the students. Daniel grit his teeth in the pain, but his face remained stern as he looked around at all the eyes on him; the eyes shaded beneath the dark of the room.

"Take it?"

"Get out of there, now!" Jac shouted. His voice made Daniel wince towards his left ear. *"Okay, I'm coming down there and I'm getting you out! Just don't give him anything!"*

"You want my power?" Daniel mumbled.

"Yes! I want it. You *don't* deserve it, and you know why? Because you're scum, you're a scummy Lowerlands being, and you don't *deserve* it." Reuben said, his fingers becoming numb in Daniel's shoulder blade.

The room stayed silent. If only eyes could talk. Nobody was enjoying this, well; nobody was enjoying this more than Reuben.

"No." Daniel shrugged Reuben's hand off his shoulder. "You're not having it."

Reuben sniggered, and a couple of people laughed along. "We'll see about that, shall we?" he said, and snapped his fingers. "Chey."

Enek was pulled backed through the ring to make room for Chey, she had something in her hand, a piece of rope. She pulled it, and the light hit her. She had something in her hands, something kicking and punching to stay. It was gagged and its hair was all over.

"Mia," Daniel said as he looked at the girl being dragged into the centre. He looked to Chey, and back to Reuben's snarling face.

"She'll be fine," Reuben said, "as long as you do one little favour for me."

Mia stopped wriggling and writhing. She let herself be pulled into the ring. She made eye contact with Daniel, and they exchanged watery-eyed glances.

"Okay," Daniel said. "What do you want?" The feeling of having power, and having never used it settled with Daniel, not only did he regret not doing anything with his power, but now he'd never be able to do anything at all. He gulped down hard in his throat and a warm tear washed down his cheek.

'I summon you! Help us! You can't let this go through. I know you can't. I know!' Jac shouted at the top of his lungs, but it was true, somewhere in the abyss of his brain he'd figured it out, no Luminary could be left without the protection of another.

Daniel fell to the ground from the force of Jac's voice, he yelped and threw his hands over his ears.

"Drama? Everyone loves a bit of drama." Reuben laughed.

"Stop!" Jac blasted the door off with a bolt of flames. The door charred in a pile of ash as he walked in. "You have to deal with this, before you dare to take anything from Daniel," Jac said, pointing to himself.

"Got yourself a protective guardian there," Reuben sniggered. "But I've dealt with this *one* before."

"That was before," Jac said.

"Before what? Before you became mister high and mighty?" Reuben laughed, and the students sniggered along out of nervousness.

Jac glanced from Reuben and to Daniel, cradling over Mia. "Daniel, you don't have to do anything he says. Mia's going to be fine."

"She is?" Reuben said.

Chey pounced out of the crowd and snatched Mia up off the ground. She wielded a golden knife up at Mia's neck. "Do as Mr. Croft has instructed, and she will live."

"How?" Daniel asked. He sat up on the heels of his feet. "How do I give you it?"

"Open your raw power up, and just will it over," Reuben replied with a grin on his face.

The room felt like it was about to drop a thousand feet below the ground. Stomachs knotted. Faces scrunched up, and teeth clenched together. One by one people left the alcove, but nobody noticed, not even when there were only a few people left.

"He can't!" a sharp roar broke through, and a tall man fell from the ceiling. He hit the ground with his fist. "Now, Reuben, you know he can't just do it. You need to have some of his blood."

Reuben's grin broadened. "Two Luminaries, and a guardian, what do I owe this pleasure?" he glanced up at the man. His face hidden by a thin purple hood. He looked at Daniel. "I have that. Right here." He picked a small vial of Daniel's blood from his chest pocket.

"You're prepared," he said.

"And you're not." He nodded to Chey and she let go of Mia and maneuvered over to the man. She held the knife to his neck.

Jac watched in awe as the man took Chey's arm and flipped her over his shoulder into the wall behind Jac. They all turned to watch as her back cracked against the stone.

Another attack charged towards him. He grabbed the boy's wrist and pulled him close. It was Jasper. "Getting boys to fight for you. You're a weak man, Reuben. Weak." He said, and pushed Jasper away.

"Would a weak man do this?" Reuben asked. He held a knife to Mia's stomach. The man took one step and the knife went deep.

Daniel watched Mia's body fall into Reuben's arms. She tried to grab the knife, but her arms fell limp. There were no vocal chords available to voice what had just happened.

"There's the incentive, Daniel, now, give me it!" Daniel watched as Reuben's lips moved, and ended in a slack-jawed snigger.

Daniel shook his head and stood. He glared at Reuben and his eyes turned red. "No," he said. A tear dropped. "You better leave, I would've done it. Really! But you can forget it now."

Reuben stood and let Mia's body drop.

The man looked at Daniel, he took a step back; he rested a hand on Reuben's shoulder, and nudged him forward. "You can take him."

"Stay away from my—" Jasper started, and Jac punched him in his face.

"I have this," Reuben said and wiggled the blood in front of Daniel. "One drip on my tongue, and I'm untouchable."

"Shut up!"

"It's true. Ask your little guardian friend, or that Luminary, and they'll tell you it's true."

"We can't intervene if he takes it," the man said. "You need to become what you are. As I should not—I cannot intervene either way." He pushed a card into Daniel's pocket before he faded out of the room.

"No, you can't leave," Jac said and reached out to him, falling in his wake.

Reuben uncapped the vial, the pop shook Daniel at his core.

"I'll do it," he said. "I'll do it now."

A dark figure propped up from behind Reuben and whacked him on his head. It was Enek. His hands still tied together, and the dirty towel was now around his neck. He tried to stay standing, and fell into a limp. "Always knew you were special," he said.

To one side there was Reuben with the vial, still between his fingers, and to the other, Mia. He looked at her lifeless body, the knife still inside.

"You can save her," Enek said, "my lord—my Luminary."

"Take her to your mum!" Jac said. He rushed around Daniel to get to Mia.

"I can deal with Reuben," Enek said.

"I can't." Daniel said. He shrugged at Jac's grasp. "She's dead."

"Daniel!" Jac grabbed a hold of his arm. "She's not."

Enek nodded. He looked over the bodies that groaned across the floor. "You best be off, they'll wake, and he's in no form to fight now," he said to Jac.

"I'll take this before we go. I don't want anything to happen now," Jac said. He snatched the vial out of Reuben's hands.

"Safe journey."

Daniel glanced up at the bruised mess Enek had become, and then back to Mia's white body. He closed his eyes, and thought of home, so much so that he could smell the meat cooking on the stove in the kitchen, and the warmth of his bed; the feelings he never wanted to wake from.

CHAPTER THIRTY-THREE

HE WAS home. He stood in the middle of the living room staring blankly ahead. Jac was stood over Mia with her hand in his. "It's going to be alright," he repeated to himself.

"Daniel!" his mother shouted. She ran up to her son and wrapped her arms around him.

"I'm sorry, I'm sorry!" he said, throwing his arms around his mum, tears wetting his cheeks and eyes.

"Why, what's going on?" she asked, taking a step back from her son.

"She has a—a knife in—in her," he gasped. "It's all my fault."

Jac shook his head. "Roan. It isn't. Really. Reuben did this."

"Erik told me. I guess he knows," she said.

Jac nodded. "I told him. It didn't go that well."

"I just froze. I could have stopped him. I know I could," Daniel said and wiped at his eyes. "Can you help her?"

"Of course I can, son. You just go and lie down, get some rest."

Daniel nodded as dawdled up the stairs to his room without taking a second glance at Mia.

When they heard his bedroom door shut, Roan rushed into the kitchen and pulled out her blue box.

"Should I take the knife out?"

"No, not yet," she said, kneeling down beside Mia. "I'm going to cut myself, and when I say so, that's when you pull the knife out." She picked a small knife from her box and held it to her palm.

"No. I have some of Daniel's blood here. There's more chance of that healing her than your blood. Isn't there?"

Roan smiled, her hands shook as she put the knife away. "Yeah. I don't know what I'm doing," she said. "It's my fault all of this, isn't it? You wanted to teach him, and I wanted him to have better. Even though you would have been the better teacher."

"No, it's fine. We just need to save her." Jac opened his hand up from around the vial he'd been pressing hard against his palm. He looked down at Mia and noticed her lips turning blue.

Jac nodded at Roan. "Now?" he asked. Roan nodded and he pulled the knife from Mia's stomach.

She twitched inwardly, but Jac straightened her out. Roan poured half the vial of blood inside the open cut. Jac parted Mia's lips with his fingers and Roan let the rest of the blood drip down her throat.

"What will happen?" Roan asked.

"She'll heal, her memory will be foggy. But she'll be attached to Daniel," Jac gulped. "Well, at least she still lives, right?" he looked up at Roan and she nodded in agreement.

"Should I stitch her up or—"

"She should heal on her own."

Daniel peered around the corner from the bottom of the stairwell. "Is she going to live?" he asked, taking a seat on the bottom step.

"She's breathing," his mother said.

"And she twitched when we removed the knife, so that's a positive sign."

"I'm going to have to take her home before she wakes," Daniel said.

"Where does she live?"

"I don't even know where it's called. But I know it's huge."

"You best take her soon, son, before she wakes. I'll pack you a bag of food and stuff; I don't want you dying out there, especially not from starvation."

Daniel almost smiled. "I'm a Luminary," he said. "Might take more than some hunger pains to kill me."

Daniel had only ever seen the inside of Mia's room once, and that was in a dream. He glanced at Jac, surprised at how he'd got all three of them safely from Templar Island into her room in the space of a minute.

"Help me put her in bed," Jac said, as Daniel glanced around the room, staring at the posters on her walls.

"Yeah," he said.

They knelt beside her; one at either side, Jac shoved his hands under her back and lifted from her chest to her head. Daniel carried the rest. They placed her on her bed, trying not to tear at the new skin forming over her wound.

"No going back," Daniel sighed. "No home or anything."

"We do have some stuff, like the castle I was telling you about. You have that. And I'm sure that with a little practice we can learn how to survive."

"Well, your optimism sure hasn't died out."

"And I can see that yours has."

"I nearly died today!" Daniel said and gritted his teeth

"But you didn't, and if it wasn't for me… you would have died, or worse, given your Luminary energy to Reuben."

"To save her. It's my fault she ended up there in the first place, so I had to do something. I couldn't just let her die."

Jac rolled his eyes. "Well you kinda did," he said. "You froze."

"Shut up! Shut up! Shut up!" he said, feeling his hands become warm. He punched Jac in his face.

Jac stumbled, he rubbed the side of his jaw and smiled. "But you didn't freeze then. You know you can do it."

"Jac, you really annoy me sometimes!"

"Sometimes I need to, and if you'd have done that to Reuben you could have cemented your place among some hard-core Luminary figures. It's not often people see them, let alone get to meet them, so you needed to tell them that you're a Luminary not to be messed with."

"There are others, right?"

"Yeah, others that we'll have to find, I almost doubted any of them would answer my plea to save you. Luckily one of them stepped up, it means they know about you, and they'll probably know more about it than either of us do."

Daniel rolled his eyes. "We can start looking tomorrow."

EPILOGUE

MIA sobbed into her pillow. She clutched at her stomach and muffled cries inside the cocoon of her duvet. The faint glimpses of what had happened the night before were seared behind her eyes, and nothing could undo what she'd been through.

"Mia," Daniel said.

She went quiet, and pulled the duvet from her face. "What are you doing here?"

"Well I couldn't—"

"No, like, you're not real! What are you doing here?"

Jac groaned on the floor and picked his head from a pillow he'd been sleeping on. "What's going on?"

"And you! None of this is real," she said, shoving the duvet to her face.

Daniel pulled the duvet. "Mia, you know me, you know who I am, right?"

"Yes! You're that freak! The creepy one who abducted me," she said.

Jac jumped to his feet. "Oh, I know what this is," he said. "It's your blood," he turned to see Daniel's jaw drop, "well, I had to use something to save her."

"Saved me?" she asked, sitting upright.

"Oh, she's oblivious," Jac smiled. "Come here, I have an idea." He sat down on her bed, and she budged away, he rolled his eyes and prodded her hard at the centre of her forehead.

"Ow!" she frowned.

"Well, she doesn't remember any of your *good times*, in fact, you're the bad guy in her eyes," Jac said.

"Leave. Now!" she batted her hands at either side of her on the bed. Her room shook. "Go!"

"What—can she?" Daniel asked.

Jac glanced from Mia to Daniel. "Looks like it."

"We can't leave her like us, she'll be dangerous," Daniel said. He tried to look in her eyes, but the look behind them was cold, and unmoving.

"Fine," Jac said. He prodded her in the middle of her forehead again. Harder this time. Her eyes closed and her head fell. "She can sleep it off."

"Is that your go to?" Daniel chuckled.

The floorboard outside Mia's boardroom door creaked. There was a knock at the door. "Are you okay?" her father called. He opened the door slightly as Daniel and Jac jumped to the floor. "Oh, you're sleeping." He closed the door.

"What are we going to do?" Daniel asked. "About her, about this, we need to find some place to hide."

"You mean live," Jac smiled. "We'll keep her under control. That's what we're going to do."

Daniel nodded. "I have to make her remember me."

COMING SOON

READ A SHORT PREVIEW

THE SCORCH OF VENUS

A BLOOD LUMINARY NOVEL

JOSEPH EASTWOOD

THE SCORCH OF VENUS

A BLOOD LUMINARY NOVEL

PROLOGUE

IT BEGAN over one-thousand years ago, but what changed eight-hundred years later, were the rules. The rules of the game were simple; you had to stay away from Templar Island, and you had to leave everything that grew there alone. Even family.

The rules changed when one of their own decided that he couldn't deal with all the rules. He'd given up, and he'd told others that it was *inhumane* for someone to possess so much power. *Inhumane*, he would cry.

Christopher lifted the black top hat from his head and threw it to the cobbles on the ground. He shook his head and a tear dripped down his cheeks. He wiped his face and spat at his hat.

"It's all about the status," he mumbled. "Status."

"Darling!" his wife threw herself out of their house and at his feet. "Don't leave. Please, don't leave."

He turned and shook his head. "I'm sorry," he murmured. "Sorry." He glanced down to Greta and pushed his top set of teeth into his bottom lip. "But I know what's going to happen if I stay like this," he said. "I'm so so so sorry."

"No, please," she cried. "Marry me!" She pulled herself up on his pants.

He shook his head and pushed her away. She slipped along the wet cobbles and fell back down to her knees.

"I'm pregnant!"

He shook his head and bit harder on his lip.

"Don't leave me! I cannot live without you!"

He snarled at her. His hand by his side quivered and he slapped her across the face. "Leave me!" he snapped.

Greta stood still. The tears that begged to bleed out of her eyes turned her face red with frustration. She gritted her teeth and rushed back into the house. "I'm keeping the house!" she finally cried and stood in the doorway.

"Good!" he turned and shouted. A smile formed on his face. He was finally happy. "It's no use to me anymore. Keep it, Greta. You'll need it for the child." He pulled at his tie and wiped the tears from his face. He untied the tie, and unbuttoned his shirt.

"What are you doing?" she cried harder.

Christopher took a deep breath and turned around to see Greta. She was holding on to the door as she trembled on her feet.

"I can't—do—this!" He fished around in his pocket and found a silver letter opening knife. He raised it to his face and it glinted in the dull light.

"We can go and see a head doctor," she pleaded. "Please, let me help you."

His fingers were stiff around the knife. He stuck it in his chest. The blood soaked the cloth around his body. But he didn't fall, he didn't waver. He stayed standing. He jabbed the knife into his chest again. And again. There was no pain. Not even a tingle or a flicker of it.

"We're having a baby," she screamed. "You can't leave us all alone."

He turned around to Greta. His chest was covered in thick slits, and blood dripped from each of them. He looked over at her. "Have the child and leave, take it away from me," he said and his form flickered out. He'd vanished. He'd teleported away.

Greta cried after him. Falling into the doorway beneath the shakes in her calf muscles.

Christopher formed in an alley way of a bustling city. He looked around to see rats squirm beneath his feet. Rain fell. He dropped the knife and glanced down at his bloody palms. He

332

washed them in the rain water.

"Hey, are you okay?" a man asked from behind Christopher. He turned to face the man. "Are you bleeding?"

"It's nothing," he smiled and tightened his overcoat. "How old are you?" he asked.

"Are you sure you're okay?" he asked.

Christopher smiled. "I'm fine. So, how old are you?"

"Twenty-four," the man grinned, "just turned. Why? Do you have a pretty daughter?"

His smile grew. "Something better. Much better."

"Better than that?"

"A life," Christopher said. "A new life."

The man chuckled. "I'll bite," he said. "Go on, it sure beats the family business," he laughed.

Christopher nodded. "What's your name?" he asked.

"Horatio Hanley," he replied.

THE SCORCH OF VENUS

A BLOOD LUMINARY NOVEL

CHAPTER ONE

REUBEN gathered himself, wrapping a brown swaddle cloth around a giant green stone as he rushed out of the forest and into a nearby barn.

"I have it," he shouted. "I have it, Marianne!"

A woman rushed out of the barn and pulled her apron off. The apron was soaked in blood. "Good. Does that mean we don't need him anymore?" she asked, nodding into the barn.

In the centre of the barn, strung by his arms to the roof was a man. His body was dirty with blood and dust. He groaned beneath the weight of his own body.

"Reuben," he coughed. "Just leave me. *Just leave me.*"

"Ha!" Reuben shouted. He rushed into the barn. "No

chance. You can still tell us where the boy is," he said.

"I can't. I don't—"

Reuben lifted his hand to him. "Enek. Shush. Say that one more time and I will kill you."

Marianne glanced from Enek to Reuben. She grinned. "Please. It's been a long time coming."

"What happened?" Enek cried.

"If you don't know where he is, then I can't share my secret with you," Reuben said. He lifted away the brown cloth from around the stone. It glittered in the dim streams of light that came in through the slabs of wood in the barn. "Do you know what this is?"

Enek shook his head. He groaned beneath the strain under his armpits. "I don't know. You can let me go."

"It's a second chance," Marianne said. "It's *our* second chance."

"From this, we can find him, in fact, we can find them all," he said. He looked up at Marianne and smiled. "Go get my wife, she'll be more than happy to hear about it."

Marianne nodded. She disappeared with a flicker.

Reuben glared at Enek. He tutted and shook his head at him. "You're going to pay for what you've done," he said. "Pay for the precious time that you've wasted."

Marianne and a smaller woman appeared in the doorway of the barn. The woman had thin white blonde hair and a hunched back. She gripped at her cardigan and pushed a white handkerchief to her mother.

"Reuben," she said with happiness pouring from her eyes. "There's a second chance." She coughed into the handkerchief and pulled it away from her lips. A pattern of blood and phlegm marked the clean white cloth. She closed it in her palm and smiled at her husband.

"Julie!" he grinned. "This man, here, he's keeping the location of someone that we need."

She wiped her eyes and scowled at Enek. She walked over to him and looked him in the eye. She turned back and looked at her husband. "But you have the new stone, you can locate him through that."

Reuben shook his head. "He's not old enough to be trapped, he'd only leave."

"I'm sure I will live," she said, she glanced back down to Enek. "And if I don't, I'll blame it on you."

"What?" Enek groaned.

"You're standing in the way of me being cured," she said. A tear ran down her cheek as she shook her head at him. "And you persist on saying that you don't know anything."

"I don't," he said. "I promise. I don't know where he is."

"Then we'll have to make sure of that," she said. She turned to her husband, and he nodded at her.

A small rivet of white fur crawled up Julie's arms from her

fingertips. She shivered in the cold, and out popped a new body, fresh from the rejuvenation that only a transformation can give. She became a fierce white cat, clean of battle scars, and primped with sharp nails. Her midnight circles for eyes stared into Enek's soul.

"Don't! Please!" he screamed.

The ivory claws poised in mid-air for precious moments before they swung, down and around, and tore into Enek's stomach. He cried out in pain as she swiped again. She jumped up from her hind legs and with both paws, one swiped at his neck and the other his face. She caught his jugular and left four clean marks across his face, tearing down his eyes, into his nose, and leaving his lip cleft.

She lapped up the blood as it spilled down his body and pooled around his feet.

"That's a good girl," Reuben said. "If only everyone knew how gracious you were, you would never have been mine."

"How long do you think she has?" Marianne whispered to Reuben.

"Two months at a push," he said. "Nothing is working on her. We've had the finest medical professions off the island," he said into a sigh. "She ends up killing them out of frustration. But it's the liveliest I've ever seen her." He smiled down at his wife.

The campus was broken. The moonlight only reflected what it saw. A deep need to be cleaned. A need to settle something so unsettling that nobody had returned to the school. Those who didn't leave where among those who had owed a debt to Reuben and his family.

...TO BE CONTINUED

final text may differ from that which is provided.

ABOUT THE AUTHOR

JOSEPH EASTWOOD was born on the 9th of June 1993, in Lancaster, England, although he's fairly certain that he's only a visitor on Earth. *Wait* unless you're the with government, in which case, Joseph is a human being with human interests, such as reading, and not dissecting human beings in order to use them in his—*ahem*—fiction.

He has many writing interests, including young adult, poetry, fantasy, thriller, and even romance, so make sure that you look at the recommended age guidelines before you pick up your next JOSEPH EASTWOOD book.

Make sure that you visit JOSEPH EASTWOOD online for *exclusive* content on your favourite books.

www. JosephEastwood.co.uk

Printed in Great Britain
by Amazon.co.uk, Ltd.,
Marston Gate.